STEPPING IT UP

The Liberty Lawrence Series: Book Two

Bea Stevens

Table of Contents

Copyright

Copyright © 2018

All Rights Reserved Worldwide

ISBN13: 978-1912913008

Spellings are in British English

Dedication

I'd like to dedicate this novel to G. Thank you for all your support and patience, and for allowing me to follow my dream. Lots of love

xxx

I'm beginning to wonder if it might have been more useful to get my 'A' level in Running instead of English. I've worked for the *Chronicle* for two weeks now and I really enjoy it. I'd like to say my feet haven't touched the ground, but that, unfortunately, would be totally inaccurate. My feet haven't *stopped* touching the ground—at a rapid pace.

I was expecting to spend my time interviewing celebrities—or at least *interesting* people. I hoped to be trying out all the latest fashions and learning new make-up tricks. It would've been nice to work with Siobhan, the beautiful fashion editor, or Tammy, one of the junior editors who has her own quirky sense of style, to put it mildly. Ha! No such luck.

They put me with Dave, who is almost seven-foot-tall, three or four years older than me and a hundred percent fitter. His skin is naturally tanned, he's bald—which he insists is by choice, but the jury's out on that one—and he's got a smile that shines in the dark, he must have Simon Cowell's dentist. I just wish he'd point that delightful beam in my direction a bit more often, instead of always rolling his eyes and frowning at me.

Dave could give Mo Farah a run for his money, he's so fast. I once spied Mo running around the track at St. Mary's University when I was on a course over in Twickenham. He winked at me, although my friend Trinny reckoned he just had something in his eye. She's not my friend anymore.

'I hope you're not planning to eat that.' Dave's just watched me place a ham and cheese sandwich on our desk.

I stare at him in dismay. 'What did you think I was going to do with it?' I hardly dare ask.

'We need to get across town.' He's already pulling on his hoodie. 'Something's going down.'

I take a quick bite of my sandwich before sealing it back in its plastic box. I suppose one advantage of bringing your own lunch is that you can eat it anytime. And I guess it will save money, as James insists. It's just such a chore.

My feet are already aching as we exit the *Daily Chronicle* reporter's office and head for the lift.

'I thought you'd take the stairs,' I grumble as he stoops to get in beside me.

'This'll be quicker as everyone's going for lunch around about now,' he says, pressing the button for the ground floor. 'Besides, I'll need my energy to get there. We're better off on foot than taking the tube at this time of day.'

My heart sinks and I look down at my Kurt Geigers. The first day I worked here I wore my Karen Millens, which have always been ideal for work. Ruined! Not only did I almost break my neck running to an impromptu press conference in Westminster—when Dave said we were in the area I didn't realise he meant it was a flipping mile and half away—but he insists on taking back alleys and muddy paths to save time. They don't save shoe leather, though.

I actually had to go out and buy some flat shoes after that. They're really nice, I have to admit, plain little pumps. I got them in nude, so they'd go with anything. They would have cost sixty quid, but they were half-price in the sale. I don't think I'd have got them otherwise. James is a bit strict about money—even mine.

They don't look like two-week-old shoes, though. And they certainly don't look nude. I sigh as we get out of the lift and exit the huge, office building. I tried my best to hide the scuffmarks, but all the dirt has stained the leather.

'Is it another drugs bust?' I'm hoping all this effort will be worth it. And I could do with impressing my new boss with a great story.

'Yep. But we have to be quick.'

I roll my eyes. *Since when has Dave ever not been quick?*

'This way,' he says, dashing through a crowd of Japanese tourists. I follow, glad I'm wearing comfy trousers and a chic light jacket, even though it is October.

'Gomen'nasai,' I say with an apologetic smile, as the tourists abruptly stop taking photos of a passing red bus and stand back to let us though. It's amazing how many languages I've learned to say 'sorry' in since I've been working with Dave. He's so tall no one's going to argue with him, so he just pushes his way through, leaving me straggling in his wake.

I wear a black, Radley cross-body bag—one that Cassie, my bestie, doesn't need any more—which houses my phone, cash, chocolate bar, and a small tablet, along with a notebook and pen—just in case. This is much more practical than the Marc Jacobs tote I used on my first day. It's a gorgeous bag, in tan leather, and held everything—make-up, lunch, Lindsey Kelk's latest novel, the usual pack of tissues, manicure set, decent-sized mirror—as well as all the stuff I've got with me now. Only trouble was when I had to make a mad dash across town it was too heavy and cumbersome to run with. I'm still using it—after all, a girl needs all this stuff—but it stays in the office now while I'm chasing stories.

Talking of chasing, I appear to have lost Dave. We were heading towards Earl's Court along the main road, but I can't see him anywhere. There are plenty of side streets he could've taken. Crikey, you'd think being so tall it would be hard to miss him, but he's got a nasty habit of just diving down some alley and vanishing.

It gives me a chance to stop and catch my breath for a minute, as I escape the lunch-time crowd and move over to lean on the wall of an office-block. I'm sure I must have lost at least four stone in the last fortnight with all this exercise. Oddly enough, my clothes don't seem to have had the memo, though. I'm even working hard to keep my carbs up, like Dave does. Actually, it's probably time I had more sugar to keep my energy up—after all, I missed lunch, didn't I? So, I delve into my bag for a Mars bar.

'You haven't got time for that!' Dave suddenly appears through the crowd, glaring at me. 'Come on, we'll miss it. Tom's already there.'

I didn't even get chance to unwrap it before I have to stuff my little bar of heaven back into my bag and take off after him.

We enter a maze of side streets and back-alleys, and I'm sure at one point we cut through someone's garden, before reaching a really nice cul-de-sac where some not-so-nice men are being led into the back of a police van.

'Over here.' Dave pulls me through a throng of onlookers to where a police spokesman in a chief inspector's uniform is making a speech. Or, at least, he *was* making a speech—it looks like he's just finished.

My heart sinks. This was my fault for being so slow. Dave's going to be mad with me. I watch as a young guy with greasy, sandy-coloured hair tries to pull away from the officer who's leading him to the van. I push through the crowd to get closer.

'I didn't do anything,' he's insisting, 'I wasn't involved.' He sounds desperate, and almost in tears.

I frown, marching over to the officer who was making the speech. 'Excuse me, why is he being arrested?'

The guy's eyebrows knit together so tightly they could make a jumper. He's clearly never heard of waxing, or even tweezers. 'He's a suspect.'

'But he's not with the rest. At least, he doesn't appear to be. Did you see their designer shoes? And the gold chains? This guy's got none of that.'

'Did you see his Rolex?' The chief inspector rolls his eyes at me. 'Of course, he's one of them.'

'I saw a pitiful *fake* Rolex. And none of his clothes are designer, like theirs were. Are you sure he's involved with them?'

Something about the guy didn't seem right. He might have been a criminal of some kind, but he appeared terrified at being lumped together with those men in the van. And I was sure he wasn't one of their gang. He just seemed so different.

'Just let us do our job, will you?' The officer says, wearily.

I catch the young guy's eye as he's about to climb into the van. He looks like he's pleading with me to do something. But what *can* I do?

***

I thought Dave would be furious with me, but when I catch up with him, he's chatting quite happily with Tom, the photographer.

'I'm really sorry,' I tell him, 'did we miss everything?'

'*I* didn't,' Tom pipes up with a grin. 'I got some great shots. In fact, I was surprised how early I was. I thought all the action would be in full flow by the time I arrived, but I got here at the same time as the cops came rolling up. I saw them knocking down the door and everything.'

Tom's about twenty-five and quite good-looking, with black hair and a neat moustache. He's over six feet tall, and far too skinny for my taste, but he seems like a nice enough guy. He clearly loves his job and takes pictures even when there's nothing to see.

'Yeah, and I managed to find out most of the facts from one of the other reporters,' Dave tells me. 'It's a good job I've got friends, isn't it?'

'Who was that, then? I didn't see you with anyone.' Tom frowns.

Dave gives him a blank look at first and then shakes his head. 'You were taking more snaps at the time, I think.'

'*Photographs*,' Tom corrects him. 'Snaps are what amateurs take. Professional photographers take photographs. The clue's in the name.'

Dave rolls his eyes. They often have this conversation. I'm sure Dave just says it to wind Tom up—and it works every time.

'It's a good job your contact at the police station's on the ball,' I remark, smiling at Dave.

'Yeah, he told me all this was going down before they'd even finished their briefing. The man's a diamond.'

'I'll say.' I can't help being impressed. Dave's got some great mates all over the place, and the guy at the station gives him some brilliant tips. It's probably how Dave's become an award-winning journalist. He's climbed the editorial ladder quite quickly and is very well thought of in the office. 'What's his name?' It suddenly occurs to me that this guy might be a friend of James.

'I can't divulge my sources,' Dave says, shaking his head. 'It's unethical.'

'Just like a cop informing a newspaper reporter that something's about to happen and where to go to get the scoop,' Tom points out, his eyebrows raised.

'Sometimes, the cops actually *need* stuff to go into the papers. It can help flush out criminals and all sorts of things.'

'So why don't they tell *all* the reporters then, get it in all the papers?' I ask. 'I mean, if they need word to get around that's got to be the best way; get it into as many papers as possible. And the radio and TV, of course. They should tell everyone.'

'They do get it out on all the media. That's what *we're* here for. To report on it to the masses.' Dave almost snaps at me.

'But they should tell everyone when they tell you, so all the different reporters can get here from the start.' I'm frowning at him now. Can't he see that I'm making perfect sense?

He shakes his head. 'You don't get it. If everyone knew then they'd all get the scoop. This way, I—I mean *we*—get the best coverage and boost the *Chronicle*'s readership. And talking of which, it's time we were heading back to get all this down on paper. We've missed the early edition, but we can get it in tonight's if we hurry.'

He turns and breaks into a sprint in the direction we came. I can just see his head bobbing above the crowd who have clearly realised there's nothing more to see and have made their way to the mouth of the cul-de-sac where several people are huddled together chatting.

I get a sinking feeling, knowing how far it is to the office. And if I don't keep up with Dave, I'll get lost. Glancing back at Tom, I'm surprised he doesn't seem to be in such a rush to leave, as he slips his mobile back into his pocket.

'Aren't you coming?' I ask, hoping he knows the way. I look back up the road and notice that Dave's already disappeared.

'Do I look stupid?' Tom asks incredulously. 'The taxi will be here in three minutes. We'll probably get back about the same time as Usain Bolt over there'—he gestures towards the last place we saw Dave, '—but without the sweat.'

My heart lightens. 'I love the way you think, Tom.'

***

I spend the afternoon writing up the story and looking over Tom's shoulder at the photos he took. Dave also writes up the story. I don't know how he does it but his has much more detail in it than my version—I suppose he must've got the information from his journalist-friends. I wish I had contacts like that. I also wish I had a row of trophies lined across the front of my desk, like Dave. He's obviously worked hard to get so much recognition.

I can't help thinking how lovely it would be to attend an award ceremony. The men all wear black tie and the women have gorgeous, designer dresses. The thought suddenly loses its appeal as I remember something.

'I just need to make a call,' I tell Dave, placing my story on top of his. I'm secretly hoping that, if the editor reads mine first, he might be so impressed with it that he won't even bother to look at Dave's. I'd love to have my name in the paper as the writer. Heck, I'd like to have my name in the paper for anything.

He grunts in response, and I dive out of the door and head for the staff room. It's late so there shouldn't be many people around. I'm right, the room's empty. Good. I quickly call Cassie, my best friend and flatmate.

'Shouldn't you be working?' She sounds cheerful.

'I meant to tell you something. I've seen the perfect dress for the policeman's ball next week,' I tell her, then bite my lip.

'It's not a bloody policeman's ball, you idiot. I keep telling you it's a charity gala night. It said so on the ticket.'

'Well, it's the same thing, isn't it?' I frown.

'No. Policemen don't have balls anymore,' she says with a giggle. 'Remember the joke? Woman pulled over for speeding offers to buy a ticket to the ball as a bribe, but the copper tells her policemen don't have balls?' She's gone off in hysterics again. She does this every time anyone mentions that joke. She thinks it's funny because James is a policeman and we haven't 'done anything' yet. She reckons... well, you can guess.

'About the dress.' I need to keep this conversation on track; I haven't got long.

'How much?' I can tell she's rolling her eyes without even seeing her.

'Just under £700.'

Silence.

'I know,' I say, 'but I need to make a really good impression. James is a sergeant, after all. As his partner I need to look the part, don't I? I can't let him down.'

'You can't let him know how much you're planning to spend on the dress, either,' she says.

'I have to. It would seem like going behind his back otherwise—and besides, he's bound to ask. You know how he is with money.' I feel a lurch in my stomach. James is a lovely guy, but he has a real thing about not spending too much. It's not as if he's poor or anything—he's got a good job and a nice little flat in Fulham. He's just waiting for the sale of his other house to go through and he'll be rich. In the meantime, he seems to think he has to hang on to every penny.

'You know what he'll say.' Cassie's right. He won't be happy.

'But wait 'til you see it,' I whine. 'It's gorgeous.'

'Tell *him* that.'

'I will. Tonight. I thought I'd go round and surprise him after work. I'll make sure he's in a good mood and then I'll just casually drop it into the conversation. Maybe after a couple of drinks.'

'It'll take more than a couple.' Cassie doesn't sound convinced.

'I've got to try. I need to wear *something*.'

'Well, good luck. Rob and I are going to the pub tonight anyway, but I shouldn't be too late.'

'Okay, babe. Have fun.'

I quickly hang up as I see Dave loitering in the doorway.

'We should just make it in time for tonight's issue,' he says.

'Great.' I sigh with relief. I really thought I might have blown it for both of us. I walk towards him.

'I'm heading out,' he announces. 'Just a bit of networking.'

'Can I come? I'd love to meet some of your contacts.' I can feel my heart pumping a little quicker at the thought. This could be my big chance. Well—it could have been if Dave wasn't shaking his head and looking at me as if I'd gone mad or something.

'No, it's just a social thing really. I like to keep in touch with them—you know, oil the cogs and all that.' He's already walking towards the lift.

'Okay. I'll just hang around here then.'

I can tell he's not even listening as he's already on his way. I wander back into the newsroom.

'What's up?' Tom looks surprised to see me.

'Dave's just gone to meet up with some more of his contacts,' I tell him, glumly. 'I wanted to tag along— you know, see how he recruits them and what makes him choose them.'

Tom chuckles. 'He's never going to reveal his sources to you or anyone else,' he says. 'Why would he? He's got friends in high places who give him the nod whenever something interesting is about to happen. That's how he gets the best stories and earns the big money. He's not about to share that with anyone, don't take it personally, love.'

I huff. Tom sounds so patronising. What makes things even worse though, is that it all makes sense. Why would Dave introduce me to the people who have helped make him such a big name? It's clearly every man for himself in this business.

'What're you doing?' I ask, watching him scroll through his screen. If I can't pick up anything from Dave, maybe I could learn a thing or two from Tom.

'Just having another look through these photos from today,' he says, idly.

'Can I look?'

'Of course.'

I'm glad to notice that he's not as secretive about everything as Dave is. I grab my lunch from my bag and go and sit next to Tom at his little desk by the window.

I recognise the house in the cul-de-sac, tucked away in a lovely little area. I wonder whose ill-gotten gains paid for it. Any of the four guys being marched out the front door and over to the police van could be the owner. They all look really smart—not at all how I expected drug-dealers to appear.

'Who's this bloke?' I ask, pointing to the sandy-haired guy who was the last one to be taken in.

'One of those scum, I suppose.' Tom shrugs.

'But he doesn't look like them, does he? I mean, look at his clothes. And his hair's greasy, and that watch is obviously fake. He doesn't look like he belongs with them at all.' I frown. The more I think about it, the less it seems like he's one of their gang at all.

'Perhaps he's a user. Probably buying off them at the time they got stung.' Tom looks disinterested.

'But why would the cops take him in as well? They'd have to have evidence of him buying the stuff off them to arrest him for that. They must know he's not one of the gang they've come to pick up.'

'I suppose so,' Tom purses his lips. 'I'd be surprised if they saw anything like that, though. I was there just as they arrived, and they were straight in and out. Picked up the scumbags and hauled them out to the van. I didn't see anyone hanging about in there to verify what they were actually doing.'

'The copper who gave the statement told me he was one of the gang, but I don't think that's right.' I remember the way that inspector spoke to me and shudder. He obviously didn't like me asking questions, but I think I had a valid point.

'Doesn't look that way to me.' Tom took a closer look, scrolling through a few pictures. The young lad was brought out a few seconds after the rest of the gang. 'I don't know what the hell he was doing inside that house, but he certainly doesn't appear to be one of that lot.' He pointed to the men in suits in the previous picture, as they were being marched to the van. 'I think you're right, Libby. Something's not right there.'

2

Dave hasn't returned when it's time to go home and I can't help wondering what he's doing—and who with. Still, I've got better things to worry about now, as I pull on my jacket and grab my bags. I'm going straight to my boyfriend's house tonight—which should be a pleasant experience, but I need to bring up the subject of spending money, which is always a bit dodgy with James. He's not stingy or anything, but he is, let's just say, *careful* with money.

I hop on the Tube and soon arrive at Fulham. It's not far to James' little flat and I notice his rusty Ford Focus parked outside. Next to it is a shiny, black Mercedes. I giggle at how different the two cars look and press the buzzer to his flat. James was finishing work at lunchtime today, so I'm hoping he's all chilled and in a good mood.

My faith wanes when I arrive outside his front door and hear raised voices. I'm tempted to turn tail and run until I realise that one of the voices is female. He's got a woman in there! My jaw tenses and I knock hard on the wooden door.

The woman's voice becomes quite shrill and I suppose she's not happy at being interrupted while she's yelling at my fella. *Tough!*

James flings open the door and gapes at me. 'Libby.'

I try to see past him to catch a glimpse of the mysterious woman I've just caught him with, but he bars my way.

'Hello.' It's about all I can manage. I clear my throat. 'Is everything all right?' I frown at him, knowing full well it isn't, but wondering if he's about to admit it.

'Come in.' He stands back and lets me enter the little hallway.

A woman with silky red hair is standing in his kitchen, drinking coffee. She scowls at me, marring her beautiful face. My stomach lurches and I feel my whole body turn hot.

'Let me introduce my ex-wife, Suzanne.' James follows me into the kitchen, clearly reading my mind.

I'm not sure whether I'm relieved that she's his ex or disappointed that she's so beautiful. A bit of both, I think.

'I'm Liberty Lawrence.' I feign a smile and hold out my hand to shake hers.

She looks disparagingly at my fingers and then treats me to a very weak handshake with her free hand.

'Libby's my friend,' James says, walking over to the kettle and making me a cup of coffee.

I feel a pang in my chest. His *friend*? Is that all? I thought—or rather, *hoped*—I was a bit more than that. In fact, just a few weeks ago I was actually convinced I was about to become his fiancée, but that turned out to be a serious misunderstanding. I get a lot of those. I still haven't forgiven James for the look of horror that crossed his face as he realised what I was thinking. Well, you couldn't blame me really—what else is a girl to think when a handsome hunk kneels at her feet with a diamond ring in his hand? See? It's not just me.

Suzanne looks unconvinced about the 'friend' thing, which secretly cheers me up a little.

'We were just discussing the house.' James doesn't look pleased about it, as he hands me my coffee. 'Suzanne's having trouble selling it.'

'The housing market's not very buoyant right now,' she says, airily. 'Christmas is on its way. No one wants to move at this time of year.'

I frown, remembering an article I read recently in *Cosmopolitan*.

'I thought it was a good time to sell,' I say. 'A recent survey showed that people are always in a hurry to buy a house if they can move in for Christmas. If they viewed now, they'd have enough time to complete before the big day, surely? I thought this would be the best time to promote it.'

James looks surprised and gives his ex-wife a questioning look.

'Maybe it depends on the area,' she says hurriedly.

'No, it was a national survey,' I point out. 'In fact, the *Daily Chronicle* is going to run a big housing feature over the next couple of months to encourage people to buy in time for Christmas. There's going to be featured homes for sale, as well as articles on makeovers and decorating. They're even going to do something on making your garden look good for the winter.'

'Well that should help.' James' mouth twitches at the edges as he peers at Suzanne who looks like she'd happily kill me right this minute. I guess this wasn't what she wanted to hear.

'We can hope.'

She's worse than I am at false smiles, I notice.

'Well, we're not reducing the price any further,' James says, resolutely. He takes his empty cup to the sink.

Suzanne nods. 'I agree. We can't afford to make a loss on it, and we need to make enough to get me somewhere decent to live.'

James frowns at her. 'Have you found anywhere yet?'

'No.' She looks despondent. 'I don't see the point until the house sells. I'll need somewhere in the same area, though.'

'Why?' He leans over and takes her cup from her.

'It's where all my friends are, silly. And work. I need to be close to the office.'

'What friends?' He looks amazed. 'I don't remember you having friends in Richmond. Most of them were in town. And you can always commute to work. You've got a decent car and the Tube's great for getting around. You're not tied at all.'

She bites her lip angrily. 'There you go again. Telling me what I can and can't do.' Her voice gets louder as she waves her arms around. 'You don't know anything about my friends. Why would you? You never took much notice of what I was doing. And there's no point in spending money on travel when I can live near to work, is there?'

I stare at her, my mouth wide open. I thought it was just James who seemed to worry about every penny, but now I see otherwise.

'But it's a waste of money if you're spending more on your house just because of the area. You're not saving anything, are you? You could get a small flat, like this one, and take the Tube to work like everyone else. In fact, there's no reason to keep the Merc. You could make some good money if you sold it.'

She stares at him, horrified. 'Why would I do that?'

'Because you don't need it.' He sounds very calm—quite the opposite of her.

'How dare you? You want me to give up my home *and* my car, now, do you? I can't believe you could be so downright selfish!' She's screeching at him now, as she grabs her Gucci handbag from the counter and stalks towards the door. 'You won't be happy until I'm poor and living on the streets!'

'Goodbye, Suzanne.' James follows her down the hallway where she waits for him to open the door.

I can't resist peeping around the kitchen door to watch her go.

'You're a cruel man, James Harper. Mean and cruel.' She flounces out, and James slams the door behind her.

I wash my own cup while I wait for him to return to the kitchen. When he does, his lovely face is tense and pale. I get the distinct impression this would be a really bad time to mention the seven-hundred-pound dress I've got my eye on.

3

Well, it looks like we're not going to have the cosy evening I was hoping for. James is really quiet and I'm wondering if I should just leave. I don't want to go, though. I want to know what's going on.

'Shall we order Chinese?' he suggests when I join him in the living room.

I nod. I'm really not in the mood to cook right now, and I can see he wouldn't be much company if we went out. At least he might be able to open up a little in his own home. 'Chicken chow mein, please.'

He phones the order through and sits next to me on the sofa.

'Sorry about Suzanne,' he says, running a hand through his hair.

'I wasn't expecting to see her. Had she been here long?' It occurs to me that she could have been with him all afternoon for all I knew.

He shakes his head. 'Not really, though any time at all's too long with Suzanne.'

I snuggle into him, and he puts an arm around me and kisses the top of my head. We haven't kissed properly since I arrived, and although James isn't overly affectionate, I feel a little disappointed.

'She's very pretty,' I remark, thinking how sophisticated she appeared.

James says nothing, which is probably a good thing. So, I continue.

'Did she just come to tell you the house still hasn't sold?' It seems to me that it's a bit of an odd thing to visit someone about. Surely, a phone call would suffice?

'Mostly.'

I can tell he doesn't want to talk about it, but I somehow think I've got a right to know if something's going on.

'What else, then?' I can't help it. I know I should respect his privacy, but something's certainly got to him.

He sighs. 'Oh, just the usual. Money and stuff.'

'Where does she work?'

'She's an admin manager at Harrow and Freeman.'

I've heard of them. 'They're an import and export company, aren't they? Based near Richmond Park.'

'Yeah. That's them.'

'She must be on good money working there, surely? Especially as a manager?' My mind drifts back to my previous 'managerial' job. I wasn't paid very well, although it was the hotel and catering industry—and I was only a *junior* manager.

'She does all right. Especially with the maintenance I give her. I don't think she's exactly starving, despite her protestations.'

I slip out from under his arm to face him, my whole body heating up. 'You give her *maintenance*? Why?'

He chews his cheek, not looking me in the eye. 'I just want to make sure she's okay for money that's all.'

'Why?'

He huffs. 'She's my ex-wife and has a large house to maintain. I couldn't just leave her to fend for herself.'

'But you caught her with another man. She's hardly by herself, is she?' There's an edge to my voice I can't avoid as my blood boils.

He shakes his head. 'No, they split up soon after I left her. She's on her own. I know what she did, and I know we got divorced, but I still...'

'Love her? Is that what it is? You still *love* Suzanne?'

He faces me now, his eyes wide and his mouth open. 'No.' He looks astonished. 'Of course, I don't love her. We're over. I told you that.'

'But you still feel a duty to pay her maintenance and let her live in that big house?' I feel like crying. This has all gone horribly wrong.

'It's not like that,' he insists, putting an arm out and stroking my hair. 'You're the one I care about now, you know that.'

'Do I? I didn't know you were still supporting your ex-wife when she's got a perfectly good job and a really nice roof over her head that you also paid for.' I feel like a sulky teenager right now, but I can't help it. This was a complete shock to me and I still don't understand it.

The buzzer sounds for the door.

'That'll be dinner.' James gets up and goes to answer it with a sigh.

I'm not sure I want to eat right now, but I can't leave with everything up in the air like this. It would only lead to us not speaking and me doing a lot of crying.

He returns with the food all plated up on a large tray, which he places on the coffee table. He also brings over a bottle of wine and a couple of glasses from the sideboard.

'Look,' he says, handing me my food. 'I only pay Suzanne a small amount to ensure she can meet the bills for the house. The utilities are quite high on a house that size, and I don't think it's fair for me to just up sticks and leave her to sort it all out. It's only temporary, until the house sells. That's why I wanted to know how much longer it would be. As soon as the house is gone, she'll be out of my life for good. She'll find her own place and get used to supporting herself.'

I get the impression he's thought this through while dishing up the dinner. I have to admit it makes sense, though. Although I've never actually seen their marital home, except in a few photos, I get the impression that it's quite lavish. Suzanne wouldn't settle for anything less, apparently.

We sit side by side eating our meal, and the atmosphere lightens a little. I find that food tends to have that effect on any situation. I've even got my appetite back—Mr Po makes a mean chow mein.

'So, tell me about your day,' James says, his tone a bit more relaxed as he pours the wine.

'It was interesting,' I admit. 'We went to a drugs bust on Withywood Way and saw the men being led out to the police van.'

He nods. 'Nasty business.'

'You know about it?' I perk up, wondering if I might garner some inside information on the case.

'I know *of* it,' he corrects.

'We missed the speech from the chief inspector, so I didn't get many details, but Dave's journalist friends filled him in. Trouble is, he doesn't share that sort of information with me. He won't even tell me who his friends are or introduce me to them or anything. I don't know how I'm supposed to pick this stuff up.'

James chuckles. He tends to do that a lot when I'm around, and I'm never quite sure why. On this occasion, I don't mind though. At least he's cheering up a bit.

'You'll get there,' he assures me. 'I'm sure you'll find out stuff he wouldn't even think of.'

At first, I think he's just patronising me, but then I remember something.

'Actually, there was something a bit weird,' I say between mouthfuls of noodles. 'After they put the four men in the van, they marched out another guy who didn't look like one of them at all. His clothes were different, he was much younger, and he just didn't fit with them, somehow. I asked the inspector about him, but he wasn't much help.' I roll my eyes at the thought of the irritable policeman. 'He seemed to think there was nothing odd about it at all, but I'm not so sure.'

James has stopped eating and is staring at me. 'How do you mean he didn't fit in?'

I put down my fork—I've never got used to chopsticks and would starve if I had to tackle the darn things again—and count out the reasons on my fingers.

'Well, first of all, his clothes were all scruffy and theirs were neat. They looked more like businessmen. Secondly, his clothes were cheap, but theirs were Armani and Ralph Lauren—and I'm sure one of the men had a Salvatore Ferragamo tie on.'

James chuckles again. I frown at him. I'm sure he's not taking me seriously at all, just like that stupid chief inspector.

'I tried to tell the copper, but he pointed out the young guy's watch—he only thought it was a real Rolex. The man's an idiot. It was obviously fake. You could see the colour rubbing off the strap even from that distance.'

I pick up my fork indignantly and resume my meal.

'Is that it? The guy's innocent because he wore a fake watch?' James' lips are twitching at the corners, and I can see the twinkle in his eyes that tells me he's teasing me again.

'Not just that.' I point my fork at him, which is loaded with a chunk of green pepper. 'I actually heard him *say* he wasn't with them. He was trying to tell the cops, but they wouldn't listen.'

James bursts out laughing, and just to make matters worse, the pepper drops off my fork and lands in my lap. *Damn!* I huff and move my plate back onto the coffee table so I can clean up the mess. It was covered in sauce and I just know it's going to stain. That's all I need.

***

By the time I emerge from the bathroom where I've been desperately trying to soak the sauce out of my trousers while also trying not to make it look like I've wet myself, James is in a much better mood.

'Come and sit down,' he says with a big grin.

I snuggle into him and am rewarded by him tipping my head up and giving me a lingering kiss on the lips. I love it when he does that. It makes me feel all gooey and tingly inside. Sometimes, it makes me feel 'other things' too.

'Are you going to look into the case?' I ask when I finally get my breath back.

His body sags a little. 'I'm not privy to every single arrest. That one at Withywood Way has nothing to do with me. Not really.'

I look up at him in surprise. 'What does that mean? *Not really.*'

He's stroking my shoulder with his thumb, and I'm not sure if it's out of affection or nervousness.

He leans forward, taking his wine from the coffee table. 'It's just that, we only get involved in certain things. And specific aspects of cases. Not always the whole thing. I'm a detective. I don't ask police constables why they arrested particular people. They do their job and I do mine.' He takes a large gulp of his Cabernet Sauvignon.

'But it's a drugs bust. Surely, you need to be involved in *that*?' I gawp at him.

'I'm not the only detective in the force, you know, Libby. Other people get involved in cases, too. I'm not a one-man band.'

He's shaking his head at me, and all I can think of is what he'd look like with cymbals strapped to his knees and a large drum on his chest with a harmonica attached. Added to that his po-face and smart clothes, and I just can't stop giggling.

He rolls his eyes. 'Now what's funny?'

'You wouldn't get it,' I tell him, reaching for my wine.

'You need to be careful following stories about stuff like that,' James says, once I've got my mouth too full to object. 'You'll be coming across some shady characters. Some of them are downright dangerous. I take it you'll be accompanied by this Dave guy on all your jobs?'

I swallow quickly before he can say anything else. I feel like he's taking the advantage, going on at me when I can't answer back. I raise my eyebrows, facing him head-on.

'Firstly, I'm only covering stories, not interviewing the criminals,' I say. 'Although... come to think of it... that would be a great scoop if I could.' I stare at him. 'Do you think there's any way—'

'No,' he says flatly. 'No way whatsoever.'

Damn! What's the point in going out with a detective sergeant if he can't pull a few strings? I suddenly get a fuzzy feeling in my stomach, which reminds me *exactly* what the point of going out with him is. He's amazing!

'Was there a secondly?' he asks warily.

I think back for a moment, trying to regain my train of thought.

'Oh, yes. No.'

'What?'

'No.'

'No, what?' He's frowning hard. He does that a lot when he's with me.

I roll my eyes. 'Keep up, Sherlock. You asked if Dave would be with me when I investigated all my stories. No, he won't.'

He looks at me indignantly. 'I thought the *police* investigated crime. You're supposed to report on it.'

'I'm an *investigative* reporter,' I remind him. 'I investigate stories as well as write about them.'

'Yes, but you're supposed to investigate what the police are doing about them. You can't take the law into your own hands, Libby. Let us do our job and you do yours.'

I huff. I hate it when he gets all condescending with me. 'Okay. So, what exactly *are* the police doing about the Withywood case? That guy's definitely not involved. Have you let him go yet?' I raise my eyebrows questioningly, wishing I hadn't left my bag in the kitchen as I could really use my notebook right now.

'You're not supposed to be asking *me* questions!' He shakes his head again—I swear it'll fall off one day if he doesn't stop doing that.

'Why not? You're the police, aren't you?'

'I'm also off-duty. And in my own home. I don't need the paparazzi round here hounding me for stories, thanks very much!'

'I am *not* the paparazzi, thank you. I'm a serious, investigative reporter and I'm just doing my job.' I feel all high and mighty for some reason.

'Well, don't.'

'What? Do my job?'

'Yes. Not tonight. You're off-duty as well, remember?'

He pulls me closer to him and I melt in his arms.

'But you will ask about that guy, won't you?' I manage before disappearing into a puddle of mush.

'We'll see.'

His lips are over mine in a nanosecond, not giving me time to reply. It's actually just as well, as I've completely forgotten what the whole conversation was about all of a sudden. James feels warm, soft, and loving. Nothing else matters right now.

<u>4</u>

I don't remember what time I got home last night but I know it was late. Cassie was already in bed. I knew I'd pay for it this morning, though, as I struggle to get up and shower for work.

My body feels stiff and I dread running around London again. I wish Dave would take the taxis like Tom. In fact, I wish Dave was a bit more helpful like Tom, too.

I'm wearing H&M trousers today with a Monsoon blouse and my little Chanel-style jacket. *Honestly, you wouldn't know it wasn't the real thing if you saw it.* I look over at my Kurt Geigers and frown.

'Can't you take them back to the shop?' Cassie says, emerging from the shower and joining me in my room. She's clearly checked my line of sight. 'They're obviously not fit for purpose.'

I shrug. 'I don't really think cross-country running is the purpose of Kurt Geigers.'

She raises her eyebrows. 'Cross-country? I thought you worked in London?'

'It doesn't feel like it when you're trudging down back alleys and dodgy footpaths,' I say, gloomily. 'Not to mention through other people's gardens.'

Cassie comes over, sits beside me on the bed and gives me a hug. She gives great hugs. She smells all clean and soapy.

'Aren't you enjoying the job?' she asks kindly.

'I am, actually. We're covering a really interesting drugs raid. I think they've arrested someone who's innocent. Or, at least, not involved like the others.' My mind drifts back to the desperate expression on the young guy's face and I feel awful that I couldn't do anything to help him.

Cassie's eyes widen. 'Wow! I didn't know you'd be involved in stuff like that. I thought it would be more like who's wearing what and where.'

'I'm supposed to be getting to that,' I assure her. 'But as I'm new I'm having a go at different things. Dave's mentoring me for now in the news office and he's more into this sort of stuff. I can't wait to work with Siobhan. Hopefully, I'll get to write more about fashion and make-up with her.'

Cassie nods. 'Actually, you're well-suited to the investigative stuff. Look at how you solved the case of the fake Louboutins *and* the stolen money at the hotel.'

She's smiling broadly, like she always does when she talks about it. I didn't really solve it, but James said I was a great help with the investigations. That's how I got the job at the *Chronicle.* A job I'm about to lose if I don't get moving.

'I've got something you could wear. Hang on.' Cassie pops back into her own room and reappears a few minutes later with her Saint Laurent Loulous. They're little, black ankle boots in cracked, gloss leather and they're a dream to wear—I've borrowed them before.

I gawp at her. 'Are you sure? They're worth a fortune.' Cassie's from a much richer family than me.

She shrugs. 'I haven't worn them in ages. You might as well get some use out of them. It'll save having to wear those again.' She gestures to my scruffy-looking Kurt Geigers, which I'd kicked into the corner of the room last night.

'Yes, but, what if they get ruined?' I frown at her.

'I told you. I don't wear them anymore. I'll have to replace them anyway.' She sounds so matter of fact, I can't resist giving her another hug.

'You're the best,' I tell her, squeezing her tightly.

The boots look great with my outfit, although, to be fair, they'd look great with any outfit. I feel much more cheerful as I throw my Radley over my shoulder and grab my Marc Jacobs.

'By the way, what did James say about the dress?' Cassie looks all eager-eyed, but I've just got a sinking feeling in my stomach.

'No time to discuss it,' I tell her, leaving the room and heading for the front door.

'What? No time last night with him, or now with me?' I can hear the confusion in her voice, but I have to go. I really haven't got time for this conversation—or the lecture that I know will ensue from it.

'No,' I reply with a shrug as I leave the flat. 'See you tonight.'

I'm glad she was only dressed in a towel as I'm sure Cassie would've followed me otherwise. She's a fab friend and I don't know where I'd be without her—or her shoes—but right now I can't afford to be late, and I know I definitely would be if I had to explain everything to her.

I'm determined not to give Dave any reason to complain about me today, as I head for the Tube. It's crammed, as usual, and I stand next to a man with really sweaty armpits. Already? The day's only just started, for goodness' sake! He's wearing a suit and carrying a briefcase, so I'm guessing he hasn't just finished a night shift somewhere, and the fact he's clean-shaven makes me think he must have had a wash recently. But the smell is sickening, and I have to look the other way to try to avoid breathing in the contaminated air in case I puke. Cassie's a lovely girl not to worry about me running the leather off the soles of her Loulous, but I think she'd draw the line at me getting them covered in vomit!

***

Dave's already at his desk when I arrive at the *Daily Chronicle*—no surprise there. He's looking at his computer screen, frowning—no surprise there, either.

'What's up?' I plonk my Marc Jacobs on the floor next to my seat and pop the Radley and my jacket on the back of my chair. I don't sit down but stand behind Dave. He's looking at some of the pictures Tom took of the drugs raid yesterday.

'They let one of them go,' Dave mumbles.

My heart leaps. 'The young guy?'

Dave looks round at me then, raising his eyebrows in surprise. 'How did you know?'

I want to tell him I've got friends in high places too, assuming that James has had a hand in this, but I daren't. James would go mad if I told anyone he'd ensured someone went free just because I asked him to. My heart flutters at the thought though. He knew I was worried about the guy, so he pulled out all the stops. I think I might love that man just a little bit more now.

'We said he didn't look like he belonged with them. Libby pointed out how different he looked from the others,' Tom interjects, looking over from his desk.

'Really?' Dave's eyebrows look like they're almost on the top of his bald head now.

'Yes.' I try to sound casual and hide the smile I feel twitching at my lips. 'The chief inspector ignored me when I told him, though.'

Dave frowns again. 'You *told* him?' He doesn't look happy.

I shrug. 'I might have mentioned it. He hadn't noticed how different the young guy looked; he just assumed he was one of them.'

Dave shakes his head with a sigh. 'Libby, we're not here to tell the cops how to do their job. We just report on what happens, that's all. You can't try to influence an arrest.' He sounds like James now, which irritates the hell out of me.

'Well, it looks like I was right, doesn't it? Why else did they let him go?' I slump into my chair.

'The four guys are well-known to the cops, who were waiting for their moment to strike. They'd got a tip-off that there was a major deal going on and had to catch all four of them together along with the drugs.' Tom wheels his chair over to the table I share with Dave.

'And they got it, I presume?' Excitement roils in my stomach to think I was actually there at the time.

Tom nods. 'Yep. Looks like they were caught red-handed. The other guy was nothing to do with them, though.' He purses his lips.

'So, why was he there?' I'm desperate to know.

Tom smirks. 'Turns out he was hiding in the attic. He'd been living up there for a few days. The gang were abroad until the night before last, and this guy managed to break in and make himself at home.'

'Oh, no!' I put my hand to my mouth. 'So, he didn't know who lived there?'

Dave shakes his head. 'Apparently not. At least that's his story. The cops interrogated him but couldn't come up with anything, and the gang even admitted they didn't know him. They had no idea he was squatting until the cops told them.'

'Of all the houses he could've chosen. What a shame it happened to be theirs.' I feel even more sorry for the guy.

'Yeah, the cops have been questioning him all night about anything he might have seen or heard while he was up there, but he reckons he knew nothing,' Dave says.

'No wonder he looked so scared—especially when they threw him in the back of the police van with the gang.' I close my eyes momentarily, imagining the scene. They'd want to know what he was doing there, and he could hardly tell them. It must have been awful for him.

'He wasn't even done for breaking and entering as there was no sign of how he got in. I don't think the cops are happy at having to let him go. Seems a bit suspicious that he was there all that time and didn't even hear anything.' Dave shakes his head. 'Doesn't ring true, if you ask me.'

I open my eyes and stare at him. 'You still think he's guilty? Of what?' I feel a little indignant about his insinuations. It was obvious the guy was innocent—am I the only one who can see it?

Dave shrugs. 'I dunno. I just don't trust him that's all.'

A horrid thought suddenly occurs to me. 'Do you think he's safe out on the streets after everyone knows he was with them? Surely other gangs might be after him?'

'He'll have gone to ground by now,' Tom assures me. 'He's probably up north or something if he's got any sense.'

'I really hope you're right.' I hate the thought of him being in danger because of the police falsely arresting him.

'Shame. It'd be a good story if we could speak to him—get his side of things.' Dave sighs.

'Expose him even further, you mean? Put his life in more danger than it already is? I should think the papers are the last people he'd want to speak to,' I protest, horrified.

'Doesn't matter now, anyway. Like Tom said, he's disappeared off the face of the earth.' Dave frowns, seemingly oblivious to how angry he's made me.

'Good,' I snap back.

I can feel their eyes on me as I fire up my computer, but I don't look at either of them. The swish of Tom's wheels tells me he's returned to his own desk, and I wish I could go over there with him. I really don't want to work alongside Dave right now. I'm beginning to think he got all those trophies from other people's misery. Perhaps, I'm in the wrong job, after all. I certainly don't want to be responsible for endangering anyone.

***

The morning passes slowly, and I'm dying to ring James and thank him for freeing that guy. I've studied the pictures of him over and over and it's blatantly obvious he wasn't involved in all that stuff. He looked terrified when they bundled him into that van, and I can see why. I can't help wondering where he is now, and I desperately want to check with James if they've got him in a safe house or something. I daren't make a personal call with Dave breathing down my neck, though, and I certainly don't want him to know I had anything to do with freeing that guy.

The office we work in is quite big and incredibly busy, with people coming and going all the time. I'm cheered up when Ben and Rob come in a bit later, smiling. Rob's Cassie's boyfriend and Ben's a lovely guy who works alongside him. Both are really handsome, too.

'Hey, Miss Marple, how's it going?' Ben grins, coming over to give me a hug.

'Great. What're you guys up to?' I ask, giving Rob a squeeze, too.

'We're about to kidnap Tom,' Ben says, as Tom starts putting some equipment into his bag. 'He's coming to take some pictures of people selling houses.'

'Well, pretending to, anyway,' Rob cuts in with a snigger. 'It's an interview with an estate agent and then a pic of someone who's recently bought a house through them. Part of this big campaign we're running.'

I wish I was involved in that. It reminds me of last night. '*Are* houses selling at the moment, then?' I ask.

'Oh, yeah. The one next door to me sold last week,' Tom pipes up, slinging his bag over his shoulder. 'And a couple of the flats in the next street are under offer already. They seem to be selling like hot cakes.'

'It makes sense,' Ben adds. 'I mean, if you're going to move you want to be in by Christmas, don't you? Especially families with kids. What sort of Christmas would they have if they've already packed all the decorations, and they're not going to get many new toys or anything when the parents are hoping to move in the near future?'

'True.' I feel a little sad at the thought of children not getting any presents because it would just be more stuff to pack and move. It doesn't seem fair, although, I suppose I can understand it. In a way. A very *unfair* way.

'What about high-end properties? Are they any more likely to sell this time of year?' I'm wondering why James' house is still on the market. It's been nearly a year, and they've already dropped the price.

'I don't see why not,' Rob says, pursing his lips, thoughtfully. 'Rich people want to be sorted by Christmas too, don't they? I'll ask the estate agent about it, actually. That might be another angle for a story.'

I smile. 'Thanks, I'd be interested to know.'

Dave glances over at me. 'Why? You're not planning on buying a mansion, are you?'

I roll my eyes. I'm still annoyed with him and I think he knows it. We've hardly spoken all morning, except for him telling me what to do, as usual. I ignore his question and just say goodbye to the others as they leave. Gosh, I wish I was going with them.

5

'We've got to go out again,' Dave declares, pocketing his phone. 'I just got a tip-off that there's some sort of domestic going on over on the Sandford estate.' He chuckles, 'Some woman's found her fella's been cheating and gone after him with a bread knife. Wants to chop off his manhood, apparently.'

I frown, remembering I've got Cassie's lovely Saint Laurent Loulous on today. I don't want to get them ruined just because of some modern-day Lorena Bobbitt.

'Is it far?' I ask, hopefully, standing up and putting on my jacket. It'll be nice to get out of the office but there are limits.

'Not really.'

I groan as I throw my Radley across my body and follow him out the door. I know what his interpretation of 'not really far' is and it's certainly not the same as mine!

'There might be some violence so you'll have to stay right back,' Dave says excitedly, as the lift takes us down to the ground floor.

I look up at him and notice his eyes shining. He's loving this.

50

'Do you know where they'll be now?' I ask as we get out of the lift.

'I've got an idea.'

Something tells me Dave's tip-off guy is more informed than the police.

'Should we get a taxi?' I suggest quickly, as a black cab passes us.

Dave frowns and I just know he was planning to break into a sprint at any moment.

'As you said, we need to stick together in case it's dangerous,' I add straight away.

He looks a little deflated, but nods anyway. Making good use of his height he hails a taxi and we clamber in. It's so nice not to have to race across town, but not so good when we end up stuck in traffic.

'We'll miss the whole thing at this rate,' Dave grumbles.

'What exactly are you expecting to see?' I frown at him, intrigued.

He leans forward. 'If this woman's as riled as I've heard there's no saying what she could do. A woman scorned is bad enough, but one with a bread knife in her hand is just downright lethal. Sounds like she's a bit of a head case, she could attack anyone for all we know. Either way, I want *us* to get the damn story.'

It makes a change for him to say 'us' instead of 'me', but I know that's what he really means. He's mad because he might not get the glory if we don't arrive in time. If *he's* heard about it then chances are other reporters will have, especially if the cops are involved. It's highly likely that someone else will get the scoop before we do.

'Has the guy actually been hurt?' I ask. 'If the ambulance and police are there we won't get a look in.'

Dave glances at his phone. 'I think he got away. They're after *her*, though. She ran out after him, brandishing the knife. There's a chance she might do something stupid with it, the state she's in.' Dave's eyes flash and he turns to the driver. 'Drop us off here, mate. We'll walk.'

Damn!

I know when Dave says 'walk' he actually means 'run' and I immediately regret voicing my concerns.

'Come on,' he says, as soon as he's paid the driver. 'This way.'

He breaks into a sprint and I try to keep up with him. The best I can hope for is to keep him in sight as his bald head bobs above the crowd. I don't know this area at all—it's pretty seedy from all accounts, and I'm actually quite nervous at the thought of getting lost around here.

It's hard to get up the road, as most people here are quite rude, deliberately barring my way, so I have to keep running out into the road to get around them. There's also a lot of litter here, and I almost trip a couple of times on bags of fast-food rubbish left in the street. I follow Dave round a corner and am relieved when the road opens out a little. There are several blocks of flats ahead, and I guess that's where we're headed. I just hope we don't have to go inside. The thought of a mad woman with a knife in an enclosed space sends jitters right through me. As does the thought of climbing stairs. The lifts never work in these places, and if they do, they're so full of urine you can't use them without the risk of suffocation from the stench.

We actually go around the back of the flats to where the police are just joining a small crowd who have congregated on some wasteland. Dave's immediately right at the front, as usual, and I try to elbow my way towards him. Again, I come up against some really horrid people who refuse to budge, and in the end, I have to go all the way round the outside of the crowd to try to reach him.

A movement in the shadow of one of the flats catches my eye and I look around to see a figure skulking along the wall, going in the direction we just came from, away from the action—which I still haven't seen, I might add.

I gasp. It's him. Attic-guy. He catches my eye and shakes his head. I pride myself on being a bit telepathic, and I understand he's telling me not to draw any attention towards him. I nod, letting him know I understand and the next thing I know he's disappeared. Just like that. One minute he's in the shadows, and the next he's gone. Or is he? Maybe he's still in the shadows but if he is, I'm blowed if I can see him.

'Libby!' Dave's spotted me and I look up to see him waving his arms, frantically.

I run around the side of the crowd and join him, staring at the empty wasteland in front of us. What on earth was all the fuss about? There's nothing there. Everyone's just staring at nothing. I look at Dave, but he's peering at something in the distance.

'What is it?' I ask.

'Shh.'

Great. Now I'm not allowed in on the secret. I look in the same direction as him, but there's definitely nothing there. I feel quite peeved and wish I'd gone after attic-guy after all. That would have been much more interesting. I could ask him all sorts of questions. *Did you see any receipts for their Armani suits while you were at the house?* Because if he did, we'd be able to see whether or not they were getting a discount. If so, there'd be a good chance the people selling them might have some sort of deal going on with them, and that could tie them in with the gang. There could be more to this than just drug dealing—as if that's not bad enough. *Did the fake Rolex come from the house?* Because if they were dealing in fake goods, the cops could find their suppliers and shut down the racket—with tons more arrests, possibly. *Did any of them talk in their sleep?* That would be a sign of a troubled mind, which means that one of them might be feeling guilty or worried about what they were up to. That guy would be their weakest link and the one the cops would most want to talk to—they'd get a lot more info from him than the hard men.

I huff as I look around at the wilderness in front of me. There's a small, muddy hill not far from where we are, and that's what everyone seems to be staring at. I wonder if this knifewoman is hiding behind it. She must be pretty small if she is.

Over to the left, there's a battered old car that looks like it's been there for donkey's years. It's even got grass and weeds growing in it. To the right, there's nothing but dried mud with bits of grass growing through in places. We'd see if anyone went over there, so she's got to be at this end. I'd have gone for the car if it was me. You could use the wing mirrors to see if anyone was coming, even though they are smashed. And there are more places to hide inside and out. Also, if the going got tough you could always pull off bits of engine or whatever and throw them at someone. Yep, the car would be much better than a little hillock with nowhere else to go.

A fence runs horizontally several feet from the hill. It goes from the back of the flats, across the wasteland and down to some houses, where it becomes the back fence for their gardens.

'Is she really behind the hill?' I whisper to Dave.

'Shh,' he says again, irritably.

I pout. It was okay for him to call me over, but I can't even whisper without being told to shush. That's not fair. And I'm only trying to do my job and find out what's going on. It seems pretty pointless just standing here staring at a stupid hill.

The cops are making us keep our distance, with more of them arriving by the minute. We're being ordered back even farther, and soon we won't be able to see a thing as the cops are starting to line up in front of us.

I hear clicking from some professional-looking photographers. I don't recognise any of them as being from the *Daily Chronicle,* but I don't know many people yet anyway, so they could be.

I can't for the life of me see what they're snapping at as nothing's happening. I'm straining my eyes but nope—nothing. One of them barges past me, squeezing in between me and Dave to get to the front.

'What are you taking pics of?' I ask, as he crouches in front of me.

'Dunno. But she's bound to make a move soon,' the guy replies. 'The cops'll flush her out.'

That's just plain stupid if you ask me. And a waste of film or megabytes or whatever it is cameras use.

I focus my attention on the car. It would make much more sense for her to hide there, and as I haven't actually seen any evidence that she's behind the hill, I can't help wondering if that's not where she is. I take a few steps closer to it. Dave's eyes are fixated on the hill, so he hasn't noticed me move.

Whipping out my mobile, I go a little closer. I'm sure I saw something stir near the back of the car. I'll bet knifewoman's planning to wait until it gets dark and then she'll make a run for it. But she'll have a long wait. It's only lunchtime. I don't know why she doesn't just give herself up if she hasn't actually done any damage.

One of the crowd tuts as I walk in front of them, so I scurry over to the edge of the mob. There're loads more people here now, most of them members of the public, but a few more reporters have pushed their way to the front. It's a waste of time if you ask me.

I feel a bit sorry for the woman. If she *is* hiding out here, she's got no chance of escape. There's nowhere to go. The look on attic-guy's face comes back to haunt me, and I wonder if knifewoman might have been threatening him. Maybe he's the cheat? He's a bit young, but then we don't know how old *she* is yet, do we? No wonder he looked worried.

Even the cops seem more focussed on the hill than the car, so I'm able to get a little closer. I take a few snaps with my iPhone. Something or some*one* is definitely over there. I can see the grass moving and it's not even that windy. Besides, it's only moving in one area.

'Excuse me, Miss, can you move back, please?' A large policeman suddenly appears in front of me and I gasp.

'I'm just—look!' I point as a small figure shoots out from the back of the car and runs towards the flats. I keep tapping at my phone, not sure what pictures I'm likely to get, but it's worth a try.

The big copper hurtles towards her, shouting to his mates, and another couple join him, while the rest have to wrestle with the crowd not to follow. Everyone's rushed over to where I am, and the cops are pushing them all back.

'I missed it!' It's the photographer who pushed in front of me. Ha. That'll teach him.

He keeps clicking as the cops return with the woman, cuffed and hysterical. She's protesting her innocence, while one of the officers carries a large bread knife in a clear plastic bag. My heart throbs. She could've done a lot of damage with that, given the state she's in. She's shaking and kicking out, but the cops are taking no notice. They frogmarch her over to one of their vans where they help her in. There are too many of them surrounding her for her to make a run for it—not that she could if she wanted to.

As soon as they slam the door and lock her in, the van disappears. The rest of the cops start combing the area, and I'm desperate to know what they're looking for. There's a group of them over by the hill while the majority are checking out the wrecked car. I venture a little closer, but one of the cops soon notices me.

'Sorry, Miss, you can't come over here. It's a crime scene,' he tells me.

Sure enough, a couple more officers are cordoning off the whole area with yellow and black tape, urging the crowd to back off.

'Looks like we won't get much now,' Dave moans, suddenly appearing beside me.

'What do they expect to find? They've got the woman *and* the knife. What more do they want?' I peer up at him. He doesn't look too happy, and I wonder if he realised how much closer to the action I was than him.

'Evidence, I suppose. Maybe they think she had more knives or something.' Dave shrugs as we watch some of the cops leave the scene and get back in their cars.

'Looks like they haven't found anything,' I say.

Dave looks thoughtful. 'I wonder who she was. I only got a glimpse of her.'

I nod. 'She wasn't very tall, about my height I'd say, and quite thin. Dark hair, almost black, I think. Scruffy, too. Her clothes were all holey except for her Nike trainers. They looked like this season's style, too. I wonder how she got hold of them.'

Dave stares at me. He does that a lot. When he's not frowning that is. 'You got a better look than *me*.' He sounds almost accusatory.

Another couple of cops give up the search for whatever it was they expected to find and make their way to their cars.

'We might as well get back.' Dave sounds really miserable.

'Okay.' *Thank Goodness!* It's getting cold, and I've wasted enough time hanging around here.

We get a taxi back to the office, but Dave hardly speaks to me. In the end, I get my phone out. He rolls his eyes, and I assume he thinks I'm texting Cassie or someone. The thought immediately reminds me of the conversation we had this morning and I shudder, seeing my message box informing me that someone's been trying to get hold of me. She's bound to want to continue interrogating me about James and the seven-hundred-pound dress, but I really don't need that right now. I ignore the message and click onto my photos.

'Were any of our photographers there?' The thought suddenly occurs to me.

'Nope. I didn't see any.' Dave sighs. 'I'd love to know who that woman was, though. And who the guy was who she went after.'

I zoom in on one of the first pictures I took, when the woman was running out from behind the car.

'Here she is.' I hold the phone up to Dave, whose tanned face suddenly looks pale.

He says nothing, but reaches out and takes the phone from me, his mouth gaping open. Then he scrolls through a few of the pictures. I hope he doesn't start looking at them all, as I've got some pretty personal stuff on there, not to mention loads of shoes. I can just see his reaction to my collection of Manolos. They're on my wish list along with some Louboutins and I can't decide which ones to buy first, so I've got pictures of all the ones I like and I'm trying to—

'How did you get these?'

'What?' I wonder if he's found the Alexander McQueens. There are some stunning styles and—

'I fucking knew it!' Dave's face is turning red with fury.

I grab the phone back off him and check which picture he's been staring at. It's okay, it's just one of knifewoman. It shows her face quite well, actually. Hmm, maybe I should think about taking up photography...

'You know who that is, don't you?' Dave's really het up over something.

'No.' I wonder if I should. 'Is she famous?' I can't remember seeing her on telly or anything, so she can't be that much of a celebrity. Maybe she's off *Crimewatch* or something.

Dave huffs. 'Millie Reynolds. Ring any bells?'

I gawp at him. I know he won't be happy when I tell him I haven't the slightest clue, so I say nothing.

Dave just shakes his head. 'Wife of Oliver Reynolds. He's been playing around for years.' He grimaces. 'Looks like she's finally found out.'

Some of my photos didn't come out too badly, and I'm delighted that Tom's actually able to use one of them for the paper, after applying some of his editing magic.

'You did well, there,' he says, nodding.

'Thanks.'

Dave just grunts, and I know he's peeved that I got into a better position than him, but it wasn't exactly rocket science. He'd disappeared for ages when we got back here. He said he had to make a phone call, but it took nearly an hour. If I went off to call Cassie for an hour, he'd go mad, but I daren't say anything. He's been in an odd mood ever since.

I write up the story in great detail, referring back to my photos for descriptions of the area and the woman with the knife, Millie Reynolds. I don't mention seeing attic-guy. Not only because it might be irrelevant *though I doubt it*, but because I don't want to put him in any danger by letting people know his whereabouts. He could still be connected with the drugs raid, for all I know. Mind you, he could be miles away by now, but still, it's not really my business. Though it would make a great addition to the story!

'How was the estate agent shoot?' I ask Tom, once I've finished and pressed 'send'.

He grins. 'It was quite interesting, actually. The boys are writing it up now. They asked about whether higher-end houses were selling, by the way, and they are. There's a big market for them, actually.'

My stomach lurches. 'Even in London?'

'*Especially* around here,' he concurs. 'The guy said some of the agents are offering incentives to vendors of high-priced homes just to get them on their books. Foreigners are crying out for them.'

I can't wait to tell James. His house should sell in no time, in that case. I wonder which estate agent Suzanne's with. One who doesn't know what he's doing, obviously, if he can't sell that house in the current market. I make a note of the name of the estate agent Tom and the boys were talking to. It might be worth James having a word with him.

It's nearly five o'clock, so we all start gathering our stuff together. Dave hasn't cheered up all afternoon, and I'm not sure if it's because of me or that Millie Reynolds. Either way, I hope he's a bit happier by tomorrow.

James seems pleased to see me when I reach his place in Fulham. I tell him what Tom said about the housing market, over a cup of tea. I love sitting in James' living room. It's quite small but it's light and airy, with high ceilings and big windows. I can't help wondering what his house is like in Richmond. I'll bet it's posh. Not that James is one to splash the cash much—although, I can see why, now that I've heard Suzanne going on about money—but he's certainly got class.

'Which estate agent are you using?' I ask, as casually as I can.

He frowns for a minute. 'Perry and Robb, if I remember correctly.'

I shouldn't be surprised. Perry and Robb are known for selling really expensive properties.

'I would have thought they were one of the best. I wonder why they can't sell it,' I muse. 'There's nothing wrong with it, is there?'

James raises his eyebrows. 'Certainly not,' he says indignantly.

'I didn't mean...' I can see I've upset him. 'I just meant that there's no reason why they couldn't sell it, is there?'

He takes another slow sip of his tea. 'No. In fact, I think I'll give them a call tomorrow. See what the hold-up is.'

'I would,' I say, decisively. 'I mean, I know Suzanne probably doesn't want to move out but...'

'That's got nothing to do with it.' His voice is sharp, and I see I've hit a sore point.

'Sorry, I wasn't implying anything,' I assure him—though he doesn't look all that assured, if I'm honest.

'It doesn't matter. I'll call them in the morning to see what the state of play is.' He sounds very business-like. He often does when he talks to me, come to think of it—even when he's off-duty.

'Okay.' I think it would be safer to draw a line under that subject, so I quickly think of another. 'Thanks for getting attic-guy off the hook,' I say brightly.

James raises his eyebrows, bemused. 'What?'

'The guy from the attic yesterday. In the drugs raid. He was set free. He wasn't part of the gang—like I said.' It feels great adding that last bit.

'I told you, it wasn't my case. I didn't really do anything, just asked what his involvement was. Someone else made the decision to let him go.' He finishes the last of his tea.

'Well, thanks anyway. I knew you must have had something to do with it.' I give him a hug. He feels all soft and manly next to me. My hero.

'I told you, it wasn't me.' He chuckles, and I feel it rumble through his body. I love being this close to him.

'Were you still working on that story, then?' he asks. I love that he's so interested in my day. Whenever I ask about his, he's always a bit cagey, and I get the impression it's all top secret. He *is* a detective sergeant, after all.

'No. This was something new. A woman found out her husband's been cheating on her, so she got a knife and threatened to cut off his manly bits. We caught up with her on the Sandford Estate.'

I think it sounds quite exciting, but James is scowling.

'You didn't have anything to do with her, did you?'

'Of course not. The cops came and took her away. Look.' I grab my phone and show him the pictures I took. Most of them are when the woman's in the arms of the cops— she didn't get far.

James looks horrified as he scrolls through the pictures, and I wonder for a second if it's the Manolos he's looking at.

'Her name's Millie Reynolds,' I tell him.

James has a face like thunder as he looks back up at me. 'You *know* her?'

I shake my head, wishing I could impress him by saying yes. 'No, Dave told me who she was. Her husband's quite a gigolo, apparently.' I shrug.

James frowns. 'How the hell does Dave know him?'

I pout, taking the phone back. 'I've no idea. I thought he was well-known.'

James is staring at me. 'Did he say how he knows all this?'

I gawp at him. 'No. I thought he was famous or something.'

James takes a deep breath, letting it out very slowly. 'No, he's not.' He smooths his beard before standing up. 'I'll make another pot of tea.'

I wait in the living room while he returns to the kitchen. I was planning to talk to James about the dress tonight. I'm running out of time. It's the ball or gala or whatever you call it on Saturday. It's Wednesday already. I wonder if I could get away without mentioning it. After all, he seems rather preoccupied at the moment. Maybe he won't notice.

'Here we are.' He offers me another cuppa and I take it with both hands. I love watching him move around, his sleeves rolled up so I can see the muscles in his arms as he lifts things. I wonder if those arms would ever lift me—perhaps over the threshold? No, I mustn't think like that. It's far too soon. James made that very clear when I misunderstood his intentions back at the hotel the other week. Did I mention I was in a wedding dress and he was on his knees in front of me with an engagement ring in his hand? What else was I supposed to think? I mean, I know he was just picking rings up off the floor at the wedding fair, but even so...

'How's Cassie?'

His question pulls me from my thoughts.

'What?'

'Cassie. Your flatmate. I was just wondering how she was.'

'Oh, yes. Fine. She's fine. Better than fine, actually. She's loving her job as a fashion designer and she's learning loads, apparently. Not like me. Dave's supposed to be my mentor but he's so secretive I'm hardly learning anything. He won't tell me who his contacts are, or how he got them. I mean, how am I supposed to find voles if I don't know where to look?'

'Moles,' James corrects me. 'Or snitches.'

Now I know he's being daft. I've heard of snitches in Harry Potter books. They're the gold ball-things with wings. I can't see how one of those would help me glean any information—even if I *could* catch one.

I decide to ignore his comments and carry on. 'It's no wonder he's got all those trophies—they should be awarded to his contacts, not *him.*' I thought 'contacts' would be a safer word to use after all that. 'Especially that copper. Did you know, he got a tip-off from someone at the station the other day before the cops had even finished their briefing about it? That's how clued-up he is!'

I didn't mean to ramble on, but I can see James is agog.

'What contact at the station?'

Damn. I probably shouldn't have mentioned that. Dave doesn't know that James is a copper, but I'm sure he didn't say anything about me not telling anyone about his acquaintances.

'Umm, I don't know.'

'But someone at the station's feeding him information?' James is clearly fuming. 'I don't suppose there's any point in me asking for the guy's name, is there?'

'I don't know,' I say again. I'm definitely regretting opening my big mouth. James seemed quite relaxed when he brought the tea in, but now, he's seething.

'No, I don't suppose you do.' He's very tight-lipped.

I'm so glad I didn't bring up the topic of the dress now.

'He won't tell me who any of his contacts are,' I explain. 'He never sees them when I'm with him. I think it's all done on the phone or in pubs or something. It's all very hush-hush, even from me.' I pause. '*Especially* from me,' I add as an afterthought. I wonder if Dave secretly feels threatened by me. Perhaps he thinks that if he introduced me to his contacts, they might like me better and tell me all the juicy stuff first. Then *I'll* get all the trophies and he'll get none. He'd hate that. Dave's so proud of those damn trophies. He's always polishing them even when they're shiny already. I think he's a bit of a show-off, to be honest.

'If someone from the station is passing information on to journalists, they'll lose their job.' James sounds very firm about that. I feel my stomach roil, hoping I haven't made trouble for anyone.

'But Dave said they *have* to pass the info on so that they can flush out the criminals.' I remember. 'He said journalists help the cops by getting word out about stuff. Things the public need to know about.'

James shakes his head. 'There's a procedure for informing the press about police business. And it doesn't involve sneaky phone calls to hacks.'

I feel a little indignant at his turn of phrase and my body bristles. I daren't retort though as James is in enough of a bad mood already. I say nothing, for a change.

He looks at me and sighs. 'Look, Libby. Journalists do a great job, and they can be a real help to the whole community, including the police. But they're not privy to certain things because it could easily prejudice a case or throw a spanner in the works if they reported stuff that shouldn't be disclosed at the time.'

'I know.' He's talking to me like I'm a two-year-old.

'That's why we have press officers and police spokesmen. They tell the press what it's safe for them to publish, without jeopardising the case.'

My mind immediately goes back to that chief inspector who'd finished his speech by the time we got there yesterday. He didn't believe me when I told him attic-guy wasn't one of the gang and look where that got him. He had to release him in the end because I was right. I can't help feeling a little smug about it.

I finish my tea and put the cup back on the coffee table. 'I'd better get going,' I say, standing up.

James frowns. 'Don't you want something to eat or anything?'

I shake my head. It's not that I don't want his company, I just feel that anything I say is going to annoy him tonight—especially if I inadvertently mention the seven-hundred-pound dress.

'I'll grab some chips on the way home,' I say, going into the kitchen for my jacket and bags.

'That's not very healthy. I've got some fresh salad in the fridge, and some nice trout.' James looks surprised as he follows me around like a lost puppy.

He's a lovely guy but doesn't seem to get that trout and salad just doesn't have the same appeal as cod and chips. The thought of food makes my stomach rumble.

'I promised Cassie I wouldn't be late back tonight,' I tell him, pulling on my jacket and heading down the tiny hallway.

'Oh, okay. Do you want me to drive you?'

'No, really, it's fine.'

'Are you sure?'

'Positive.' I'm getting the impression even *this* conversation is irritating him a bit.

'Well, thanks for coming over. And I'm sorry about... you know.' He takes me in his arms and locks his luscious mouth over mine in a searing kiss. I've no idea what he was apologising for—the atmosphere between us? Talking to me like I'm an idiot? —but somehow it doesn't matter when he kisses me like that. My stomach burns and I feel all fuzzy.

'Take care,' he says, finally freeing my lips.

'I will,' I promise.

I practically skip down the steps and out of his building. I'm glad we left on good terms, as it was getting a bit tense in there tonight. I wonder if it was because of Suzanne and all that business with the house. It obviously put him on edge. I hope he calls the estate agent tomorrow and sorts out what's going on. Something just doesn't ring true with that woman, especially after what Tom said today.

7

I pop into the chippy on the way home. I've already rung Cassie, who's at home on her own as Rob's watching a football match with his mates. She's really excited when I tell her I'll bring fish and chips back with me.

'I shouldn't, I'll never keep this weight off,' she tells me, but still asks for a large portion.

While I'm waiting for the food to cook, I look around at the notice board. There's all sorts of stuff on there, sofas for sale, flats to rent, and several advertisements about missing cats and dogs. My eye's drawn to a poster about a new gym that's opening up not far from where we live, and I quickly take a photo of it for the details. If Cassie's really bothered about putting on weight she might like to go, and I'd love to be fit enough to keep up with Dave.

***

I check my boots before I step into the flat and am relieved that they look as good as they did when I left this morning. Despite what my bestie said about not needing them anymore, I'd hate to ruin them for her.

'Yay!' She's thrilled to see me—or is it the food she's so excited about? —and has already opened a bottle of wine. Actually, she's already drunk half of it, too, I note.

We sit in front of the telly, eating our supper out of the paper and drinking Merlot. Cassie's in a much better mood than James was, and I'm glad to be home.

'I'm stuffed,' she moans, rubbing her belly. She's managed to finish all her food, but it looks like she might be regretting it a little now.

'Oh, I've got this.' I pull my phone out of my bag and scroll to the picture of the gym advert. 'They're doing special introductory offers,' I tell her. 'What do you think?'

She gapes at me. '*You* want to join a gym?'

I don't know why she seems so surprised. 'I thought *you'd* want to, so I'd keep you company.'

Her lips twitch a little with amusement. 'That's very kind of you.'

I sigh, rolling my rubbish into a ball. 'Okay, I also thought it would be good to be able to keep up with Mo flipping Farah,' I admit. 'I feel awful holding him up when we go off to chase stories, and he gets really huffy about it. Maybe he might like me a bit more if I wasn't so slow.'

'Fair point.' Cassie pouts. 'When does it open?'
'Monday.'
'Great. We'll go then. It might be fun.'

I get the impression it will be much more fun for her than for me. Cassie's already slim so will look lovely in one of those Lycra outfits I've seen in the sports shop window. I, on the other hand, am a little bit larger than her—not much—and am hoping I'm not about to make a fool of myself. *It wouldn't be the first time, though I know you'll find that hard to believe!*

My trousers are feeling a bit tight, so I change into my pyjamas. Cassie's already got hers on—which might be how she managed a large portion of chips tonight—so she clears away the rubbish and opens another bottle of Merlot.

'How was James?' she asks when we're both lounging on the sofa with our drinks.

'I think he's a bit worried about his house not selling,' I tell her.

Her face shines. 'Oh, yeah. Rob told me you were asking about the housing market. He said the estate agent reckoned there was no reason why a nice house in Richmond wouldn't sell within weeks of going on the market. He couldn't keep them on his books long enough. I don't know what the problem is with James'.'

I shake my head. 'Nothing. He said it's in perfect condition. They even dropped the price, and it still won't sell. He just wants to be rid of it *and* rid of Suzanne. I think things might be a bit easier for us when she's off the scene.'

'I can imagine,' Cassie says, thoughtfully. 'Is everything okay?' Her voice is soft, and I know she's concerned about me. I really like James, but we seem to have these 'misunderstandings' every now and then that crop up and ruin things.

'He seems a bit preoccupied,' I tell her. 'I don't know if it's work or Suzanne, or the house or whatever, but he didn't seem all that happy tonight.'

'Maybe he's just tired,' she offers, patting me on the arm. 'Everyone gets like that sometimes. And he has a tough job.'

I nod, grateful for her support. 'Yeah. Hopefully things'll look better tomorrow.'

'He was okay about the dress then?' she asks, suddenly quashing my new-found enthusiasm.

'I daren't bring the subject up while he's feeling like this,' I admit.

Her eyes widen as she stares at me. 'You haven't told him? Libby, it's only a couple of days away. He's going to have to know sooner or later.'

She sounds a bit like my mum now, which irks me a bit. I bite my lip.

'Actually, he might not.' I take a large glug of my wine before continuing. 'I was thinking I might just buy the dress on my credit card and then return it afterwards. They won't have to know I've worn it, will they? Especially if I leave the tags on.' I hardly dare look at her face for a reaction.

She huffs. 'I suppose people get away with that sort of thing all the time,' she says, thoughtfully, 'but *you...*'

She trails off, and I know exactly what she's thinking; *I* never seem to get away with anything. I don't know if it's because I'm too honest or just too unlucky. But I'm determined it'll work this time. It has to. My relationship with James depends on it. And besides, I already sent my mum a picture of me in the dress from the changing room in the shop the other day, and she agreed I looked lovely in it. Mum doesn't say that about many things I wear, so I took it as a sign. I *have* to have it, even for just one night.

'I wish you were coming,' I say, wistfully. 'I just know it would be more fun.'

'It's a charity gala, Libby. It's not meant to be *fun*.' Cassie giggles.

'It'd better be or I'm not going.' I pout, childishly.

'What? And give up the chance to wear a fabulous Jovani dress? And spend the evening with that handsome copper of yours?' She feigns astonishment, putting her hand to her mouth.

I laugh. She's got a point. I take my phone from the coffee table and scroll to the picture of me in the dress. It's absolutely gorgeous. The colour's called 'blush', which is a sort of peachy pink. It's got sparkles all over it and the plunging neckline makes it look sexy but not trashy. It's the sort of dress you could get married in if you wanted to—not that I'm thinking along those lines, of course. It skims down the body making me look really slim, and I'm sure I'll find the perfect shoes to wear with it. Cassie's going to lend me her cream fur jacket, which will look stunning over the top—and keep me warm. I've already got a hair appointment booked, and Cassie and I are going to have a massage in the afternoon, too. That should get rid of all the stress of working with Dave. I tried to get James to have one, but he wasn't keen. It's a pity as he could do with relaxing a bit.

'It is beautiful,' Cassie concedes, looking over at my phone.

'I can't believe the price. I've seen loads of Jovanis for over a thousand quid, so this really is a bargain. It's like it's meant to be,' I tell her.

'I just hope James sees it that way.' Cassie doesn't sound convinced.

'He won't know how much it cost. I'll just tell him it's something I had in my wardrobe. He doesn't know anything about designers. He'll assume it's from River Island or something.'

'Are you sure?' Cassie obviously isn't.

I nod decisively. 'Positive.'

***

I always hate Thursdays. They're a sort of nothing day. Once you've got over Wednesday—hump day—you want to be looking forward to the weekend but Thursday sort of blocks your way. Fridays I can understand. Some people dress down and some knock off work early. There's a point to that. It's the gateway to the weekend. But Thursday? What on earth is that all about?

I decide to wear a skirt for a change, with some thick tights. The Saint Laurent Loulou ankle boots will look good with it, and I pull on a thin jumper. I was hoping to dress up every day in this job, like Siobhan who does the fashion pages. I've got some lovely suits and dresses that would look ideal for work, and some stylish heels to go with them. It's just not practical in this department, though, when I have to hurtle across town at a moment's notice to report on a drugs bust or theft or whatever.

I'm a bit miffed, though, as the other girls who work in our office manage to dress nicely for work and I'm sure they do the same job as me. The only difference is they get to travel by taxi or Tube, not run across town burning shoe leather.

***

Dave's his usual, miserable self when I get into the office, and I smile as brightly as I can manage. Tom appreciates my cheerfulness and beams over at me.

'Morning, Libby. You look nice.' He picks up his camera, and to my surprise, takes a photo of me.

'Thanks,' I say, on both counts.

No one's ever spontaneously taken a picture of me, as far as I know, and I hope I looked okay. I didn't get the chance to check my lippy, or pout, or stretch my neck or anything.

'What's happened about Millie Reynolds?' I ask Dave as I take my seat at the end of his desk. 'Have the cops still got her?'

'Nope.' He doesn't sound too happy about it.

'So, she hadn't actually hurt her husband, I take it?' I switch on my computer.

'No. Just threatened him, but there were no witnesses.'

'Right.'

'None that would admit to it, anyway,' Tom calls over, clearly noticing that Dave's not very talkative this morning.

'The man's a flaming idiot,' Dave grumbles. He huffs, tapping his pen irritably on the desk. Unfortunately, he's left-handed so I can't even reach over and yank it out of his hand. I hate that noise and I'm sure he knows it.

'Where is he now? Do you think she'll take him back?' I know *I* wouldn't, but you often hear of couples like this staying together despite everything.

Dave snorts. 'No.'

'Good. I wonder where he went,' I muse.

'Probably with one of his other women.' Dave's clearly not happy with the situation, and I wonder if he's actually more of a gentleman than I gave him credit for.

***

I'm glad when Ben and Rob pop into the office a while later. They only work next door, but I wish they were stationed in here with us. The other reporters in here don't talk to me and Dave much. I get the impression they're a little jealous of Dave, so I feel a bit ostracised by association. I plan to get around them, though. I just need to figure out a way.

'Are you still working on the housing market boom?' I ask Ben, who pulls up a chair next to me.

He and Rob are on a coffee break so have come to spend it with me, which is lovely of them. Unfortunately, Dave doesn't believe in stopping for coffee, so it feels a bit awkward.

'It's hardly a boom,' Rob says, perching on the other end of the desk. 'More a bit of a surge, I'd say.'

'Well it's not surging very far in Richmond,' I tell him. 'James' ex can't sell their house for toffee. She reckons no one's interested.'

Ben frowns. 'Is there something wrong with it? Richmond's a lovely area.'

'I know,' I say with a sigh. 'James said it's in perfect condition. They had it redecorated and everything.'

My stomach roils a bit. I wish so much that they could sell the house and move on. I'm sure that's what was stressing James out last night. He doesn't need this on top of everything else. Mind you, it makes a change from *me* stressing him out. And on that subject, I've decided I'm definitely *not* going to mention the Jovani dress. He's got enough on his plate. Besides, what he doesn't know won't hurt him.

'Maybe we should take a look,' Rob says, thoughtfully. 'We could go round there and suss the place out.'

I gasp at the idea. 'Would you? She'd never suspect anything. You could just pretend to be interested in buying it. Have a look around and see if she's done something to sabotage it so it won't sell. I'm sure she just wants to keep living there because it's so nice.'

Ben's giggling now. 'You'll have to pretend to be gay then, bro. Why else would two guys be looking at buying a house together?'

Rob frowns. 'We could say that *one* of us is looking to buy it. The other's just coming to give an opinion.'

'It's got four bedrooms,' I say, remembering what James told me. 'You could say it's for your family.'

'Yeah, we'll do that. I'm looking at it for my fiancée and the baby. You're my best mate coming to give advice.' Rob nods, decisively.

'Hang on, why can't I be the one who—' Ben looks indignant, but clearly has second thoughts. 'Oh, okay, never mind. We'll go with that.'

I'm relieved. I'm not sure how good Suzanne's gaydar is, but with Ben's perfectly manicured nails, coiffed hair and waxed eyebrows it doesn't take a genius to suss that he's not straight. He really is good-looking, as is Rob.

Rob smirks. 'Drink up, then, mate.'

While they drain their coffees, I scribble down the address. I've seen a picture of the house and it looks stunning. It's no wonder Suzanne doesn't want to leave. James showed me the sales details and it's got everything—including a dressing room. It's the sort of thing I'd like, but maybe not that big. I'm not keen on cleaning and I can imagine a place that size would take all day to dust.

'Here you go.' I hand it over to Rob, who's beaming at me.

'Great. I love undercover work. Best part of the job.'

Dave snorts, suddenly reminding us of his presence—as if we could forget. He's been huffing and tapping all morning.

'You need to get that seen to,' Ben tells him, feigning an earnest expression. 'It sounds painful.'

The boys get up and leave, chuckling.

'Maybe we can get some work done, now,' Dave says, just loud enough for them to hear.

Ben gives a really loud snort in reply, and I hear them both burst out laughing as they go down the corridor.

I try to hide my smile.

'That *was* work,' I tell him. 'It's all part of their series on the housing market.'

Dave shakes his head. 'It's got nothing to do with us.'

I want to tell him it's got everything to do with me, but I know it'll only make him grumpier.

'It's still for the *Daily Chronicle,*' I point out. 'We should all work together.' I stick my nose in the air and finish my coffee, which isn't that easy, actually, as I have to put the cup up higher to reach my mouth and I almost spill coffee down my lovely Monsoon jumper.

Tom chuckles. He often does that. His desk isn't far from ours, so he listens in to our conversations and joins in. It's good because he's on his own over there, so we're company for him. Also, Dave's so moody, I'm glad I've got Tom to talk to sometimes.

Dave seethes, standing up. 'I've got to make a call,' he mumbles, and leaves the office.

I roll my eyes. I'd love to just leave the desk and go and have a chat with Cassie or James whenever I felt like it, but the rule is that personal calls aren't allowed except in emergencies. It seems to be a different rule for him though—unless he's talking to one of his golden snitches again.

8

With Dave out of the way, I take the opportunity to search the web for some shoes to go with my Jovani gown. I know it means running my credit card up a bit more, but that's what it's there for, isn't it, emergencies? And this is for James' work event so it's definitely important, isn't it? Especially with his promotion. He's only recently been made a sergeant, and he has to sort of prove himself to keep the rank. I think he's doing really well at the moment—especially with my help—so I want to really wow his superiors on Saturday, so there's no doubt he can stay a sergeant.

I find a nice pair of Louboutins and sigh at the price. They're almost £1000. I consider whether I could just wear them for the night and then return them. They'll know they've been worn, of course, because of the soles, but maybe I could claim I bought the wrong size? Na, they'd only say it was my own fault.

I quickly tap back to the Word document I'm supposed to be writing as Dave reappears. He's got a face like thunder. In fact, it's worse than thunder, it's a whole storm.

'What's up?' I know he won't tell me, but I ask anyway.

'Nothing.'

Told you.

'Is there any news on that guy who was hiding in the attic?' I ask, hopefully.

Dave grunts. 'No. Why would there be? He's nobody.'

'Nobody's nobody,' I reply, indignantly. I have a strange suspicion that's how he sees me—a nobody who's just a nuisance.

'Well said,' Tom calls over.

I smile at him, glad of his support.

Dave rolls his eyes.

'I'm going out,' he says.

I jump up, glad of some action. 'Great. Where are we going?'

'You're going nowhere. I said *I'm* going out,' he says firmly.

I gawp at him as he switches off his computer.

'We're supposed to be a team. I'm supposed to shadow you, remember?' I'm sure he forgets I'm here half the time—or at least, he tries to.

He shakes his head. 'This is private. You can't come. You can write up that story, though. It needs to be in tonight's paper.'

I frown at him. 'But aren't *you* supposed to be writing it, too? They're picking the best one, aren't they? That's how it normally works.'

He shrugs. 'Well, I'll see how I'm fixed for time later. If not, it's a good chance for you to get your name in the paper.' He gives me a really patronising look and rushes out.

I huff. I'm writing an article about the number of potholes in the roads around Knightsbridge. Apparently, the council are working flat out to get them filled, but it's causing huge traffic delays. They don't usually mend them at this time of year, except in emergencies, but they've been inundated with complaints, apparently, and I have to write the story giving both sides of the argument. I don't know what's worse, the potholes or the roadworks. Tom's shown me some of the photos he's taken of the problem, and the roads really are in a state. It's because of the change in weather, apparently, and shrinkage of the tarmac, and cars running over the cracks and making them bigger—something like that, anyway.

'I'm going to get some quotes for this article,' I tell Tom, as a brilliant idea pops into my head.

'About potholes?' He frowns at me.

'If it's important enough for an article, it's important enough for the public to have their say.'

I'm very proud of the way I'm handling the subject, even though my mind is whirring with which shop I'll go to first. Harrods is bound to have some lovely shoes to go with my ballgown, and I might even get a little bag to match. Selfridges is having a sale, too, so that's definitely worth a look. It's a shame this article isn't on fashion as I'd much prefer to do the research for that instead. Anyhow, this way I can kill two birds with one stone. *Not that I'd actually want to kill any birds, of course.* I'll ask a few people about the roads while I'm there. I don't know why I didn't think of this before. Actually, I do. Dave would never go for it.

The town is really busy, as usual, just how I like it. The crowds just add to the atmosphere of excitement, with everyone busy deciding what to buy next. I get the buzz as soon as I step out of the taxi. I'm just near Brompton Road, so it makes sense to slip into Harrods first.

I took the opportunity of interviewing the taxi driver about the roads on the way over here. I've got a few quotes, though I'm not sure if I'll be able to use them. The *Daily Chronicle* enforces a limit on the amount of expletives we're allowed to use in one article.

It's like my feet already know the way, as I tackle the crowds and go straight to the shoe department. They've got a brilliant selection here. The first to take my eye is a gorgeous Jimmy Choo, velvet platform shoe. It's a bit chunky to wear with my ballgown, unfortunately, but it's a lovely shade of pink and has crystals all down the heels. I'm also tempted by the Romy 60 in pink suede, which is a more classic shape and looks so elegant. I'm not sure that it's the same shade as my dress, though. It looks a bit bright. The same style is available in silver glitter, I notice, and my heart leaps when I pick one up. I quickly try it on. It feels heavenly, and I automatically straighten my back a little as the height of the heel elevates me—well, on one foot anyway. My eyes light up as I spy the same style in the even higher Romy 85. I reach out and grab one, putting it on the other foot. I might be walking a little wonkily, but my feet look fabulous. I'm torn between the two heights—I'm also finding it hard to stand in them. Perhaps I should have tried one at a time.

A stern-looking assistant is heading my way, so I quickly put the shoes back. She's got a suspicious look on her face, with narrow eyes and a tight mouth. Do I *look* like a shoplifter? Maybe she thought I was about to make a run for it in the shoes—chance would be a fine thing. I could hardly walk in them, let alone run.

I hastily slip back into my Saint Laurent boots and move away from the display. My eye immediately lights on a different arrangement. Valentino Garavani has just brought out the Patent Rockstud Pump 100 in the most beautiful two-tone pink. I gasp at its beauty. I really want to stretch my arm out and pick one up, but I don't want to get fingerprints on it. Not because the assistant will use the prints in a case against me—not that I *am* planning on shoplifting, of course—but just because I don't want to mar their brilliant shine. They're four inches high and have these sweet, pyramid-shaped studs planted all around the edge, on a strip of lighter-pink leather.

I feel rather giddy with excitement. There are so many fabulous designs to choose from. I glance back over to the Jimmy Choos. I'm really tempted with the glitter pumps, which will go with anything. That would make them an investment rather than a purchase. That's allowed. It's the sensible option. But the Garavanis are gorgeous too. And they'd look great with trousers as well as dresses. Hmm, so would the Jimmy Choos. Why is it all so difficult?

That miserable assistant still has her beady eye on me. She's standing by the Jimmy Choos but she's still looking my way. I feel a little uncomfortable, to be honest, so decide to make a move. Butterflies are racing in my stomach with the thought of all these shoes—and I haven't even got around to bags yet.

Maybe I need to sit down with a nice cup of tea and have a good think about it. I smile at the shop assistant in a very non-shoplifter sort of way and leave the store.

It's gone colder outside, and I can hear drilling nearby. That reminds me about the story I'm supposed to be writing about the roads. *Damn.* I follow the sound and come across a group of men in hardhats who are working on a cordoned-off section of road.

I whip out my tablet and take a quick picture of the scene. I know it's not half as good as Tom's, but I think it makes me look more official if I take a picture, and besides, it'll help me with descriptions later. An old guy is drinking tea near the barrier that butts onto the street. He's wearing a high-visibility jacket like the others, but somehow it looks scruffier on him. I quickly take his photo, which makes him turn and look at me.

'Hello, I'm Libby Lawrence from the *Daily Chronicle*,' I tell him with a bright smile. He doesn't smile back. 'I'm writing a piece on the potholes and subsequent roadworks that are causing problems in the area. Do you have any comment to make?'

He frowns at me, and I wish I had one of those microphones to point at him to make me look the part. I quickly tap on my tablet, trying to look efficient. When I look back up at him, he's still frowning.

'I can see you've got a tough mission, filling all these holes. Do you have anything I can quote for the paper?' I'm trying to look bright and cheerful but inside I've got a horrid, sinking feeling.

'I'm just doing my job, lady.' His voice has a sharp edge, and I can see he's annoyed. Probably someone else who thinks I'm just a nobody.

'I'm just doing my job,' I repeat as I type his comment into my tablet. 'Thank you, Mr...?' I look up but he's gone back to work with the others. Typical.

Feeling a little deflated, I look around to see that one or two passers-by are watching me. I wonder if they recognise me as being a famous reporter. On second thoughts, I haven't even got my name in the paper yet, let alone my face, so it's hardly likely. They're probably just wondering what I'm doing talking to miserable workmen and tapping stuff into my tablet.

'Hi,' I say, approaching a well-dressed lady with bags of shopping. 'I'm Libby Lawrence from the *Daily*

Chronicle. Would you like to comment on the roadworks that are going on around here to fix these potholes?'

She's looking at me like I'm an alien. I get that a lot.

'The question is,' I say, raising my voice as a few more people look my way, 'Are you *for* the potholes or *against*? If you're against, how do you feel about all the roadworks that are slowing down the traffic in this busy part of London? Is it a necessary evil, or just a nuisance?'

Even more shoppers have gathered around me now, and I feel a rush of excitement. I didn't know I could command attention like this. And these people are perfect strangers.

First, I hear mumblings and then their voices get louder.

'Fix the roads properly in the first place and we won't get potholes,' a man shouts loudly.

'Yeah.' There's a chorus of agreement.

'Thank you. And your name is...?' I quickly write down the comment, not even sure who said it.

'Stop blocking the roads during rush hour.' another man shouts.

Again, there's a cheer of support.

'Get rid of the holes. They're tearing up our tyres!' It's a woman this time, but now everyone's talking at once so it's hard to tell which one said it.

'Yeah. My tyre was in shreds the other day after I'd been down here!' agrees someone else.

'They're just causing chaos!' a man booms from the throng.

'They have to do that to mend the blooming roads!' someone else points out.

'Well, they should do it at night when we don't need to be here.' someone retorts angrily.

'We do!' Oh no, it's the guy in the high-vis jacket who's 'just doing his job'.

I glance over and see all the workmen looking my way. The crowd is quite huge in front of me, and they're all shouting at once and raising their hands to make their point. This wasn't supposed to happen. I only wanted a few quotes.

'Well, do it quicker then,' someone replies.

A couple of the workmen have just walked around the barrier. They don't look happy. They're confronting some of the horde.

'We do our flaming best,' one of them yells. 'Our job would be much easier if we didn't have to put up with stupid motorists honking their blooming horns at us while we're trying to work.'

'Your job's easy anyway,' someone pipes up. 'All you do is shovel tarmac into holes. A trained monkey could do that.'

'Or an untrained one,' someone interjects.

'Oy! Watch what you're saying about us.' Another of the men behind the barricade has joined in now. In fact, he's coming over, too.

'I don't know which is worse, them potholes or these arseholes,' a large man jeers as the workmen down tools and stride towards us.

The air's filled with shouting and taunting. The crowd's got much bigger and even some of the cars have stopped in the road and the drivers are joining in the argument. I can see fists being clenched and a lot of pointing going on. Not to mention a few ruder hand gestures. I take a few photos of the scene—sans rude gestures—as surreptitiously as I can before shoving the tablet back into my bag.

As a couple of policemen arrive, I decide it's time to go. The whole mob's in uproar, with yelling going back and forth between the workmen and the shoppers. No one notices as I sneak through the tumult and walk as inconspicuously as I can up the road.

It's a relief to reach Lancelot Place and I manage to hail a passing taxi and ask the driver to take me back to the office.

'You were lucky to get me. Looks like there's a massive hold-up on Brompton Road,' he grumbles. 'We'll have to go the long way round.'

'Oh, really?' I'm trying to sound disinterested.

'Yeah. Some sort of riot, I heard. They've stopped the traffic. As if it's not bad enough already down there with the state of the roads. They've had workmen down there every day this week—night-times too. It's a blooming shambles, if you ask me.' I watch the back of his head shake and I'm glad I *didn't* ask him.

I'm keeping my tablet safely tucked inside my bag, and just for once, I'm *glad* I'm not a famous reporter who everyone recognises.

9

It's actually a relief to return to the office and I slump down at my desk. Dave still hasn't returned, which is probably a good thing if he's still in a bad mood. I've had enough of bad-tempered people for one day. Tom's not here, either, probably out on a job somewhere.

I flick on my computer and go over to the machine for a coffee, though I could really do with something much stronger with the awful day I'm having. My rumbling stomach reminds me that I missed lunch, so I delve into my Marc Jacobs for my lunchbox.

'Hi, it's Libby, isn't it?'

One of the girls from the other end of the office pulls up a chair and sits down while I chomp away on my ham sandwich. At first, I feel a little embarrassed that I've brought my lunch from home, but then she produces a tinfoil package that she opens to reveal a bread roll— filled with tuna, if my nose doesn't deceive me. It looks like one from the canteen, though, not home-made like mine.

'Yeah. Lovely to meet you.' I've seen her several times. It's the one who gives me dirty looks, so I'm surprised that she's being friendly. She might just have an unfortunate, resting bitch face that she's not aware of, but she does seem to glower a lot.

'I'm Bethany. You're new here, aren't you?' She tucks into her lunch. She's really well dressed, in a pair of loose-leg sandy-coloured trousers, which she's teamed with a cream blouse. I think I recognise the blouse as a Chloe, but I'm not sure about the trousers. They look nice, anyway, almost matching the colour of her shoulder-length hair. I think I might look into getting some like them, actually. They're all floaty and look quite expensive. Which they probably are.

'Yes, just a couple of weeks. I've seen you around but—'

She sniggers. 'It's hard to talk, isn't it, with all the others here?'

I look down to where she works and notice the rest of her team have disappeared.

I nod.

'They don't like us fraternising,' she goes on. 'I don't know why. We're all working for the same paper, aren't we?'

'Yeah. We should be working together,' I say between mouthfuls of my lunch. I wish we *were* working together—she and her friends get to wear heels all day, unlike me.

'Absolutely.' She peers over at my screen. 'What're you working on?'

I roll my eyes. 'It's a piece about potholes, of all things.'

She looks surprised. 'What's so interesting about them?'

'Nothing, really,' I admit, shaking my head. 'It's just something Dave thought would be a good idea for some competition he's taking part in. I didn't take much notice, he just seems to compete for anything going, by the look of all these.' I gesture to the trophies lined up along the front of the desk.

'Yeah, I never understood that kind of mentality,' she says. 'So, why's he got you writing about potholes for a competition? It's hardly nail-biting stuff.'

'It has to be something to do with the council, I think. And I suppose it's a bit unusual that they're filling potholes in October. Usually, they save up roadworks for the better weather, but these are deemed an emergency—probably because it's Knightsbridge.'

Bethany looks thoughtful. 'There was an accident involving a cyclist and a pothole last year,' she muses. 'The guy went straight over his handlebars and into the path of an oncoming truck. It was all caught on CCTV. He was really badly hurt and sued the council for quite a lot of cash. That might be why they're worried now.'

I gape at her. 'I didn't know that. I can't believe Dave didn't tell me.' Hurt engulfs me, swiftly followed by anger. 'So much for teamwork!'

'I think he just wants all the glory,' Bethany says conspiratorially. 'That's how he's got all these stupid trophies, by walking all over everyone else.'

'Hmm, well he's not going to walk all over *me*,' I tell her, defiantly.

'Good for you,' she says with a nod.

'If this competition's got to have a story involving the council, it's probably being run by them,' I muse with a frown. 'So Dave'll be looking to put a positive spin on the story from their point of view.'

'Makes sense,' Bethany agrees, screwing up her tinfoil.

'But if this is because they don't want to get sued again, then they're not actually filling the holes to provide a service, more to cover their backs.' I fume. Dave should really have given me all the facts. I was doing my best to cover both sides of the story to give an unbiased view, but this changes things.

'Well, I'll leave you to it,' Bethany says, as Tom returns.

'Thanks for that,' I say, smiling at her.

Tom's not smiling. In fact, he looks really miserable as he plonks his camera on his desk and slumps into his chair.

'What's up?' I hardly dare ask.

'There was a big story and I missed it that's all,' he says gloomily.

I tuck my lunchbox back in my bag. 'What was it?'

'A massive riot outside Harrods,' he says. 'Apparently there was this raucous argy-bargy going on about the roadworks down there. Members of the public were up in arms about it, and some of them were having a go at the guys who were trying to fill the potholes. There were quite a few arrests, apparently.' He frowns at me. 'Weren't you going down that way? I'm surprised you didn't see anything.'

I stare at him, my whole body heating up.

He sighs. 'I'm going to be in the doghouse for missing out on this. I really could've done with some good pictures of the action. All I got was the aftermath. The cops had already carted away the troublemakers when I got there, and the crowd had dispersed. Even the workers had gone.'

I whip out my iPad and scroll down the photos. I was right in the middle of the action and got some great shots of people waving their fists about. I slowly go over to Tom's desk.

'Are these any good?' I ask, tentatively.

His eyes widen as he takes the tablet from me. He swipes through them.

'How on earth did you take these?'

'It all kicked off while I was down there,' I admit. 'I just took some snaps in case they were any good.'

He stares at the screen. 'Good? You're a genius! I'm sure I can do something with this one.' He points to one where I was surrounded by angry shoppers. Some of them appear to be staring right at the lens. At me!

'You took a hell of a risk getting that close to the mob,' he says, shaking his head. 'That lot look ready to kill.'

A thud in my stomach reminds me just how angry they looked. It was quite terrifying.

'Do they know what started it?' I ask slowly.

Tom shrugs. 'Search me. I'll give my mate Bill a call over at the *Gazette*. He owes me a favour.'

As he reaches for his phone, I feel a twist in my belly. If anyone finds out I caused a riot, I'll not only lose my job—I could go to prison. James will be furious, and my parents will disown me.

'Billy, it's Tommo.' While he makes the call, I creep back to my desk.

Listening in to the conversation it sounds like Bill didn't get much gen on the subject, and I slowly relax as I stare blindly at my computer screen. I'm wondering if I did the right thing handing over the photos, but Tom looked so dejected at having missed out on a good story, and I'd hate to see him get into trouble. He's a nice guy. I'm not sure quite how nice he'd be if he knew the whole debacle was my fault, though. *Which I'm sure it wasn't.*

He puts the phone down and disappears with my iPad.

'Won't be long,' he promises.

I grab another coffee and decide to research the story Bethany was telling me about. There doesn't seem to be anything about it anywhere, which is frustrating to say the least.

She's back with her team now, all huddled together around one computer screen. I daren't go over and ask her for more details. Instead, I quickly write a report about what she told me. At least I've got the bones of the story, which I've headed 'Pots of Trouble'. I go on to describe what happened—leaving out the bits about me, of course—up until the police arrived. I can't help wondering who the 'troublemakers' were that the cops removed. Surely, they must have been doing something wrong to warrant being arrested? The police don't just wade in and grab anyone who happens to be in the middle of the mêlée, do they? I wonder if James knows anything. I shoot him a quick text:

Heard anything about a riot in Knightsbridge today? Several arrests, apparently. L. xx

'Look at these!' Tom rushes in with my iPad, and I guess he's been doing some fancy jiggery-pokery with my snaps. He slots a memory stick into his computer and taps a few keys.

I go over to see what all the fuss is about. To give him his due, the pictures are really impressive. Much clearer than the ones I took. The colours are vivid, and the detail of the angry faces of the mob makes them appear even more frightening than I remember. My stomach lurches again.

'I'll get these done for tonight's edition,' he says with a grin. 'Hope you've got your story ready.' He gives me back the iPad and I return to my desk.

'Nearly,' I promise, a little nervously. I've got some quotations that I'd jotted down, so I add them to the article. All I need now is the name of the guy Bethany was talking about, and a few more details to authenticate it. Glancing over at her, I'm disappointed to see that she's deep in conversation with another of the girls she works with. They've all been giving me odd looks since I started here, and I was beginning to think they all hated me until Bethany approached me today. Maybe she's the only one who likes me, though? Her friends just seem to be ignoring me. I daren't go over and butt in on their very important and possibly highly confidential discussion.

As Dave still isn't back, I go through to the staff room and call Cassie. She always cheers me up. Well, usually. When she's not expecting me to confess to James about the price of the dress I'm going to get for the gala dinner-ball-thingy.

I scroll through the pictures on my iPad, intending to bring up the one of the lovely Jovani dress, but something catches my eye. I enlarge the image. Oh. My. Goodness.

'Libby? Are you there? Is everything okay?'

I'd forgotten that I'd rung Cassie. I quickly put the mobile to my ear.

'Cass. You'll never guess what's happened.'

'What? Is it about the dress?'

I shake my head—as though she can see me. 'No, it's... hang on.' I quickly get up and close the door, glad that I'm the only one in here again. 'It's Dave.' I then go on to explain about Harrods and the horrid shop assistant, those lovely Jimmy Choo glitter pumps, and then the Valentino Garavanis in the two-tone pink.

'And Dave was there? In Harrods?' Cassie sounds confused for some reason.

'What? No. He was in the café just down the road,' I explain. *Why would Dave be in Harrods?*

'Oh.'

I tell her all about the interview with the workman and the riot that happened afterwards—not that there was any connection, of course.

'Anyway, in the end I was just aimlessly taking snaps and that's how I caught him. He's in one of my pictures, I've got it here. He's sitting in the window of the café eating a Cornish pasty, by the look of it.' I zoom in a bit more. 'Or it could be an apple turnover,' I concede.

'So, isn't he taking pictures of the action in the road?' she asks, and I swear I can hear her eyebrows rising down the phone.

'Nope. He's not taking a blind bit of notice.' I shrug. 'What sort of a reporter is it who sits there with all that happening around him and doesn't even look up? He looks quite chilled, actually.' He's almost smiling.

'Are you sure it's him?' she asks.

I stare at the image. Even sitting down he's towering above the people around him, and I'd recognise that bald head anywhere. 'Of course. But why would he...? Hold on a minute. I'll bet he's got his reporter friends taking photos and he'll just buy them off them. Then he'll get the story from one of them and send it straight to the chief editor. *Damn*!'

Just when I actually thought I'd got the inside scoop on a good story *and* had the chance to submit it before him, he's gone and beaten me to it again.

'Libby? Are you okay?' Cassie sounds concerned.

I slump back in my chair like a rag doll. 'Not really. I thought I'd be able to get my story in the paper for once, get my name in lights, but I can't. He'll have sent his in electronically from the scene. I'll bet it's all ready to print now, they won't need to even look at mine.' A heavy lump settles in my stomach and just for once I wish it was from eating too many dumplings.

'Oh, hon, I'm so sorry,' Cassie says.

'It's not just me, either,' I tell her, gloomily. 'Tom did a lot of work to make my pictures look good and now no one'll see them.'

'You can show *me*,' she says eagerly. 'I'd love to look at them. All of them. Even the one with Dave eating a big samosa, or whatever it was.'

'Thanks, Cassie.' I really appreciate her support. 'I suppose I'd better get back to work. I'll see you tonight.'

I click off my phone and stare at the picture of Dave. He's in the background, just behind the roadworks. There's no way he couldn't have noticed all that ruckus right outside the window. He's holding up his pastry in his left hand, about to take a bite. There's a coffee mug to the right of him, but I can't see if there's anyone sitting there or not as it's too blurry. I seethe. I wonder how many more of his stories he gets like this; enjoying long lunches and then buying the copy from other reporters. No wonder he gets all those trophies.

I quickly switch off the iPad as someone opens the door.

'There you are!' It's Dave. And he doesn't look happy.

I'm not too pleased, either. I want to snap back, *I could say the same to you*, but instead I just stand up and follow him back to the office, biting my tongue all the way.

'We just made it!' Tom greets us excitedly.

'What?' My brain's turned to mush.

'Tonight's edition' he says. 'I hope you don't mind. I saw you'd finished your story, so I sent it down with the photos.'

10

A massive boulder lands in the pit of my stomach. I stare at the screensaver flashing around my computer. I'd left the story on there when I went to ring Cassie. But it wasn't finished.

'So, *you* sent it down?' Dave's voice is like gravel and he stares daggers at Tom.

Poor Tom had looked so pleased with himself a moment ago but now looks completely crestfallen.

I narrow my eyes at Dave, who doesn't notice as he's still scowling at Tom. But why? If Dave sent his story through earlier, they won't even bother to look at mine. Then it hits me. *Had* he sent his in? Or have we pipped him at the post? That's what this is all about— my story landed on the editor's desk before his. Ha! That'll teach him to disappear all day.

I stand a little straighter as I'm flooded with righteousness. It's a good feeling and one I don't get very often, so I have to make the most of it.

'Is there a problem? *You* asked me to write the article, after all,' I point out. I'd be looking down my nose at him right now if he wasn't so damn tall.

That angry glare of his is suddenly focussed on me. Oddly enough, I don't feel so righteous now, more... scared.

'I asked you to write a piece about the council's roadworks in Knightsbridge,' he says slowly, through gritted teeth.

The room falls silent and I glance over at Bethany to see that she and her team are all gawping at us.

'And I did.' I try to sound confident, but my voice is a bit squeaky. 'I wrote the story from both sides, got the quote from the workman and some from the people affected by the work.' My legs feel a bit wobbly and I'm shaking now. I want to sit down but I daren't move for some reason.

'So, you're saying you wrote an evenly-balanced article?' Sarcasm drips from his mouth, and I suddenly feel sick.

'Well...'

'And you checked all your facts?' He raises his eyebrows so high that if he had hair it'd be covering them now.

Someone sniggers from the other end of the room, and I look over to see it's Bethany. Now she's whispering something to the other girls and they're all sniggering too. My whole body heats up. I close my eyes as realisation hits me. *She lied.*

'Where the hell did you get all that rubbish from?' Dave raises his voice, making me pop open my eyes again.

The team at the other end of the room are all laughing hysterically now, and I just want the ground to swallow me up.

'S-someone told me about it. I was going to check all the facts before I submitted the story, but—'

'But you decided to take a break instead?' Dave sounds vicious. I've decided I don't like him, after all.

'I was in shock,' I mumble. 'I needed a few minutes to calm down after being caught in the middle of the riot.'

Dave snorts. 'That'll be the riot caused by some stupid reporter asking daft questions, I suppose?'

Shit. He knows. But I couldn't possibly have been the cause of all that, surely?

'I don't know what you're talking about.' I know it's a lie but he's not exactly being honest, is he? After all, when's he going to admit that *he* was there, too? Scoffing his lunch while Rome burned, so to speak.

'She took some good pictures,' Tom pipes up.

The girls are still giggling as they walk past us and leave the room. It's the end of the day and they're all going home. I only wish I was. I'm so tempted to blurt out that it was Bethany who fed me the fake news story, but I know it wouldn't do any good. She'd only deny it. And her friends would obviously back her up. *Bitch*.

'Those pictures are the only reason you've still got a job,' Dave says flatly.

I gape at him. 'What?'

'I've just had a right dressing down by Phil Peerless, the chief editor, because of that stupid load of rubbish.' Dave's back to the gritted teeth again. I wouldn't mind but they're not exactly even. His front ones protrude a little and the one two back on the left actually looks a bit wobbly. 'What the hell were you thinking, writing something you had no proof of?' he goes on, 'first rule of journalism—check your facts.'

'I told you, I was *going* to check everything. I just thought I'd get the bones down while I had the facts in my head, and I was going to verify them before submitting the story. Only, I couldn't find anything...' I sigh, feebly.

'I wonder why!' Dave's really hacked off.

'Give her a break. She hasn't been here five minutes,' Tom calls over from his desk. 'And it was my fault, anyway. I shouldn't have sent the story down without checking first. It was just that the deadline was...'

'Well, if she'd been sat at her desk like she should have been it wouldn't have been a problem, would it?' Dave snaps.

Tom sighs. At least he tried.

'I'm sorry,' I mumble. There's not much else I can say.

'You're just lucky I've saved your damn job!' Dave says. 'If I hadn't been caught up at the police station all day, I'd have been here to keep a closer eye on you.'

Now I *have* to sit down. 'The police station?'

Dave puts his hands on his hips. He towers over me even more when I'm sitting. 'Yeah. Apparently, they've had a tip-off that I've been getting information from one of their colleagues through the back door, so to speak. Now who would have told them that?' His eyes are on fire as he stares at me.

My mouth drops open, but no words fall out.

Tom gives a sharp intake of breath. 'Ooh, man. That's serious. I suppose it's to be expected when you're doing so well, though. Any of those journos could have a jealous streak. Is someone holding a grudge for something?'

Dave tears his gaze from me and peers over at Tom, who's packing his things away.

'Why would they hold a grudge?' He's frowning hard.

I look at the row of gleaming trophies. I suppose it's just possible that another journalist might be envious of all his success. I wonder if he won them all fair and square. At the back of my mind, I can't help remembering that conversation I had with James the other night, though. I told him Dave was getting insider information from the station. Surely, he wouldn't...?

'I dunno.' Tom shrugs. 'Why does anyone do anything? We're only human. And we *all* make mistakes.' He says the last bit really slowly, staring into Dave's face.

To my dismay, he then grabs his jacket and heads out the door. I really didn't want to be left alone with Dave, especially in this mood.

The big guy sits down with a huge sigh. 'You'd best get off home, too,' he says.

'I really am sorry,' I tell him as I switch off my computer. It suddenly occurs to me that he thinks I'm apologising for grassing him up to the cops, so I quickly add 'For messing up with the story. I shouldn't have been so gullible. And I honestly *was* going to check the facts.'

'Well, at least you got your name in the paper,' he says.

I almost drop my Marc Jacobs. 'What?'

'They removed all the bits about the guy with the bike and the court case—you know, all the libellous stuff that would've shut the whole paper down—but left in your description of the riot. Looks like you got a good view and those pictures were spot-on.'

There's a lurch in my stomach. 'Tom did something with my snaps,' I admit.

'I know. He's been credited as well, don't worry. It was a good piece—although if it transpires that it was all a set-up by one of our journalists it'll be a completely different matter.'

I gawp at him. 'No, it wasn't,' I mumble. 'Goodnight.'

***

I have to stand on the Tube back home, just to add to my misery. I thought I'd be really chuffed to actually get my name in the paper but it's a bit of a hollow victory. Not that I had anything to do with that debacle in Knightsbridge, of course—I don't know how Dave could even suggest such a thing—but I feel really stupid for falling for that rubbish Bethany 'bitch-face' told me. I could have got the whole paper closed down if that'd gone to print—the council would be sure to sue— and then where would I be? And not just me, either. Everyone. Not that I'd worry about Bethany bitch-face losing her job, of course, after all, it'd be *her* fault. But what about Rob and Ben? It was good of them to put in a good word for me at the paper in the first place, the last thing I'd want is to be responsible for shutting the whole place down.

I'm not going to see James tonight. I feel too miserable and don't want to make him feel any worse than he already does. Besides, I haven't caught up with the boys since they went to look at his house in Richmond and I'd rather explain it all to him once I've got the complete story.

I struggle to get to the doorway once the Tube stops and for one awful minute it looks like it's going to take off again before I can escape. I don't know why they're so intent on 'mind the gap' down here, they'd be better off minding the old woman with the huge brolly and twenty-six shopping bags who insists on blocking the aisle when everyone's trying to get off. And to make matters worse, she has the nerve to tut at me as I try to get past her—as though *I'm* the one in the wrong.

I'm cheered up by a call from Cassie as I'm making the short walk from the Tube station to our flat.

'Ben and Rob are here,' she tells me excitedly. 'They've got some news for you about James' house.'

'Great,' I reply.

'And they've brought dinner,' she informs me. 'Indian.'

'Even better.'

I can hear them all gabbling excitedly as soon as I open the front door. The pop of a cork immediately lifts my spirits even further, and I leave my jacket and bags in the hall to quickly go and join them.

'Are we celebrating?' I ask, as Rob hands me a glass of something fizzy and expensive.

'I'd say. You got your first article in the paper, didn't you?' He grins at me. He's really handsome and I can see what attracted my bestie to him—not that he's as dishy as James, of course.

I smile at them all. I didn't expect them to notice, really, especially as the guys hadn't returned to the office since they went to Richmond.

'And there's more,' Ben says, waggling his eyebrows mysteriously. 'Come and sit down and we'll tell all.'

Cassie giggles, picking up the tray of food and following us into the living room.

'It's a superb house,' Rob says as we all sit down.

We've got two lovely, squishy sofas and he and Cassie cuddle up on one while Ben sits cross-legged on the floor, leaving me to sprawl out on the other one.

'I've seen pictures,' I tell them. 'Is it as big as it looks?'

'Practically a mansion,' Ben replies, airily, as we all tuck in.

'Yeah, I had to pretend to be an entrepreneur with business overseas to make it look feasible that I could afford it,' Rob pipes up.

Cassie frowns. 'Or you could have said *I* was.'

'You were too busy with the twins,' Ben says with a chuckle.

'And the other one on the way,' Rob adds, tearing at some naan.

'That's why you couldn't go with him,' Ben says. 'I just *had* to step into the breach and help out my dear friend.' He puts the back of his hand to his forehead dramatically.

'Oh, poor you.' Cassie giggles.

'So, I assume Suzanne was home?' I ask, as bubbles zoom up my nose.

'Oh, she was home all right,' Ben says with a smirk.

'And?' The suspense is killing me.

'And so was her boyfriend,' Rob cuts in.

I stare at him. 'What boyfriend?'

'The tall one with the light-brown hair,' Ben informs me.

I frown. 'She never mentioned a boyfriend.'

'No, I'll bet she didn't,' Ben goes on. 'And I'll bet no one mentioned the son, either.'

My whole body heats up as I gawp from Ben to Rob, then to Cassie.

Her eyes are as wide as mine.

'Whose son?' My voice is a little croaky.

'She referred to him as *ours*,' Rob says softly.

'As in hers and the boyfriend's?' Cassie clarifies.

Rob bites his lip. 'The guy wasn't in the room at the time.'

'So, it could mean either he or James is the dad?' She's speaking very slowly, while my brain is spinning like a top.

'They only split up a year ago. How old is he?' I can feel a huge lump in my throat and it's hard to get the words out.

Ben sighs. 'It was something about having his own room whenever he came home,' he explains. 'There wasn't a nursery, just an ordinary spare room.' He shrugs.

'James has got a son,' I wail, suddenly losing my appetite. 'That explains why he's paying maintenance.'

Rob stares at me. 'What?'

'Let's just make sure of our facts before we get upset,' Cassie suggests. She comes over and gives me a hug.

Tears are already streaming down my face.

'Did she say how long they've been together?' I ask the boys when I finally find my voice again. 'She and the boyfriend, I mean?'

They roll their eyes.

'We didn't ask,' Rob admits.

Hmm, I suppose it's not a very masculine topic of conversation, more's the pity. I wipe my eyes.

'That would explain why they need such a huge house for just two of them,' Rob pipes up.

'Is that why they don't want to move out, do you think?' I ask, giving a loud sniff.

'Possibly,' Ben concedes. 'It might also explain why they were trying to put us off buying it. According to Suzanne, the area's not as nice as everyone thinks. She reckons the local schools are awful.'

'No.' Cassie looks outraged. 'That settles it, then. We can't possibly send the children there.'

We all gaze at her and she turns red. 'Sorry, I was just getting into character.'

'There's no need,' Rob reminds her. 'You're not likely to go there, are you?'

Cassie sits up straight, gawping over at him. 'I think I *should* go and see the house you're thinking of moving our family into,' she says, indignantly. 'It's not just *your* decision, you know.'

'It's no one's decision,' Ben says with a chuckle. 'Keep up. It was just a bit of a story, remember?'

She looks disappointed. 'Oh, yeah.' She pouts. 'Shame, I quite fancied stuffing a cushion up my top and going for a good poke around.'

I give her a big hug, glad I'm not the only one who gets a bit carried away sometimes.

11

My mind's still whirling when I get up the next morning, though that could be partly due to the amount I had to drink last night. The guys insisted it would make me feel better—which it did, at the time.

I've decided not to worry about the 'son' situation until I'm sure of my facts. After all, if Suzanne can deceive James about not having a boyfriend, it's just possible she's been deceiving house-hunters about how many people are in her family.

I pull on my woollen Karen Millen dress, which looks great teamed with thick tights and the Saint Lauren ankle boots, and leave my hair down for a change. I've got that 'Friday feeling', especially as I'm going to fetch my new outfit for tomorrow night's 'do'.

James is going on a course today until tomorrow afternoon, which is probably a good thing. If I sat down for a natter with him tonight it would be impossible not to mention Suzanne and the house—and their son.

'Don't forget, the guys said there was no sign of the elusive son.' Cassie reminds me as we enjoy our tea and toast in the kitchen. 'I mean, no matter what age he's supposed to be, you'd expect to find *something* of his lying around.'

'I think it's her that's lying,' I reply, decisively. 'I'm sure she hasn't even told James about having a boyfriend.'

'Well, don't let it spoil your romantic evening tomorrow,' Cassie says, giving me a warning look.

I frown. 'Of course, I won't.'

She doesn't look so sure, and I really wonder if she thinks I'm some sort of blabbermouth. Not that I *am*, of course.

'I might be back late,' I tell her, stuffing my lunchbox into my Marc Jacobs.

'Are you getting the dress today?' she asks. 'The Jovani?'

'Yes. But it's only to borrow. I'll take it back afterwards.' I know it's a bit dishonest, but everyone does it. Well, everyone who can't afford to splash out seven hundred quid on a gorgeous dress, anyway.

She says nothing, but I can feel the doubt emanating from her.

'See you later,' I say, grabbing the Radley and heading for the door. I don't need to hear any negative thoughts today. It's Friday. That means it should be a good day. I'm sure there's a law about it, somewhere. I might ask James.

The Tube is packed, as normal, and I have to run the gauntlet of sweaty armpits to get off at my stop. I hope the smell doesn't permeate onto me, and quickly whip out my J'adore and spray myself as I head towards the office.

Dave's grumpier than ever. Doesn't he know what day it is? I guess he's still mad at me for yesterday.

'Morning.' I sigh as I put my Starbucks coffee on the desk before taking off my jacket. I decided to pick up my drink at the Tube station today to save time when I got here. I thought it would mean getting to the office a few minutes early, which I was hoping would impress Dave. Unfortunately, I got held up in a queue and then the barista got my name wrong on the cup. He was calling out for Lily—how was I supposed to know he meant me? Anyway, now I'm a few minutes late instead of early, and I don't think it's helped Dave's mood at all.

I quickly switch on my computer and shuffle through my notebook, trying to look efficient and busy.

'Morning, Libby.' He's even more tight-lipped than usual. I inwardly curse myself for the umpteenth time for being so naïve and believing all that crap. Talking of which, I glance down to see Bethany bitch-face smirking in my direction before giggling with those other two girls she works with. I narrow my eyes at her, telepathically telling her that I'm onto her and she won't get away with it a second time, though I'm not sure she understands. Cassie and I often communicate like that, but unfortunately not everyone's as gifted as us.

'What're we working on today?' I turn my attention back to Dave, who's just sat at his computer staring at the screen. 'Any more stuff about potholes?'

I'm secretly hoping for an excuse to nip over to Knightsbridge and pop into Harrods for another look at those shoes. I was thinking about them last night—no surprise there—and I'm concerned that the Valentino Garavanis might be the wrong shade to go with the dress, as they're more pinky but the dress is a bit more peachy. The Jimmy Choos would work well, though, and I also had another thought—how about some nude coloured Christian Louboutins? You can't go wrong with them, and if I get some with a bit of sparkle, they'll look great for the event. Louboutins are my all-time favourites, and I don't *have* to get the most expensive ones—although, even if I did, they'd be an investment, wouldn't they? I actually own a brand-spanking-new pair of Follies Strass 'pumps', which are absolutely adorable. They've got this mesh overlay with sparkling red crystals dotted all over it, which makes it look like you've got little rubies scattered all over your toes. They just won't go with the dress, though, unfortunately, or they'd be perfect for tomorrow night.

'Nope,' Dave says, shaking his head. 'That's all done now.'

'Oh.' I can't hide my disappointment.

'The cops are looking for that guy who was hiding in the attic at Withywood Way, though,' he continues. 'Turns out the gang claim he's been stealing from them, and the cops want to question him about a couple of burglaries. He's gone to ground, though, of course.' He rolls his eyes. 'I knew they let him go too soon.'

My stomach burns, and I hope James won't be in trouble over his release.

'Well, they would have had to let him go if they had no evidence,' I say, defensively. 'You can't just keep people locked up without a good reason, you know.'

Dave raises his eyebrows at me. 'It was a bit suspicious that he was found in the attic of a drug dealer's house, though, don't you think?'

I shrug. 'Not if he thought the place was empty— or, at least that the occupants were away.'

Dave frowns now. 'But there must be plenty of other houses with no one at home. Why didn't he pick one of those? Why *this* house?'

'He probably thought it was just any old house,' I say, obstinately. 'There was nothing to suggest who lived there, was there?'

'Those in the know would know,' Tom pipes up.

I gawp at him. I was hoping he'd be on my side.

'Well, he's obviously *not* in the know, is he?' I reply before taking a large gulp of my coffee.

Dave snorts.

I roll my eyes.

Tom just shrugs and gets back to squinting at his computer screen.

I take it as a victory, although I can't help wondering if attic-guy *did* know something about the house. I shake my head, annoyed that the guys have planted an element of doubt in it. I was sure attic-guy was innocent—he even *said* he was—but now I can't help wondering. And it's not a *good* kind of wondering, either.

***

I spend the morning investigating attic-guy, who, it turns out has a name, Alfie Reynolds. One of the reporters from the *Gazette* found that out, much to Dave's annoyance. There's no mention of whether or not his name is short for Alfred, although, I hope not. He looks like an Alfie. Tousled hair, scruffy clothes and actually quite good-looking, though far too young for me. Not that I'd be interested anyway, of course.

According to the *Gazette*, Alfie's homeless and was squatting in the house. When the occupants returned, he hid up in the attic. It makes sense. Even if it was a bit cramped up there it would have been much warmer and dryer that living out on the streets at this time of year. I still can't help wondering what he was doing on the Sandford Estate the other day, though. He certainly didn't look happy. And what was his relationship with Millie Reynolds?

Whenever Dave stops breathing down my neck for thirty seconds, I click onto the Christian Louboutin website. They've got some wonderful shoes, as always, and I'm spoiled for choice. I know they're expensive, but I've got this credit card and I've worked out that if I pay more than the minimum payment it will cut down on the interest. Plus, of course, once you make a payment on one of these, you get to use the money all over again.

My heart always beats much faster when I'm looking at shoes—especially Louboutins, my absolute favourites—and I'm getting quite hot.

My stomach suddenly burns as I stare at the screen. I'm gaping at a pair of New Very Prive Quadro Lurex high heels. I've always wanted a pair of Very Prives. They're a peep-toe style with a very elegant stiletto. These ones are almost five inches tall. There's a platform sole, though, so they don't feel as high—or, at least, the ones I tried on in Selfridges didn't—and I can actually walk in them. I'm not sure if these are a bit higher, though, as the ones I was trying were just Very Prive, not *New* Very Prive. I can't see much difference in the style, to be honest, but the *New* edition don't seem to have as many different colours and spikes and things. These are really classic, and I absolutely adore them in both black and nude. The ones that have caught my attention are nude but with a pattern in quadro lurex and specchio leather. Believe me, they are gorgeous.

'Time for lunch.' Dave's voice pulls me from my thoughts and I'm almost reluctant to switch off the lovely shoes.

I quickly squint at the price before flicking off the screen and a heavy boulder lands in my stomach, immediately extinguishing all the lovely hot flames. Six hundred and twenty-five pounds! Normally, if I squint the price doesn't come up that high. Or, at least, I don't *think* it does. When it's a bit blurry, I can usually guess at the figures, which are always a lot lower than six hundred and twenty-five pounds. Maybe I misread it? I did squint rather more than usual. And I flicked off the screen far too quickly to read it correctly. Phew. That's what happened, I'm sure of it.

'Are you okay?' Dave's frowning at me again.

I nod. 'Of course.'

'Enjoy your lunch.' With that, he leaves the room. Probably off to run a marathon or something. I'm sure that's all he does in his free time. Run. I inwardly balk at the thought, but then I remember that Cassie and I are joining the gym on Monday. I wonder if that'll make me want to spend my lunchtime running all over the place.

I pull on my jacket, imagining myself sprinting across London in my New Very Prives. How elegant would that look? I might have to practice first, though. I'm sure there must be a knack to running in five-inch Louboutins. Maybe I could take them with me on Monday night. How great will I look on the treadmill in my heels? I'll bet everyone will start copying me. It'll become the 'in thing'. That's it—I'll be Libby Lawrence the trendsetter.

I grab my Radley and head out of the office. My skin tingles and my stomach feels a little jittery as I make my way to Knightsbridge and pick out the Jovani dress. I gape at the label. There's a bright red 'SALE' sticker on it, announcing '£50 off'. My heart rate quickens. It's a sign. An omen. Now I'm certain it was meant to be. Some otherworldly force—namely the Goddess of Sales and Reductions—is telling me I must buy this dress. Now.

Quickly, I take it up to the counter and whip out my credit card. The sparkles twinkle under the bright lights as the assistant carefully wraps the dress in tissue and places it reverently into a bag. For a second, my breath hitches, dreading it being one of those brash 'SALE' carrier bags, announcing to the world that, although I've shopped in a swanky boutique, it was only when everything was reduced. Although my bank manager, MoneySaving Expert Martin Lewis, and my dad would all be proud of me for snapping up a bargain, my street cred would instantly plummet.

'There you go.' The assistant, Scarlett, according to her name badge, hands me the bag and I sigh with relief that it's a normal one.

'Thank you.' I tuck my card back into my purse and head out the door before she can change her mind about the price.

In my mind, I can just hear her shouting after me 'Sorry, there's been a mistake. That dress wasn't in the sale, after all. You owe me another fifty quid.' It's a recurring nightmare I have each time I bag a bargain. That, and the one where the alarm goes off as I reach the doorway and everyone in the street as well as the shop watches me being carted off by a couple of security guards who don't believe I've paid for my shopping.

'Louboutins next,' I mutter to myself, pushing all the negative thoughts to the back of my brain. The thought cheers me instantly and I squeeze my Radley a little tighter, telepathically assuring my credit card that it'll be okay, I'll get it paid off soon.

The New Very Prive Quadro Lurex heels beam at me from under the spotlight in the middle of the display at Harrods. I hold my breath, taking in their beauty. I have never seen anything so lovely, and they will look perfect with my dress.

'Can I help you, madam?'

I jerk around, reluctantly hauled from my veneration by a narrow-eyed shop assistant. It's her. The one that spied on me looking at the Jimmy Choos and Valentino Garavanis yesterday. She still has that suspicious look on her pinched face today, giving me the urge to turn and run out of the shop. But I don't. Why should I feel guilty when I've done nothing wrong? Instead, I take a deep breath, straightening my back a little.

'Yes. I'd like a pair of those, please. Size seven.' My voice is clear and crisp, attracting the attention of a couple of browsing shoppers.

She frowns. 'You mean, the New Very Prives?' she clarifies, disbelievingly.

I nod. 'Yes. In the Quadro Lurex.'

She gapes at me and I give her an expectant stare in return.

Then I clear my throat, casually swinging my carrier bag over to the other hand, giving her a clear view of the logo of the boutique I just bought the Jovani in. She glances at my shopping and her eyes widen.

'Is there a problem, Clarissa?' An older lady with immaculate hair and make-up sidles over to us, looking quizzically at the assistant.

'Um.' Clarissa still looks unsure.

'I just asked for a pair of those in a size seven,' I interject. 'I don't have long, though, so if there's a problem...?' I glance at my watch.

'Of course not.' The older lady gives me a wary smile. 'Clarissa will fetch them for you now.'

'Yes, of course.' Clarissa scurries away, under the hard stare of her boss.

'Is there anything else we can get you?' the older lady asks me, the fixed smile still on her lips. It doesn't reach her eyes, though, I notice. 'A handbag, perhaps? We have some exquisite clutches you might like.'

I'd love a new clutch, but I've already got my eye on one of Cassie's that I'm sure she'd let me borrow for the occasion.

'No, thank you. Just the shoes.' I feel quite proud of myself. Not only have I just saved fifty pounds on the dress, I've also saved several hundred by not buying a bag. I'll be quids in at this rate. Ha—eat your heart out,

Dad, Martin Lewis, and whatever my bank manager's called.

Clarissa finally returns with the shoes and my heart leaps as she holds them up to me.

'Would you like to try them on?' Her thin lips are very tight as she asks.

'I'll leave you to it,' her boss says, before walking away. I can imagine her having some stiff words with Clarissa later. Good. I feel like I'm in that scene from *Pretty Woman* when Julia Roberts returns to the shop that she was snubbed at before and shows the assistant all the expensive shopping she just bought elsewhere. Only this time, the woman who doubted me, namely Clarissa, is having to serve me—and she's clearly not happy about it. Ha!

"Six hundred and twenty-five pounds, please,' she says, placing the box into a large bag.

'Of course.' My heart thumps like mad as I pull out my credit card. I can almost feel the plastic melting between my fingers as it cringes up at me. It seems I hadn't misread the price on the computer screen, after all.

I force myself to smile as I slot the card into the machine, praying that it gets accepted. It seems to take ages for it to authorise and I spend the time looking around at the bright displays, avoiding Clarissa's eye. With all the money I've saved today, I might be able to buy something else...

'Thank you.' Her clipped tone makes me jump for a second and I peer at the screen, breathing a huge sigh of relief when I read the words 'Transaction complete. Remove card'.

I beam at Clarissa, who forces herself to smile back in a very tight-lipped, reluctant way. Giggling to myself, I head for the door and hurry back to the office. Mission accomplished.

12

Despite not having had time to eat, I consider my lunchtime a very fruitful one. I get back to the office just in time to see Dave sit at his desk, and I can't help noticing the envious looks I receive from Bethany bitch-face and her friends when I enter the room with my shopping bags.

Dave also glances down as I tuck my treasures under the desk. 'Doing something nice this weekend?' he asks.

'Yes, actually,' I reply, going over to the coffee machine. Talking as I pour my drink means I need to raise my voice slightly, and I can feel Bethany bitch-face and her gang watching me. 'I'm going to a gala dinner in Mayfair tomorrow night with my boyfriend.'

I return to my desk, feeling a little smug at the gasps I can hear from the girls, who suddenly appear very interested in their work and not looking at me at all.

Dave grunts. I take it this sort of thing doesn't impress him, which doesn't bother me in the least. The fact is it impresses the girls at the other end of the office, and that's all I'm bothered about.

Treating myself today has changed my whole outlook on life. I got up this morning feeling depressed that Dave was annoyed with me, Bethany bitch-face had made a fool of me, and James may or may not have betrayed me by having Dave questioned about his contacts and by having a son he hadn't told me about.

Now, newly empowered, I've decided to make Dave proud of me, somehow exact revenge on Bethany and her friends, and get to the bottom of what happened with James before I accuse him of anything. Very grown-up. I'm proud of myself already. And all because I bought myself a new dress—reduced in the sale—and a new pair of shoes that were actually an investment rather than a purchase. The fact that I managed to get one up on that snooty Clarissa at the same time made it worth spending every penny of the six hundred and twenty-five pounds. I wonder if I'd feel any more determined if I'd bought a new bag, too...

It's unusual for Dave and me to be stuck in the office all day, and I can't help wondering if he hasn't been able to use any of his contacts because of the police sniffing into his business yesterday.

A commotion from the other end of the room makes me look up from my screen and I gape as Bethany and her friends all rummage into their bags, pulling out flat shoes, which they quickly swap with their heels before heading out the door. They must be going somewhere off the beaten track, as it were, as they usually take a taxi. Maybe that's what I should do? Just bring a change of flat shoes so I can wear my heels all day. I'd much prefer to do that. I don't know why I hadn't thought of it before.

My mind starts whirring with all the outfits I could be wearing to work instead of limiting myself to whatever will go with flat shoes or boots. It's as though someone has just flung open my wardrobe doors and invited me to step inside and pick whatever I want to wear—which is how it should be, in my view. When I left my job at the hotel, I was relieved to not have to wear a uniform anymore, and had looked forward to choosing what to wear. I had no idea I'd be limited to sensible ensembles because of having to race around town all the time. Maybe I should think about getting some new power suits or bodycon dresses? I can see another shopping spree on the horizon.

It's not until Dave clears his throat and gets up for another drink that I realise my fingers have inadvertently clicked on net-a-porter.com and I'm aimlessly browsing through the latest fashions. I quickly switch back to the newspaper reports I was examining.

'Any luck?' Dave asks as he walks behind me to the coffee machine.

'Not yet. Alfie's obviously not a habitual burglar. None of the recent crimes have given any mention of him.' We were hoping to establish whether the guy had a criminal record—after all, he had broken into the house in Withywood Way, hadn't he? If he was a criminal, even just a petty one, he could be linked to the drugs in that place. That was Dave's theory, anyway, so I had the donkey work to do. Personally, I still believe he's innocent.

Dave plonks a cup of coffee next to my computer and glances at the screen.

'He was either very unlucky or very stupid to get caught in that house,' he says with a frown.

'He's only a kid,' I remind him. 'I vote for unlucky.'

With a grunt, Dave returns to his seat, sipping his drink.

'Thanks for this,' I say, lifting my cup.

Another grunt. I swear he comes from a family of pigs. Talking of which, I remember I was going to try to get back into his good books.

'Have you any family locally?' I ask, airily.

He looks over, taken aback. 'My sisters are both in Chiswick and my brother's over in Fulham,' he says. 'Why?'

I'm surprised at his suspicion.

'I just wondered,' I say, casually. 'My family are all in Kent.'

'Oh.'

Well that went well. Not! I don't know why I bother. I was only trying to be sociable. Trying to make him like me. A bit.

I sigh. Tom's out on a job so it's only me and Dave in the office right now. Awkward doesn't cover it. I decide the best thing to do is try to immerse myself in my work. The shiny trophies catch my eye. Maybe if I could crack a case, I might earn one. Ooh, how great would that look on the mantelpiece? Well, if we had a mantelpiece. We could keep it in the centre of the coffee table in the living room, I suppose. Everyone would see it when they came to visit, and it would be a good topic of conversation whenever we had nothing else to talk about. Actually, I can't remember the last time I had nothing to talk about. There's always *something*. Oh, well, now there'll be my trophy to discuss as well, won't there? And Mum and Dad will be so proud. They'll tell all their friends. 'Oh, yes, our Libby's an award-winning journalist in London, you know?' I can just hear them now.

Actually, what I can hear is Bethany bitch-face and her friends trudging back into the office. They look totally pissed off. Probably didn't change their shoes quickly enough and missed the story they were pursuing.

'I've never been so insulted in all my life!' Bethany bitch-face is yelling to the others.

I smirk. Sounds like a challenge to me. And I never back away when someone throws down the gauntlet. My ears prick up as I stare at my screen, pretending to be engrossed in my work.

'You? It was *me* he was referring to.' The blonde-haired girl looks most indignant that her friend thinks she's the target for the insult. *Whatever that might be.*

'Sophie's right, Bethany. The guy actually pointed at her and told the cops she was the one who started it all,' the darker-haired girl says as they all change their shoes.

'Yeah, he called me a troublemaker and said I should be locked up for starting a riot!' The blonde, Sophie, looks most annoyed.

The word 'riot' hits a nerve inside me, and I start to get a bit hot. It seems to have piqued Dave's interest too, and he swings around to face them.

'Are you girls okay?' It's the first time I've seen him speak to any of them.

'Not really,' Sophie says, sinking into her chair. 'We just went to Knightsbridge as Joanna Lumley was opening a new clothing department in Selfridges, and almost got arrested.' Her voice rises as she finishes her sentence.

Joanna Lumley? *The* Joanna Lumley? In Selfridges? Damn, I knew I should have gone there for my Louboutins. I can just imagine bumping into Joanna. Such a classy lady. I'm sure we'd have loads in common. She'd probably invite me for coffee,and we'd get to know each other properly. I could tell her how 'absolutely fabulous' I thought she was, and she'd laugh hysterically. She'd love me. I'd have to take her home to meet my mum and dad. Apparently, Dad had a real 'thing' about her when she starred in something called *The New Avengers* in the 1970s. And Joanna could tell

Mum all about the new clothes she's promoting. Perfect. Mum could do with a bit more glamour in her wardrobe.

'It wouldn't have happened if we'd got there on time,' Bethany points out, scowling at her friend. 'We should've taken a taxi.'

'It wasn't my fault. I heard that some of the roads had been closed yesterday because of the rioting in Knightsbridge. How was I to know they'd opened them up again?' Sophie moans.

'Yeah, we missed Joanna, so we thought we'd get the reaction of some of the shoppers in the area. She was promoting a range of designer clothes for more glamorous over-fifties, so we just stopped some people to ask what they thought.' The darker-haired girl rolls her eyes.

'You should have seen your face when that big guy approached us, Carol-Anne,' Bethany scorns.

'Well, I didn't know what he was on about. He just started yelling something about damn reporters causing chaos in the streets,' Carol-Anne replies indignantly.

'But we'd hardly asked anyone anything!' Sophie wails. 'The ladies up by Selfridges were all too busy trying to get in for their bargains so we went down by Harrods. There are always lots of discerning over-fifties down there.'

'Yeah, mostly foreign, though,' Bethany says, shaking her head.

'Not all of them,' Carol-Anne interjects. 'Anyway, the cops soon appeared once that guy started yelling his head off and then no one wanted to speak to us.'

'Because you were asking a few middle-aged women about fashion?' Dave frowns incredulously.

'He was a workman who didn't like journalists,' Sophie says. 'Accused me of being a troublemaker. I hadn't even said anything.'

'You must've just *looked* like a rabble-rouser,' Carol-Anne says with a snigger. She goes over to the coffee machine.

'Flaming cheek!' Sophie gapes at her, but her friend just giggles.

Dave frowns and I can almost see the cogs turning in his bald head. *Oh, no!*

I'm desperately trying to think of a way to change the topic of conversation, but something tells me it's too late.

'So, it was just Sophie he accused of stirring trouble?' Dave clarifies.

'Yeah. But the police seemed to think we were all guilty by association,' Bethany replies quickly.

'But it was Sophie the workman picked on,' Carol-Anne points out, taking three steaming mugs back to their desk. 'He said he recognised her.'

Part of me feels quite flattered. Sophie's really pretty, so if it was the 'just doing my job' guy—as I strongly suspect—thinking that she's me then that's a compliment, right? Somehow, I don't think Dave sees it that way, as his face turns towards mine.

I shrug innocently.

He narrows his eyes. 'So, this guy thought he recognised Sophie as an upstart who started a riot down there recently? That's interesting.' His tone speaks volumes, and I just pray that his mouth doesn't.

I can feel all my earlier resolve dissipating as the euphoria I'd enjoyed after my shopping spree is replaced by a feeling of impending doom.

'Hi, Tom,' I say, brightly. I only saw him coming up the corridor towards the office, but I welcome him anyway, grateful beyond words for the distraction.

He looks surprised as he finally enters the room. 'Hi.'

'Good shoot?' I ask.

'Yeah, quite good.' He's looking around at everyone, clearly unnerved.

No one else speaks. *Damn!* And they're all looking at us. *Double damn!*

'Was it anything interesting?' I ask Tom, trying to keep the conversation going.

'Er, not really.' He frowns at me, quizzically.

I don't usually ask what he's working on, so I can see that this might seem a bit odd for him, but I just wish he'd co-operate. How hard can it be to just hold a normal conversation?

He turns his back to me while he pours himself a coffee. My face is burning as I try to think of some way of deflecting the attention from myself. My mind's gone numb. In the end, I get up, leave the room, and head for the ladies' loo.

I lock myself in a cubicle and sit down with a sigh of relief. I check the time. Another hour to go. Why couldn't this be one of those firms that close early on a Friday? Then I could escape all the drama, go off and enjoy my weekend, and by Monday it would all be forgotten about. No such luck.

I pull out my phone and text James: *'Hope you're having a nice time.'*

No reply. He must still be on his course. I wonder if it's any fun. I once went on a customer service course over in Twickenham. It was residential and we stayed at the university where it was taking place, St Mary's. That's when I saw Mo Farah, actually. Though he wasn't on the course. He was on the running track. Anyway, it was like my old days at uni, with all us girls sitting around in our pyjamas in the evening, drinking hot chocolate and eating biscuits. We talked and played daft games like 'spin the bottle' and 'never have I...' until the early—or not so early—hours. Then we nearly fell asleep in the classroom the next day. It was pretty boring stuff, to be honest, about how to be polite when talking to guests.

Somehow, I can't see James and his colleagues playing 'spin the bottle' in their pyjamas all night. Nor sitting around eating biscuits and drinking hot chocolate. They'll be staying in a posh hotel, for a start, and probably spending their evenings swotting up on the next day's lectures. The thought of James in his pyjamas sends funny shivers through my stomach and I suddenly wish he wasn't so far away. I miss him.

The sound of the door banging pulls me from my thoughts and I suddenly remember where I am. Checking the time on my phone, I realise I've been in here nearly half an hour. After stuffing the phone back in my pocket, I quickly pull the flush so as not to arouse the suspicion of whoever just came in, and open the cubicle door.

'Oh, hi. You'd been gone a while. I came to see if you were okay.' It's Sophie.

'Thanks. That's really nice of you,' I say, surprised. 'I've got a sore stomach. Time of the month, I think.' I rub my belly with a wince, just to back up my story.

She nods as I wash my hands and I think I've convinced her.

'Have you worked here long?' I ask her before running my hands under the dryer.

James Dyson must have forgotten women actually like to hold conversations in the loos, as the racket from the machine totally drowns out her reply. It's a shame because I really wanted to know. She seems much nicer than Bethany. Of course, I can't ask her to repeat herself once I move away from the dryer, so I just nod, as though I've understood every word and follow her back out the door.

Dave gives me a strange look when we return to the office and I rub my stomach. Being a man, I know he won't ask questions. I'm right. He just gives a knowing nod and says nothing.

I thank Sophie before resuming my seat and stare intently at my computer screen. I've no idea what they were discussing in my absence, and I'd rather keep it that way.

I immerse myself in researching Alfie for the next half hour until it's time to go home. I still haven't found out anything about him, but I'm not bothered. It's the start of the weekend now and I've got much more important things to think about.

13

Saturday afternoon finds me waxed to a gleaming shine, eyebrows perfectly shaped and tinted, and my face covered in the most expensive gunk I've ever smelt while having a full-body massage. Cassie is on the bed next to me, groaning contentedly while she enjoys the same treatment.

My mind has gone to complete mush, with all thoughts of work, Bethany bitch-face and credit card bills completely obliterated.

'I'll bet you can't wait for tonight,' Cassie murmurs.

Immediately, a vision of James Harper pops into my head and I hum contentedly.

She giggles. 'I'll be staying over at Rob's tonight, so you'll have the place to yourselves,' she goes on, the delight evident in her voice.

Another hum escapes my throat. Where did that come from? I didn't mean to reply to her. I was just thinking about James and... Well, okay, enough said.

Cassie chuckles again and I try to ignore it. I concentrate, instead, on the woman who's running her oil-covered hands up and down my spine. I've gone all lax like a jellyfish, and she's doing heavenly things to my body. I'd like James to do heavenly things to my body. With or without oil. The thought makes me hum again and I pop my eyes open in shock.

Cassie's laughing even louder now, and I'm glad I can't look at her. We've both got our gunked-up faces resting in the holes in the massage beds—or, at least, I *assume* she has as well, as the only things I can see are the shiny black floor tiles beneath my bed.

My masseuse finishes her ministrations and tells me to roll over, which takes a lot more effort than I expected. My body feels heavy and languid and I could just drift off to sleep. Except that Cassie's just rolled over, too, and I can feel her giving me a knowing look. Luckily, the face mask is green, thus neutralising the scarlet glow that I can feel rising up my body and ending at the tip of my head.

Cindy, my beautician, comes back into the room armed with a hot towel that she places over my face. It feels heavenly. It's also a relief that it will cover any of my blushes, as my face will be red after the treatment anyway. The perfect cover-up. I wish there was a hot towel handy every time I become embarrassed. Which is quite often, actually, though you'll find it hard to believe.

Hair and make-up follow, and a couple of hours later I'm transformed into a really sophisticated-looking lady sporting an elaborate up-do with a few sparkles entwined, and make-up so perfect I won't dare eat or drink all night.

'The lipstick's designed not to transfer onto glasses or cups, or to fade when you eat or drink,' Paula, the make-up artist informs me, as though reading my mind. *I thought it was only Cassie who could do that.*

'Great,' I reply, then realise it would have been more befitting of a lady to use 'splendid' or 'indeed'. I'll have to remember that for later. I don't want to let James down in front of his colleagues and bosses.

***

I stare in my bedroom mirror one last time, as I hear the rattling of a diesel engine outside. He's here. I knew he'd be prompt, but I still feel even more nervous now that he's arrived.

I hear Cassie buzzing him up as I take a deep breath and a long look at my reflection. The dress is stunning, as are the shoes. Cassie's short, milky-coloured fur jacket sets the whole outfit off perfectly, and I feel like a million dollars. Even though I say it myself—or at least, think it—I *look* like a million dollars. I pick up Cassie's Louboutin Vero Dodat clutch from the bed and run my fingers nervously over the leather before leaving the room.

'She won't be a minute,' Cassie assures James as I arrive in the living room doorway. He turns to face me. I gasp. He looks totally edible. I've never seen him in black tie before—actually, I've never seen him in *any* tie before—and it really suits him. What's more, he genuinely looks comfortable in it. Most celebrities I've seen on the red-carpet fidget and fiddle with this sort of attire, but not James Harper. He looks like he was born to wear this kind of style.

His mouth has dropped open and his eyes are wide, irises darker than ever. He looks gorgeous with just his right eyebrow raised in what I hope is appreciation.

'Hi.' I suddenly feel really shy and continue to take deep breaths to stop myself shaking.

He manages to close his mouth and his lips turn up in a sensual smile, dimples appearing in his cheeks.

'Wow,' he mouths.

Cassie beams at me with a reassuring nod.

'Hi.' James' voice sounds a little croaky and he immediately clears his throat. 'Ready?' He strides towards me, offering me his arm.

I nod, take his elbow, then turn back to say goodbye to Cassie.

'Have fun, Cinderella,' she says with a grin.

'You look beautiful,' James murmurs as soon as we're out of earshot.

'Thank you. You look lovely, too.'

He chuckles as we arrive at the taxi and he opens the door and helps me inside. I sit back into the plush leather and wait for him to join me.

'Are you excited?' I ask him, as the taxi whisks us through Chelsea.

He frowns a little in thought. 'That's not exactly the word I would have used,' he admits, 'but I'm certainly looking forward to spending the evening with you.'

I blush. He's sitting by my side, holding my hand, and has hardly taken his eyes off me since he got in the car. He smells lovely, too, and I snuggle in a little closer, careful not to crease our clothes.

James lets go of my hand and puts his arm around me. My skin tingles as I feel his fingers graze the bare skin of my back.

'Hang on a sec,' he whispers with a frown.

A little disconcerted, I wait while he fiddles with something on my back.

'That's got it.' He sits back, contented. Then he hands me a small piece of card.

Suddenly realising what it is, I try to cover it with my fingers, but he doesn't let go at first. *Damn.* It's the price tag off my dress. I'd left it on, tucked up under the shoulder. It must have fallen down.

His face falls as he stares at it. '*How* much?'

'It's okay,' I whisper back. 'Look.' I point to the bit that says £50 off, but I can see he's still focussing on the part stating £699.99.

Even in the dimness of the taxi I can see the colour drain from his handsome face. *Think quick.*

'It's Cassie's,' I lie. 'I've borrowed it for the night. And the jacket. And this.' I hold up the gorgeous Louboutin clutch. *Well, two out of three ain't bad, right?*

He lets out a long breath. He already knew I was borrowing the fur jacket as we'd discussed it in front of him the other day. So, he obviously considers it plausible that I'd got the dress on loan, too. Logical.

'Oh.' He nods with a relieved smile.

I don't feel quite as relieved, knowing that I now have to figure a way of returning said dress without the label attached. I smile back, taking the offending item from his hand and tucking it into the clutch. I'll have to think about it later.

***

The event is being held at the Hilton on Park Lane, which towers over the streets of Mayfair, its columns of blue lights beaming way up into the night sky.

'Here we are,' says the taxi driver, pulling up right outside the entrance.

I feel like royalty as James climbs out and comes to open the door for me to disembark. Praying that I don't get my heel caught on the door sill, I take his hand and slowly pull myself up.

There's a buzz of excitement as people mill around the pavement. Women in sumptuous ball gowns straighten their skirts while men fiddle with their bow ties. My heart thumps wildly as I cup my hand in the crook of James' arm and allow him to lead me through the large front doors of the hotel.

I gasp as I take in the opulent foyer. Twinkling lights shine overhead and the floor has a magnificent starburst pattern in the centre. My Louboutins click impressively as I follow James' lead and we go over to one side where it's not so crowded.

James removes my jacket and hands it to a woman who gives him a ticket and takes the fur off towards reception. The wooden panels and furniture are highly polished and gleam under the bright lights. Pride fills me, being with such a stunning partner, and I remember, not for the first time, what a lucky girl I am.

We enter a large bar area where a waiter approaches us, carrying flutes of champagne on a silver platter. James accepts one for each of us, and I relinquish my hold of his arm to take mine from him.

'James. How splendid!' An older, portly man beams as he comes to join us.

'This is Superintendent Griffin,' James informs me.

'Oh, I think we can dispense with the formalities tonight,' the man gushes kindly, offering me a pudgy hand. 'Andy. Just call me Andy.' He gives me a massive smile. 'And you must be Suzanne. Lovely to meet you, my dear.'

I feel myself turn hot as he takes my hand in his and gives it a hearty shake.

'No, sir, this is Liberty,' James corrects him, calmly.

The superintendent looks flummoxed for a second and then lets out a laugh. 'I'm so sorry, my dear lady,' he says, his face turning crimson. 'My mistake.'

He looks sincere, and I smile at him.

'That's all right,' I assure him, giving his hand a small squeeze, 'and you can call me Libby.'

'Libby,' he says, as though engraving my name on his memory. 'I will.' He nods very definitely, and I feel myself warming to him. He's white-haired, with a thick beard and moustache to match. He reminds me a little of my granddad.

A very elegant lady, whom I presume to be his wife, joins us. Her dress is in rich, green taffeta with silver crystals adorning it, and a neat, boat neckline. The emeralds in her drop earrings twinkle under the lights and she has the confidence of an older woman.

'Ah, there you are, Elizabeth.' Andy leans in to kiss her on the cheek. 'You remember James Harper, don't you?'

'Of course.' She smiles and holds a hand out to shake James'.

'And this is Libby,' Andy says, gesturing towards me with his glass. His eyes twinkle as they meet mine, and I can see he's proud to have got my name right this time.

'Libby, how nice. I've just seen... er...' She has a rather limp handshake, I notice, and she's frowning a little. She looks behind her and then back to me, then to James, as though slightly perturbed.

She's a beautiful-looking woman and I hope I look as good as her when I'm in my sixties. She hardly has any wrinkles—I might ask her what she uses later.

'It's a fantastic venue, isn't it?' I reply, not sure whether to call her by her Christian name or not. I suppose I should if I'm calling her husband Andy, but she hasn't exactly told me to, and I'd hate to offend her. Oh, dear, it's all a bit confusing and I really don't want to embarrass James—or myself.

She smiles. 'Yes. Have you been here before?'

'No, but I've—'

My words are cut off as someone starts tapping a glass very loudly.

'Ladies and gentlemen.' I can't see who it is from here, but Andy groans.

'Oh, gawd, not Hinchley. Whoever let him in?'

Everyone's gone quiet to listen to the announcement, so Andy's remark can clearly be heard by the crowd, who give out a few astonished gasps. Everyone around us has turned to stare at the poor man, who is nonchalantly taking another gulp of his champagne.

Someone clears their throat noisily, and I can only assume it's the Hinchley guy again. Apart from that, the room is deathly silent.

Andy looks up at me with raised eyebrows, clearly at a loss as to what the fuss is all about. The whole situation coupled with his innocent expression makes me want to laugh and I can't stop a giggle escaping.

Andy smiles at me. James frowns. Elizabeth looks bemused.

My clutch is tucked under my arm and one hand holds my glass, so I quickly put my other in front of my face. It's no good. The more I try not to laugh, the more I snigger. I try to cover it with a cough, but it just makes my champagne slosh in the glass and I'm worried it'll spill all over my dress. That would be disastrous as I won't be able to return it tomorrow if it's stained. The barb from the label is still scratching my back, but I keep reminding myself it'll be worth it when my credit card bill comes in minus the six hundred and fifty pounds.

I try to pretend I'm clearing my throat as the giggles continue to engulf me and end up giving a loud snort instead. Mortified, I stare at the floor. I can feel everyone staring at me and I daren't look up.

'Oh, come on, man, get on with it. Is the food ready yet or what?' Andy's voice booms over the titters caused by my faux pas.

I slowly raise my head. Andy has taken a step back, and I can clearly see the man he's talking to. Like the other men, Hinchley is dressed in a black tuxedo, but his has a huge, satin cummerbund wrapped around the waist. His face is bright red and he looks furious. Poor Andy, I'm sure he didn't mean to be rude. I give the old man a sympathetic smile. When I look back at Hinchley, I'm stunned to see that he's looking right at *me*. Frowning. Hard. Come to think of it, he looks slightly familiar. I narrow my eyes, trying to remember where I've seen him before. His scowl reminds me, and I feel a lurch in my stomach. Oh, no. He's the chief inspector from Withywood Way.

'Yes,' he says, through gritted teeth. 'Dinner is served.'

Everyone starts murmuring as they slowly make their way into the large restaurant.

'Come on. Don't want it going cold, now, do we?' Andy urges us to join the throng, and I glance up at James. He looks slightly bemused but steers me towards the crowd.

'You're with us tonight,' Andy tells me, excitedly.

'How lovely.' I'm truly relieved. He seems such an amiable character, and I'd much prefer to spend the next couple of hours with him than some stuffy, boring old know-it-all. Or worse—Chief Inspector Hinchley!

'We have Alex and his wife, Jenny, too,' Andy calls over to James.

'Oh, good.' James smiles, then whispers to me, 'Her name's Janine, not Jenny.'

'Right.' I giggle. 'Understood.'

'What about Betty and Harold? Did you get them?' Elizabeth asks her husband.

'Drat. No, sorry, old thing. Table only seats eight. I got Ernest Farrell. I want to pick his brains about a vacancy they've got coming up in forensics. Think it might be ideal for Daniel Britten, what do you think?'

'Good idea,' Elizabeth agrees cheerily. 'What's his wife's name?'

'Daniel's?'

'No, silly, Ernest's.'

'Ah, now, I know this. It's Samantha. Or Susan. Actually, I think it's Penelope, come to think of it.'

'Penelope? You're sure, Andrew?'

He shakes his head. 'Not really. It's that sort of name, anyway.'

The *female* sort? I wonder, stifling a giggle. That narrows it down. Not!

We've finally reached the doorway of the large room and I look around at all the circular tables full of people chattering and laughing.

Waiting-on staff are lined up around the edges of the room, and I surmise we're about to be served banquet style, which is understandable given the number of diners. There must be about two hundred and fifty guests, I'd imagine. I'm glad I don't have to serve them all.

'I got us a corner table by the window,' Andy announces.

'Oh, good. I can't stand being too warm,' Elizabeth replies, fanning herself already.

'R.H.I.P.,' Andy confides to me, tapping the side of his nose.

I assume my confusion must have shown as he goes on to explain, 'Rank has its privileges.'

'Oh, of course.' I beam at him. He's a handy guy to have around.

'Plus, I gave a rather hefty backhander to Parsons, the guy who organises the seating plan,' he adds quietly.

I can well believe it. This man's a legend.

He takes the lead, heading towards a table tucked in a corner by the window. Most of the diners have now found their seats, so I feel a little self-conscious as we follow the portly old man between the tables. Suddenly, he stops short.

'Hang on a minute. That's not right.'

'What is it, dear?' Elizabeth sounds a little perturbed.

'That flaming Hinchley fellow's got my table!'

'Surely, you must be mistaken. We must be on another one?' She sounds calm, but there's no mistaking the concern on Elizabeth's face as she looks around the restaurant.

There are now only five empty seats—and they're all on Chief Inspector Hinchley's table.

14

We approach the table, and sure enough, the little name plates by the empty chairs bear our names.

Andy clears his throat. 'Seems to have been some mistake,' he says, frowning at Hinchley.

The chief inspector raises his eyebrows disinterestedly. 'Really?'

'Yes. I was told we were sharing with Farrell, the forensics chap. We had something to discuss.' Andy can't hide his disappointment as he looks around the table, though he manages a nod to the couple who are sitting next to Hinchley.

'There must have been a change of plan,' Hinchley replies with a look of apathy.

'Just sit down, Andrew,' Elizabeth urges, as people on nearby tables look over at us.

'Can't have dinner with him. The man's an arse,' Andy mutters as we all take our seats. 'I'll be getting my money back from Parsons, you mark my words.'

I'm happy to be sandwiched between James and Andy, while the seat next to James is empty, followed by Hinchley, then a woman I presume to be Janine. Next to her is her husband, Alex, if I remember correctly, then

Elizabeth. I'm not so thrilled to be sharing with Hinchley, however, but can't help sniggering that his partner obviously hasn't turned up.

James introduces me to the chief inspector, who narrows his eyes as he mutters, 'How do you do?'

'Very well, thank you. How do *you* do?' I reply with a sweet smile.

'And this is Janine and Alex,' James goes on. *Thought so.*

Janine, a very thin lady in red, with short black hair and glasses, gives me a friendly wave across the table, and Alex raises his glass to me, saying, 'Lovely to meet you.'

Hinchley rises to his feet.

'Oh, gawd, not making a speech now, are you?' Andy grumbles.

Hinchley throws him a look of disdain and then peers over towards a woman in a beautiful, sparkly dress who's approaching our table. My heart sinks when I notice that the dress she's wearing is a Jovani. *My* Jovani. The exact same dress as mine but the midnight blue version. To be fair, the colour suits her, as she has beautiful red hair, which she also wears in an up-do.

She arrives and stands, smiling broadly at us as we all look up at her. When I say *look*, I should probably make that *gape* as I recognise her.

'Ladies and gentlemen, may I introduce my partner for this evening, Suzanne Harper.' Hinchley throws a supercilious smirk towards me and James, while Suzanne beams at everyone as though she's a Hollywood superstar being presented on the red carpet.

James' body stiffens beside me and he, along with the other men, stand up politely. Suzanne nods and takes the seat next to James before everyone else sits down again.

'James, what a pleasant surprise.' She smiles at him with all the grace of a crocodile about to devour its next victim.

'Hello, Suzanne. I didn't realise you were coming tonight,' James replies. 'You've met my partner, Libby, haven't you?'

I manage to beam at her. I'm used to plastering on a fake smile and being nice to people I dislike, as I had enough practice working in a hotel recently.

'Suzanne, how nice to see you again.'

'Well, now, I didn't expect to see *you* tonight. I trust you're keeping well?'

'Yes, thank you.' My teeth are gritted, smile intact. *Like hell she wasn't expecting to see me. I'll bet she saw my name on the card when she swapped the place names over. Cow!*

'Oh, yes, *you're* Suzanne, aren't you?' Andy bellows next to me. Then he frowns, giving me an odd look. 'But I thought you...'

'How lovely to see you again,' Elizabeth interrupts, smiling at Suzanne.

'No Felicity tonight, Chief Inspector?' James asks pointedly when the greetings are over.

'No, I'm afraid she couldn't make it. She's come down with the most awful cold. Luckily, Suzanne agreed to step in for her.' Hinchley smiles at his partner for the night.

'How kind of you,' James says, glaring at his ex-wife.

'Oh, it was the least I could do,' Suzanne replies with a sickly smile. 'Felicity and Leonard have always been such good friends to me. I couldn't bear to think of him having to come to the event alone.'

'I see,' James says, his jaw tense.

'Such a thoughtful woman,' Hinchley adds, lifting his glass.

Suzanne chinks her glass against his with a smile and they sip their drinks.

'You're a sergeant, too, aren't you, Alex?' I ask, taking advantage of the fact that the 'golden couple' now have their mouths full.

He smiles at me. 'That's right. James and I were promoted at the same time. Just a case of hanging on to the position now, eh, James?'

'You're right there,' James replies with a relaxed grin.

'Oh, you've both got nothing to worry about,' Andy insists, picking up his glass. 'In fact, I propose a toast. To the two best sergeants the force has ever seen!'

'Hear, hear,' I add, raising my glass with a bright smile.

We all take a drink, although Hinchley and Suzanne don't say anything. Not one word of encouragement. *How rude!*

'And we mustn't forget,' Elizabeth says, 'that behind every great man is a great woman.'

'Of course,' Andy says, smiling at her fondly. He raises his glass. 'To all the great women.'

There's a chorus of 'to the great women' and we all take another sip of champagne.

'So true.' Suzanne looks over at James pointedly as she adds her tuppence worth once everyone has their mouths full. I was right before—*cow!*

James tenses beside me again, and I feel sorry for him as he was actually beginning to relax until his ex opened her mouth again. I can see it's going to be a long night.

Luckily, the food arrives, and we all tuck in. We're starting with seared scallops, one of my favourites. My mouth waters as I gaze at the plate. It's served with fennel and mangetout salad. It's absolutely delicious, and I hear myself groan with pleasure. *Oops!*

'I like a woman who appreciates good food,' Andy assures me with a smile as I blush profusely.

'I do,' I admit, grateful for his good nature.

'Yes.' Suzanne throws me a condescending look, making my blood boil. 'So, we see.'

James clears his throat, as though warning us not to make a scene. *As if I would!*

I ignore her and continue with my salad. She's trying to insinuate that I'm fat, I just know it. *Flaming cheek!* She's not exactly Twiggy herself. I have to admit she is a *bit* slimmer than me—but then she's also older, so that accounts for it, right? Besides, there's a difference between being slim and being downright scrawny.

The beef arrives shortly afterwards, and my heart lightens. I keep a close check on myself to ensure I don't make a sound this time as I enjoy the food.

'This is lovely,' Andy declares, attacking his meal with great gusto.

I smile at him. 'It is,' I agree, 'isn't it, James?'

When I turn to face James, I'm disappointed to find him murmuring something with Suzanne. She gives me a condescending look and continues the conversation as though I haven't spoken.

'Sorry,' James says, suddenly realising I'm awaiting a response. 'What were you saying?'

'Andy and I were just admiring the food.'

'Oh, yes, very nice.' It's then that I notice James has hardly touched his.

'As I was saying,' Suzanne says, turning his attention back to her.

I'm determined not to let her ruin my evening, so I smile over at Janine, who is sitting directly opposite me.

'So, Janine, what do you do?' I ask.

She looks a little surprised, but also thankful that I'm speaking to her. Hinchley's obviously not good company, and Alex is discussing foreign holidays with Elizabeth and Andy.

'I'm a secondary school teacher,' Janine replies, her eyes lighting up.

'Ooh, I wanted to be a teacher when I was little,' I say.

'You can't. Only grown-ups can be teachers,' she informs me with a smile.

I laugh. For some reason I didn't expect her to have a sense of humour. I can see I'm going to get on well with this woman.

Andy's clearly been listening in to our conversation as he guffaws, making everyone on our table and a few neighbouring ones turn to look at him.

'What did you want to be when you grew up, Andy?' I ask, glad that the atmosphere has lightened.

'A fireman,' he replies. 'I really fancied going around with the sirens blaring, making everyone get out of the way to let me through. Then I saw how dangerous it was and decided I could get the same effect by joining the police, so I did.'

'Isn't that a dangerous job, too?' I ask.

'Not if you're sitting behind a desk all day. Isn't that right, Hinchley?' Andy looks over at the chief inspector who scowls at him but says nothing.

'Of course, when I was younger, coming up through the ranks I had my fair share of action,' Andy goes on. 'Got shot once during a riot.'

'Oh, no.' I quickly place my knife down and put a hand to my mouth. 'Was it bad?'

'Just a graze,' Andy assures me. 'Nothing I couldn't handle.'

Elizabeth pats his arm. 'Such a brave man.' Pride oozes from her face.

'It would be a different story these days,' Andy goes on. 'Too many drugs about. People getting high and then attacking innocent parties. I don't understand it.' He shakes his head.

'Yes, it must be quite scary when you're dealing with drug users,' I say, looking questioningly at Hinchley.

'We don't have an easy job,' the chief inspector tells me bluntly. 'Especially with all the *interference* we have to cope with.' His eyes bore into mine and I get hotter.

I take a deep breath. 'I don't think anyone has an easy job these days,' I reply.

'You can say that again,' Janine says.

'Okay. I don't think anyone has an easy job these days.' I grin as she and Andy erupt into laughter.

'I like you,' Andy says, lifting his glass.

I chink mine against his. 'I like you, too.'

'I like you three,' Janine adds, holding her glass up to us.

We all chink together like the three musketeers with their swords, giggling.

Hinchley rolls his eyes. He'd never be one of the musketeers. Too stiff and serious. Even d'Artagnan had a sense of humour.

***

I look up at James as the waitress whisks my plate away. He looks tense. Annoyed. Suzanne has been muttering to him all the way through the main course, and I think it's taken its toll. As he reaches for his glass, I catch his eye.

'Lovely meal,' I say, smiling.

'Yes.'

Suzanne leans into him again, but I cut her off before she can speak.

'Do you know what we're having for dessert?' I ask, snuggling a little closer to him.

'Why, are you still hungry?' Suzanne interjects with a sneer.

I'm not really hungry, although I do love anything sweet. I was just making conversation, though I shouldn't really need to make small talk with my boyfriend, I realise. I plaster on my fake smile and raise my voice a little, leaning forward.

'Goodness, Suzanne! Did you say you're still hungry? You must have a healthy appetite—isn't that right, Andy?'

Andy guffaws and the others titter politely.

'No. That's not what I...' Suzanne's protest is cut off by the waiting-on staff suddenly reaching over to put our pear soufflés in front of us.

'Pear soufflé, warm salt caramel fudge and cinnamon ice cream,' Andy declares. 'My favourite!' He looks over to Suzanne. 'This'll fill you up, dear,' he says, cheerily.

Suzanne just stares at him.

James and I exchange a little smirk before eating our sweets. I feel warmth spread through my body at being so close to him—I just wish his ex-wife wasn't so close to him, too.

Andy's certainly enjoyed his meal tonight, and something tells me he probably had a hand in choosing the menu as well as the seating plan. He wastes no time in finishing off his soufflé and puts down his cutlery with a contented sigh.

'This is lovely, isn't it?' I say to James once I notice Suzanne has just taken a mouthful of ice cream.

'Not as lovely as you. Did I tell you how beautiful you look tonight?' His eyes twinkle as he gazes at me, and I get that funny jittery feeling in my tummy again.

'You did, but you can tell me again if you want to,' I tease.

He opens his mouth, and I'm sure he's about to repeat himself for fun, but Suzanne butts in.

'Oh, James, I meant to tell you something,' she says, leaning forwards.

James' face clouds over for a second and then he turns to face her. 'What is it now, Suzanne?'

She looks taken aback by his attitude but continues anyway. 'I thought you'd want to know we had some viewers at the house the other day,' she tells him. 'But of course, if you're more interested in your friend there, I shan't bother.'

James sits a little straighter, his interest piqued. 'Did they put in an offer?'

Suzanne gives me a supercilious sneer before continuing. 'Not yet, but it looks hopeful. Nice family. Young children, that sort of thing. Husband works abroad a lot. They seem pretty wealthy, so hopefully they'll pay the full asking price.'

James sags a little in relief. 'That's good.'

I'm not so sure. 'What was the wife like?' I ask, smiling. 'It's normally the wife who has the final say. If she liked it, you might be in luck.'

Suzanne narrows her eyes at me, making it clear that she doesn't think it's any of my business. James looks questioningly at her, though, so she doesn't have much choice but to reply. 'She wasn't there.' Her voice is clipped.

That confirms my suspicion about who the viewers were.

'Oh.' James looks disappointed. 'Mind you, if the guy went there unaccompanied, maybe he wants it to be a surprise for her?'

'Well, he had another man with him. A friend. Said the wife was heavily pregnant so wasn't able to come.' Suzanne looks thoughtful.

I'm glad Rob and Ben did such a good job in convincing her they were genuine, but I'm intrigued as to why she wants James to think they might buy when she tried so hard to put them off.

Our coffees arrive, and I slip my fingers over James' as we both reach for the cream at the same time.

'Of course, I'll let you know if they make an appointment for a second viewing,' Suzanne says, obviously trying to keep James' attention.

A thud in my stomach makes me pour a little too much cream into my cup, and James frowns at me. I stare back at him. *She's trying to keep your attention*, I try to tell him telepathically, but he doesn't seem to understand. It's only Cassie who seems able to communicate with me that way, unfortunately. *She's keeping you dangling on a string.* Still no reaction. Then he turns back to face her as she goes on about the house.

I take a slow sip of my coffee—which is actually rather nice with extra cream. I know what Suzanne's game is; she'll keep James thinking that they're going to get an offer any day soon, so he won't get suspicious. As long as he thinks they're just waiting for the lovely family to get back to them, she's got every excuse to keep contacting him. She must know he can't have a real relationship with me until all this is tied up, so she's stalling. *Bitch.*

After the meal, most people go through to the ballroom, where the music is already playing. However, as Suzanne is still talking with James it's a little awkward for Hinchley and me to go anywhere, so we stay put. Either side of the couple. Who aren't a couple anymore. *I wish someone would remind Suzanne of that!*

My heart sank when Andy and Elizabeth followed Janine and Alex out the door—after Andy making me promise to dance with him later. I wanted to go with them but thought better of it.

I lean right over to catch the chief inspector's eye while the other two are talking. 'Did you organise all this?' I ask him with a bright smile.

'Not exactly,' he replies, curling his lip.

'Well, it's very nice,' I offer.

He rolls his eyes and looks away.

'You and Suzanne are obviously very close,' I say.

That got his attention. He glares at me incredulously. 'She happens to be a friend of the family, yes.'

'How nice.'

He's still staring at me, huffing like a traction engine. He clearly doesn't know what to say. Not that I'm insinuating anything, of course. At least, not *really*.

'It was good of her to step in tonight,' I say, casually, adding, 'Two lonely people brought together.' I give a wistful sigh.

'Lonely? I'm not lonely. I'm married, for goodness' sake.'

I glance at him as though he's just pulled me from my thoughts. 'Oh, yes, so you are,' I say a little louder than I should. 'But *she's* not.'

15

The chief inspector quickly suggests following the others to the ballroom, so we all get up and leave the table. The Wellington Ballroom is on the first floor, so I quickly link my arm through James', and we take the lead. I'm hoping that we might lose the others on the way there, so we won't have to spend any more time with them tonight, but they're practically snapping at our heels.

'This is beautiful,' I say as I gaze up at the massive golden chandeliers. Only the ones near the entrance are lit, as a wooden dance floor has been erected at the other end of the room where a few people are already performing some interesting moves. Small tables are dotted throughout the room, and I'm determined we'll be sitting on a different one to the couple behind us.

'Oh, look!' Suzanne's exclamation draws the attention of everyone on the tables near the entrance and several who are just mingling. She's pointing at me. 'I didn't realise we're wearing the same dress! How odd is that?'

There is laughter all around us and people are nodding and pointing at me. I just want the ground to swallow me up. I consider running for the ladies' but it's too late. Everyone's noticed, thanks to 'Gob Almighty'.

'What are the chances of that?' I smile although I'm dying inside. *Dying to strangle that bitch!*

'Oh, I like it in this colour,' one of the ladies says, and suddenly they're all deciding which looks the best!

One or two get closer to examine my sparkles and my blood boils even more.

'What about these?' I kick the woman taking up my space in front of me, showing off my Prives.

'They're Louboutins,' one of the women marvels, while the one with the bruised shin narrows her eyes at me.

'The latest style,' another chimes in. She's pregnant and is wearing some lovely Kurt Geigers. Obviously, a woman of taste.

'New Very Prive Quadro Lurex,' I say as they all crowd around me for a good look.

'Gosh, I bet they're expensive,' someone comments. I don't recognise her shoes at all.

'Not too bad,' I say, aware of James' sudden interest.

'Beautiful,' they all mutter, nodding.

'I'm Libby, by the way,' I say brightly. Next thing, I'm shaking hands with Melinda, Bryony, Tiffany, Cheryl, Maisie, Aashi, Lydia, Michelle, Veronica, and goodness knows who else. They're a really friendly bunch and want to know all about me, my work, my clothes...

'This is my boyfriend, James,' I say, surprised at the bewildered look on his face.

'Hi, James,' they chorus.

'Hello.'

'And what do you do?' Maisie, an older lady, asks him.

'How about a dance, Libby?' Tiffany asks, and they all cheer and head towards the other end of the room.

I look back to James and point to the dance floor. He nods, still speaking with Maisie.

We all pile onto the wooden tiles and the DJ immediately swaps Tom Jones for The Weather Girls, eliciting a rapturous cheer and an oddly harmonised rendition of the song sung at full pelt and with some interesting actions.

The women, ranging in age from about twenty to seventy, if you include Maisie—who eventually joins us—are lovely and welcome me into their throng with open arms, literally.

I was expecting a string quartet or ballroom dancing or something, but this is amazing. The DJ plays some really great music and we're joined by loads of other dancers. The atmosphere's electric. Even James comes to join in after a while, having removed his jacket and bow tie and rolled his sleeves up a little, exposing his muscular, tanned forearms. Delightful. He twirls me around the wooden floor and my head spins deliciously with all the champagne, loud music and dancing.

After a while, we leave the others and go to find some more Bollinger.

'Come and join us,' Veronica insists, and we sit at a small table with her, Tiffany, and their partners, Liam and Craig.

Liam, Tiffany's boyfriend, turns out to be a real laugh as he regales us with some hilarious stories about when he was working on a cruise ship. I don't see James laugh very often, so it's lovely to see him so relaxed and happy.

About an hour later, I really need the loo, so I peel myself from James' arm, which he's had around my shoulder ever since we sat down, and head for the ladies'.

The toilets are as luxurious as the rest of the hotel, with dim lighting, thick carpets and a host of soaps and hand creams to choose from. Luckily, I don't have to queue as there are only a couple of women in there right now, and I'm soon back at the vanity unit washing my hands with the softest, luxury soap I've ever used. The hand dryer is efficient but quiet—one you could actually use while holding a conversation—and then I decide to check my lipstick. It's not supposed to come off, I know, but I never quite trust these things.

The door opens and I turn, knocking my Louboutin clutch onto the floor. I bend down to retrieve it and my heart sinks when I look up to see Suzanne standing above me with her hands on her hips.

'Got a job scrubbing floors, now, have you?' she sneers.

Just how does one scrub Axminster?

'Yes,' I say airily. 'This is the new uniform. Oh, I see you're working for the same company. Come to help, have you?'

I put my purse and lippy back into the clutch, along with a couple of tissues, and stand up to face her.

'Think you're funny, don't you?' Suzanne purses her lips angrily.

'I have my moments.'

She takes a step closer, and I suddenly notice a small piece of card under her silver Dior sandal. *Shit!* The price tag off my dress must have fallen out of my bag.

Trying to ignore her steely gaze, I turn back to the mirror and proceed to touch up my lipstick. I'm glad to see that my hair has stayed in place all evening—despite some really fancy moves on the dance floor—and my make-up still looks good. I don't really need to reapply the lippy, but I'm just buying some time before I can reclaim the label Suzanne is still standing on.

'You've got a bloody nerve,' Suzanne replies.

I smack my lips together before turning back to face her. I'm disappointed that she hasn't moved yet.

'What?'

'You heard me. You're not a policeman's wife. You shouldn't be here.'

'Neither are you,' I remind her. 'Should *you* be here?'

Her eyes flash as she stares back at me. 'At least I *was* a sergeant's wife.'

'And now you're with a chief inspector. Does that mean you've been promoted?'

She presses her lips together tightly. 'I'm not *with* him. He's just a friend.'

'Oh. That's right. You came together because his wife's ill and your boyfriend's... er?' I try to walk past her as I speak, but she spins around, taking a step towards the door.

She notices the exposed piece of card at the same time I do, and snatches it up before I get the chance. *Damn!*

While she examines it, I use the distraction to brush past her and open the door. Several people are milling about in the corridor, and a few look around as I step out.

'Ha!' Suzanne's hot on my heels and she yanks my arm, spinning me around to face her. 'You got your dress in the sale, I see.' She holds up the ticket and everyone goes quiet around us.

My whole body burns, and I just know I'm turning red. *Where's a green face mask when you need one?* I take a deep breath, my mind whirring.

'Of course,' I say, 'didn't you?' I raise my eyebrows at her, forcing myself to steady my breathing.

'Absolutely not!' she scorns. 'I *always* pay full price for everything.' She sticks her nose in the air.

'More fool you,' I say. 'There's no shame in saving money.'

I hear a few murmurs of approval from the people loitering around us.

'Some people have no shame anyway,' she says, flicking her hand towards me as if shooing away a fly.

My blood's past boiling point now. I've had enough of her tonight.

'You're right,' I say as coolly as I can manage. 'I paid for my dress myself with my own hard-earned money. I didn't have an allowance from my ex-husband that I could squander on new clothes while he thought he was paying utility bills for my house.'

Gasps can be heard all around me, Suzanne's being the loudest.

Her face turns red and her jaw is tenser than ever. 'What did you say?'

'You heard me,' I reply. 'Your ex is working his socks off to pay for his own tiny flat as well as supplement bills for your massive house in Richmond. And all the time you're frittering away his cash on seven-hundred-pound frocks and Dior shoes. Furthermore, you're putting potential buyers off by telling them the house is in a horrid area with useless, local schools—and all so you can continue living the life of Riley with your new boyfriend.'

The air is filled with gulps and murmurs, which start to get louder as more people come to witness the action.

'How dare you?' Suzanne screams at me.

'What? Tell the truth?' I can't believe she's screeching her head off in a corridor of the Park Lane Hilton in front of all these people. *Some people have no shame!*

'Oliver is just a friend.' she insists.

'Chief Inspector Hinchley's just a friend,' I point out, 'but *he* doesn't leave his razor in your bathroom and show potential buyers around your home, does he?'

If looks could kill, I'd be six feet under by now.

As if in slow motion, I watch in horror as Suzanne grabs a glass of red wine from one of the spectators and throws it down my dress. I'm sure my heart stops beating for a moment. *I'll never be able to return it now!*

There's a collective hiss from the crowd, who seem as disbelieving as I am that she'd do such a thing. Some move closer to get a better view of the damage.

'That's enough!' A man's voice stops everyone in their tracks and silence falls over us as James strides through the crowd carrying my jacket.

Despite my reeling mind, I manage a pious expression for Suzanne, who just glares at James.

'Time to go,' he says, holding out my fur for me to put on.

'Thank you,' I say, giving Suzanne a supercilious grin. *Gosh, it feels good!*

'Did you hear what she said about me?' Suzanne demands.

'Every word.' He looks tense again.

'It's slander.' She scowls at me.

'It's the truth.' I scowl back.

'Leave it, Libby.' James' voice is so curt I'm actually shocked.

'She's been lying to you, James. Keeping secrets and...'

'I said leave it.'

My stomach roils with horror. He's chastising me. In front of her. In front of everyone.

'We're leaving. Now.' His face is as dark as thunder, his jaw clenched.

'So, it's okay for her to live with her boyfriend while you support them both and let them live in your lovely big house in Richmond?'

'Not here, Libby.' He puts a firm hand at my back, urging me to leave. But I'm not standing for this.

'Or is it someone else you're supporting?' I turn to face him. 'Someone like your *son*, perhaps?'

***

Without waiting around for his excuses, I turn and rush out the door, hail a taxi, and head for home while tears stream down my cheeks. James' shocked face haunts me. I couldn't work out whether he was confused because it wasn't true or devastated because it was. Either way, I hadn't given him time to argue with me.

I pull a tissue from my clutch and begin dabbing at the wine stain on the journey home. There's no way I can return the dress now, but at least I'll be able to wear it again if I can remove this mess.

It's a relief when we pull up outside my home, and I quickly pay the driver before rushing into the building. I can't let anyone see me in this state.

As soon as I get into the flat, I throw the clutch onto the sofa, kick off my Louboutins and peel off the jacket. Luckily, the wine went down the skirt part of my dress so none of it touched Cassie's milky-white fur. I'm already unzipping the dress as I head for the kitchen.

Thankfully, I've managed to remove the worst of the splotch. Taking a clean, white tea towel, I place it under the dress, then dampen another towel and continue blotting the wine with it. Next, I grab the table salt from the cupboard and pour it over the affected area, praying that it doesn't scratch the crystals as it soaks up the stain.

I have to wipe mascara-mixed-tears from my face with the back of my arm, mindful of not marking the dress any more than it already is. Once my blurred vision is back to normal, I can see that the salt seems to be doing its job in lifting out the stain. Relief starts to seep into me for the first time in what feels like hours, and I notice I'm shivering with cold, standing in just my underwear. I daren't stop blotting the dress, though, so continue dabbing and removing the salt crystals along with the blemish.

When I've finished, I wash the affected part of the dress in cool water and wrap it in a towel to remove as much liquid as I can. It takes a couple of gentle squeezes to get the majority of moisture from the fabric before I lay the dress out flat to dry.

Only then do I allow myself the luxury of going into the bedroom, stripping off the rest of my clothes and diving under the warm shower.

Relief at removing the stain mingles with regret that things ended so badly with James and fresh tears mix with the shower's powerful jet. The heat of the water coupled with the late hour make me yawn, and I quickly finish getting washed before hauling a large towel around me and heading for bed.

***

I didn't expect to sleep so soundly but don't wake up until I hear a key turning in the front door. It's already light and the birds are singing. Cassie's chatting happily, and I hear a couple of male voices that I assume belong to Rob and Ben.

Taking a deep breath, I dive into the bathroom and get ready. I pull on a pair of comfy jeans and a T-shirt, and tie my hair in a ponytail, glad that it's only Sunday.

They're all standing in the kitchen, giggling, when I go through. Rob has a copy of the *Daily Chronicle* in his hand.

'Hi, we brought breakfast,' Cassie announces, pointing to a couple of McDonald's bags on the table. She frowns. 'Is everything okay?'

She's looking behind me and I realise she expected me to have company last night. *Some hope!*

'Yes, fine.'

'I'll have the extra bacon McMuffin if no one else wants it?' Ben volunteers.

I push one of the bags towards him then pull out the contents of the other.

'Was it a good night?' Cassie asks, walking towards me.

'It was very... eventful,' I reply. 'What about you?'

'We all went to the cinema. There was a really scary film on, though I only actually watched half of it,' she says with a grin.

'It wasn't scary.' Ben rolls his eyes, stuffing the spare McMuffin into his mouth.

'Well, it was more... I don't know... *menace* than horror,' she concedes.

'And talking of menaces,' Rob says with a grin. 'Have you seen this?'

We all follow him through to the living room where he spreads open yesterday's newspaper on the floor while we put our drinks on the coffee table.

'It only went in last night. Ben and I stumbled on this story by accident yesterday.' He grins, and I glance at the article. 'I think it's something you were working on the other day.'

I wrack my brain—which still feels a bit mushy from all the champagne, if I'm honest—trying to remember what I was doing last week. It feels like a lifetime ago after the events of last night.

Wronged Wife Wields Knife in Threat to Cheating Husband's Manhood

'Did you find out who it was?' I ask, immediately scanning the text for more information.

'Oh, yeah, we found out, all right.' Ben grins wickedly. 'Read on, McDuff.'

I do as he says, reading aloud. 'Police were called to Hanover Heights on the Sandford Estate recently to stop a woman carrying out her threat to cut off her husband's "manhood" after finding he had been cheating—in more ways than one!

The would-be victim has now been named as Oliver Reynolds, a con man who it is suspected has cheated several women out of large sums of money, while sleeping with them and falsely gaining their trust.

Reynolds, 34, has been accused of making false promises to Alice McGurk, 49, from West London, in April of this year when he proposed to her before she offered him £11,000 to subsidise his non-existent company. Ms McGurk said in a statement to the police "I feel so stupid. I trusted him. He let me think he was a successful businessman. I wanted to marry him. And all the time he was already married and didn't have a penny to his name."

Ms McGurk is believed to not be the only woman to have fallen for Reynolds' lies and police are investigating similar cases, which may be connected. He is thought to have had at least two other girlfriends since Ms McGurk threw him out of her West London home.

It is still not known who told Reynolds' wife, Millie Reynolds, 33, of her husband's adultery, although the police are following leads on several suspects including Ms McGurk and her brother, Frank Thomasson. Police are also eager to speak to the Reynolds' teenage son who disappeared last week after being cleared of any involvement in a drugs raid at Withywood Way, West London.

Investigations are ongoing.'

My stomach is burning, and I don't know how long ago my jaw dropped.

'He's got to be Alfie Reynolds' father.'

'Who?' Ben frowns at me.

I swallow hard, my mind racing. 'There was this young lad who was at the Withywood drugs bust. I knew he wasn't involved,' I begin.

'I remember,' Cassie says. 'You said so at the time.'

'His name is Alfie Reynolds. And I saw him again at the Sandford Estate when the woman—who must be his mum—was hiding behind that car with a knife. The cops came and took her away, but no one else had a clue Alfie was there. I *knew* he had to be involved somehow.'

'So, *he* probably told his mum,' Rob says, his eyes flashing.

'What a bastard.' Ben doesn't mince his words. 'The old man, I mean, not the kid. I wonder how many other poor women he's conned out of their money. And I can't imagine what his wife and son have been put through.'

A niggling doubt at the back of my mind suddenly turns into a full-blown panic.

'Have you seen a picture of this Reynolds guy?' I ask the boys.

Ben shrugs. 'Nope.'

Rob shakes his head. 'There's probably one on the internet somewhere, I'd imagine. There just wasn't time to source one for the article. Why?'

'Because Suzanne Harper's new boyfriend is called Oliver,' I blurt out.

Cassie grabs her laptop and they all start trawling through the internet while I scoop up the rubbish from breakfast. Gut instinct tells me it's the same man, without having the guys confirm it, but I keep quiet.

Something else is eating away at me, too. It's Oliver's son who Suzanne was referring to, not James'. Part of me knew he wasn't a father—I just wish that part of me had taken over last night before I accused him in front of all his colleagues and their spouses.

I check my phone once I've stuffed the rubbish into the recycling bin, and am disappointed, though unsurprised, not to have a message waiting. James must hate me now. I might have lost him his promotion. And I've probably just thrown him right back into the arms of his ex-wife.

I want to cry but at the same time I feel angry. James spent almost the whole meal talking with her last night when he was supposed to be with me. I must admit, Andy and Janine were really fun to spend time with, but I'd have liked James to have joined in, too. And did he know Suzanne would be there? I'd already guessed it was she who had tampered with the seating plan, swapping around the place names—especially as Andy had it all worked out so beautifully. *Bitch.*

'It's him!'

The triumphant chorus from the living room jerks me from my thoughts and I go in to see them all beaming up at me.

'It's definitely the guy who was showing us round the house,' Ben says, looking up at me.

They're all sprawled on the floor, the newspaper now a crumpled heap, cast aside in favour of the laptop.

'Thought so.' I nod.

'We should tell James,' Cassie says. 'Is he coming over?'

'No.'

'Is everything okay?' She stands up and hurries over to me.

'Not really,' I admit.

'Oh, no.' She looks as disappointed as I feel and gives me a warm hug.

'I think someone should tell him, though,' I say, fighting back tears. 'If I say anything, he'll think it's just sour grapes because of Suzanne, but she needs to be warned about Oliver Reynolds.'

'I just hope he hasn't conned her out of any money.' Ben says exactly what I'm thinking.

'Oh, no.' Another thought occurs to me. 'What if he's been pressuring her to get more money from James to fund his non-existent business?'

A heavy thud hits the bottom of my stomach as I recall berating her for gleaning money from her ex-husband to pay for her expensive clothes and shoes. What if I got it all wrong? *Surprising, I know, but it has actually happened before!*

'We definitely need to speak to James,' Cassie says.

'You guys go. I've got something I need to do,' I tell them as brightly as I can manage.

'Are you sure?' Cassie frowns at me. *I get that a lot.*

'Yeah.'

Cassie gives him a call to arrange to go over, then we all fetch our coats and pile out of the door at the same time.

'Need a lift?' she offers as they head for her car.

'No, thanks, I'm fine.' I wave to them, breathing in the cold air.

A brisk walk might just clear my head.

'What on earth happened?' I mutter to myself as the cool breeze blows away the cobwebs in my brain. It's also blowing up my trouser legs, giving me goosebumps on my knees, but we won't go there. I wish I'd worn straight jeans instead of boot leg now.

There aren't many people about, and I can hardly hear myself, let alone be overheard, so I continue.

'On Friday afternoon I had all that resolve. I was going to step it up. Make Dave happy, get my own back on Bethany bitch-face *and* be grown-up about the James situations. Now what's happened?'

The cogs whir in my head as I struggle for the answer. Nothing's forthcoming. I try walking a bit faster, hoping it might help my thoughts sort themselves out, maybe my brain works on a dynamo effect—but I start getting a bit sweaty, so conclude that was a bad idea. At least my brain told me that much. It also suggested taking a taxi the rest of the way, so it's starting to work.

I get dropped off in the high street on the Sandford Estate. It's not as busy as last time I was here, and I take a proper look around. There are several charity shops—one of which has a lovely pink jacket in the window—and a pound shop within the first few feet I cover. Litter is still widespread, and the people seem as unfriendly as they did the other day, but it doesn't worry me. I think I'm getting used to hostility.

I get to the area by the blocks of flats. Some children are playing on the rusty old car, pulling bits off it and throwing them at each other. Nice. The mound where Dave and everyone else seemed to think Millie Reynolds was hiding has now been taken over by a group of scary looking teenagers, smoking and giggling. Makes me wonder just *what* they're smoking, but it's none of my business. *Besides, I did mention they were scary looking, didn't I?*

There's a rowdy game of football being played over by the nearest block of flats, the wall of which seems to have become one of the goals—I'll bet the occupants love that!

I stroll over, looking for Hanover Heights, the block where the Reynolds live. It's not hard to miss. Loud music is blaring from one of the downstairs flats where the window is wide open, and I can hear yelling in the background. A young boy of about three or four is swinging on the main front door, holding onto the handles and wrapping his legs around the door, shouting 'wee' over and over. I *think* that's the sound of him enjoying himself and not an indication of something more sinister but judging by the dribbles down the front of the door I can't be too sure.

Unfortunately, the number of the flat wasn't given in the newspaper—we're not allowed to divulge details like that—and I'm in two minds about asking the 'wee' boy if he knows the Reynolds.

While I'm contemplating what to do, someone runs past me. At first, I assume it's one of the footballers, but then I recognise his hair.

'Hey, wait a minute.'

The guy stops and turns around, frowning at me.

'You're Alfie, aren't you?'

He frowns even harder. 'Who are you?'

'I'm Libby. Do you remember me?'

His grumpy expression tells me he does.

'Can I talk to you a sec?' I'm trying to sound all casual, but he's still scowling at me.

'What about?'

'Look, can we go for a coffee or something? I'm paying.'

He still looks suspicious.

Then I remember Dave and his contacts. I pull a £10 note out of my purse and hold it up to him.

'I'll pay you for your time.'

I thought he'd be pleased. I'm sure that's how they do it on the telly. And Dave must pay for his information, surely? But Alfie just looks mystified, and I wonder what he actually thinks I'm hoping to pay him for.

'I just want to talk to you,' I explain.

He looks a little relieved, but still narrows his eyes at me.

'Come on, I'll tell you on the way.' Cajoling seems to work, but he still snatches the tenner out of my hand before he comes with me.

We find a 'greasy spoon' just off the high street and sit at a rickety table in the corner. I'm not sure how clean the cups will be, so I opt for a bottle of Coke and a straw, while Alfie chooses a large hot chocolate with extra cream, a plateful of chips, two doughnuts, a chocolate brownie and three bags of crisps for later. I watch silently as he heaps his fourth spoonful of sugar into his drink.

'You were at that house,' he accuses me, the suspicion still not leaving his eyes.

'That's right. I spoke to the cops. They let you off, didn't they?'

His expression changes to one of surprise. 'You did that?'

I shrug, not wanting to lie. 'I had a word.'

'Oh.'

If I was expecting a thank you, I'd have been sorely disappointed.

'You weren't involved in the raid, were you?' It suddenly occurs to me that I might have got it wrong—after all, it has been known.

'Drugs?' he sneers at me. 'God, no.'

'That's what I said.' More relief than I'd care to admit washes over me.

'Were you really just squatting in the attic?'

He nods, his mouth full of chips lathered in red sauce, which drips down his chin.

'I thought so.' I sip my Coke, hoping he'll elaborate once he empties his mouth.

He doesn't do either. Just shovels even more chips in and continues to chomp.

'So, don't you have a home?'

He shrugs. 'Sometimes. Me dad chucked me out, though.'

My heart lurches. 'Why?'

Another shrug.

'What about your mum? Didn't she want you at home?' I hate to think of an unwanted child, left to fend for himself on the mean streets of London.

'It was 'cos of her,' he says, incredulously.

'What did she do?' I frown.

He shakes his head. 'You don't get it.' His mouth is still full, and bits of chip fly out each time he speaks, but I'm trying to ignore it and just keep a safe distance.

'So, your dad threw you out because of your mum?' I clarify.

He sneers at me. 'No.'

'What then?'

He gives a huff, and I swing my chair back on two legs to avoid being splattered by the barrage of chewed chips that shoot out along with his rancid breath.

'Dad's seeing some bit of posh. I threatened to tell Mum. He threw me out so I couldn't say anything.' He makes it all sound so reasonable.

'That's awful. Has it happened before?'

He nods. 'This time, I told her, though.' He grins. 'She waited for him to come home, then threatened to chop his dick off with the bread knife.' He chuckles. Then frowns. 'You were there, weren't you? I saw you.'

I nod. 'Yeah. I think your dad might be seeing a friend of mine in Richmond now.' I use the word 'friend' for fear of arousing suspicion, though in my head I put it in quotation marks.

'Sounds right,' he says with a nod. 'Another posh bird. They're always posh. And rich.'

'Would you know if he's taken any money from her?'

He starts on the chocolate brownie. 'Probably. He pretends he's got money and a great business. Then he tells them he's waiting for some cash to come from abroad or somewhere. They always offer to tide him over until it comes through. Works every time.'

'Does your mum know about it?' I can't believe he's so blasé on the subject.

He looks at me as though I'm stupid. *I know, right?* 'Not about the other birds,' he says. 'Well, until this one. But what can he expect if he throws me out? I'm not gonna just stand by and let him walk all over the pair of us, am I?'

'Of course, not.'

'Mum thinks he's got a business, though. That's how he gets away with sleeping around. She thinks he's away with work. When he comes back, he's got money. He even gave her new trainers last time. Mum doesn't ask questions.'

The first doughnut faces the black hole that is Alfie's mouth, and I know it's not worth asking anything else for a moment or two so I sip my Coke, trying to make sense of it all.

'Took me ages to twig,' he goes on, licking his fingers. 'I mean, I knew he was up to *something*, but I didn't know what. Then I saw him over in West London when he was supposed to be abroad. Had some real Bobby Dazzler wiv 'im. Bright red hair she had, beautiful. He's always had a thing for redheads—tried to get Mum to dye her Barnet once but she refused. Anyway, they didn't see me. I was watching through the restaurant window. She paid, of course.' He rolls his eyes.

'Of course,' I echo.

'I asked him about her when he finally made it home. Not in front of Mum, though.' He sighs. 'That's when he threatened me. Said if I breathed a word of it to 'er indoors he'd kill me. I reckon he meant it an' all.'

'Oh, no.' The thought sickens me.

He curls his lip as though he couldn't care less.

'I never said a word, but somehow Mum got suspicious. She's not as stupid as he thinks. Then he accuses me of blabbin' to her. Chucked me out, he did. Told me not to come back.'

'So, you went to live in that house and got caught up in the drugs raid?' My stomach churns knowing the danger he'd unwittingly put himself in. He's still only a kid, after all.

'Yeah.' He's just finishing his second doughnut, jam squirting everywhere.

'After all that malarkey, I thought I'd be safer at home—at least while Dad wasn't there. That's why I told Mum. Thought if she knew she'd chuck *him* out. Then I could move back in.' He grins. 'Hadn't reckoned on her hacking off his bits, though.'

'She didn't actually do it, did she?' I suddenly feel alarmed.

'Nah. Fucking coward ran off, didn't he? Made it safe for me to move back in, though. Don't reckon he'll be back in a hurry.' He gives a triumphant laugh.

I shake my head. I've got to hand it to him—he's a shrewd kid.

He stuffs the crisps into his pocket, crushing them, no doubt, and we head back towards his home.

'I remember seeing you,' he says, as we near the flats.

I swallow hard. I daren't tell him I'm a reporter after everything he's just told me. Not that I'm planning on putting all his personal business in the paper, of course.

'You were with that bald guy, weren't you?'

I'm about to admit to it when he adds 'the bouncer'.

I stop walking and stare at him. 'What?'

'Don't deny it. Is he your boyfriend? I've seen 'im on the door of a couple of clubs in town.'

I don't know what to say, so I just smile. *Surely Dave can't be moonlighting?*

'Will your mum be home now?'

'Yeah.'

'Good.' We walk a little closer to his tower block. 'Well, it was nice talking to you. See you around, Alfie.'

'Okay.' He looks quite happy as he waves and then runs the rest of the way to Hanover Heights.

I check out the pink jacket in the window of the charity shop on the way back up the high street. It's really lovely, with sweet little pearl buttons down the front. Unfortunately, I can't see the ticket with the size on, and the shop doesn't open on Sundays anyway.

There aren't many taxis in this area, so I have to walk quite a way before I see one and can actually rest my feet. I pull out my mobile as the driver chunters on about the latest football results and open a message from Cassie.

Hey, babe. Told James about you-know-what. He had his suspicions something wasn't right with Suzanne, so he's gone over to confront her about it. Said he didn't really get the chance last night after you mentioned *it. Turns out he knows of Oliver Reynolds already. Will tell you more later. Xxx*

I lean back in the seat and let out a long sigh. No word of James missing me or being upset about last night or anything. He doesn't care. Well, fine. Two can play at that game!

17

I open my wardrobe with fresh eyes the next morning. It's the start of a new week, a new beginning and a new me. Mondays aren't usually this exciting but today is different. Cassie and I are going to the new gym tonight, so I'm taking my kit with me to work and I'll meet her at the venue. It'll save time travelling and makes perfect sense.

As I'm taking my Nike trainers with me, I can change into them if I need to run across town, too. I'm going to wear my black and white Karen Millen skater dress and a pair of Jimmy Choo Hoxton 100 knee-high boots in black leather—boots courtesy of Cassie as I'm still saving up for a pair. They're high-heeled and look great with the dress—or anything else for that matter— and I feel so good in the outfit that I've done my make-up extra specially well and put my hair in a half-up, half-down style with a pretty, sparkly clip.

I've decided to buy lunch today despite what James Harper thinks about it being a waste of money. This means I can take a really pretty little handbag—I've gone for the black Kate Spade I picked up last summer in the Harvey Nicks' sale—as I can stuff my make-up and paperback into my gym bag. I've got a black Adidas by Stella McCartney—looks great and holds loads.

'Wow, look at you!' Cassie whistles admiringly as I strut into the living room.

I twirl with a giggle, making my dress spin out around me. At least I'll be able to run in it if necessary, whereas anything tighter would be constrictive.

She smiles. 'Did James ring you last night like he said he would?'

'Um...' I'm not sure how to tell her I switched my phone off to avoid the call.

'Don't tell me he let you down?' She frowns. 'He promised me. After all that stuff you found out for him as well.'

'Maybe he'll call today,' I suggest. 'He might have been busy with Suzanne and all that Oliver Reynolds stuff.'

She nods, but I can tell she's not impressed with him. I just hope she doesn't call him up to tell him what she thinks. Hopefully, she'll be too busy. Then it'll all blow over and we won't even think about it.

'Got to go,' I say, pulling on my black woollen jacket.

'Okay. I'll be staying home tonight after the gym,' she promises. 'Sorry about last night. Hey, you'll have to tell me all about what happened with your dress.' She eyes it still lying on the towel on the kitchen counter. 'In fact, I want to hear about the whole night—James was very cagey about it all, and you...'

'See you at the gym,' I shout, cutting her off as I rush out the door.

I know she was desperate to know what's happened, but luckily Ben had taken her and Rob out for dinner last night as a thank-you for letting him tag along to the cinema with them on Saturday. Then they'd gone back to Rob's for the night, so we didn't get to talk. She must have asked James, but it sounds like he didn't tell her anything either—no surprise there—so the poor thing's dying for some gossip. Maybe I'll feel more like talking about it tonight. Or perhaps, we'll be so tired after our workout at the gym that we'll both just go home and flop. Fingers crossed.

It's gratifying to get so many admiring glances on the Tube for a change, and I feel great as I walk into the office. Everyone stops talking and they all just stare at me.

'Morning,' I say with a bright smile and remove my jacket.

Even Bethany and her chums are gawping at me. Then two of them leave the room, while Sophie continues to stare my way.

When Dave finally puts his tongue back into his mouth, he clears his throat and mutters, 'You'll never run in those boots.'

'Actually, running isn't in my contract,' I inform him. 'I need to 'travel to the necessary destination using the quickest means possible' when following a story.' I used my fingers for quotation marks, just to prove I know what I'm talking about. 'For me, running isn't usually the quickest means to get anywhere.'

Dave scowls. 'Well, you can make your own way by Tube if that's what you want but I'm telling you now, you'll miss out on everything. You'll never get a good story relying on public transport to get you to the scene of the action. Ask them.' He points to Sophie's desk.

'That's okay. I've got my trainers with me if I need them,' I reply, switching on my computer.

He looks relieved. I knew that would rile him. Not that it isn't true. I checked my contract. But he's quite right, I'd never get a good story if I had to wait for the next number twenty-seven bus or whatever. I need to get a car. I'm saving up.

Tom chuckles. I think he enjoys seeing Dave on the back foot for a change.

'Here.' He places a coffee in front of me and I smile.

'Thanks, Tom.' That's a first.

He goes off to pour one for a guy who's just arrived to fix the CCTV. Goodness knows why, but we've got cameras everywhere in this building—and on the outside.

Shortly afterwards, Carol-Anne and Bethany return and start whispering with Sophie at the other end of the room. I don't even want to know what they're on about. I think Sophie might be okay, though she's not the sharpest tool in the box, and I'm not sure about Carol-

Anne yet. We all know about Bethany bitch-face though, and I've noticed she seems to be the ringleader.

'I saw the paper on Friday,' I say to Dave as Tom returns to his desk. 'That piece on Oliver Reynolds.'

'What about it?' Dave frowns.

'It sort of ties in with our story about the Lorena Bobbitt woman over at the Sandford.' My stomach roils with excitement, and I'm relieved when Dave actually tears his eyes from his computer to look at me for a change.

'So?'

'Did you read the article?' I ask, pulling it up on my screen. 'The cops are looking for a kid who went missing after the raid at Withywood Way. The guy *we* know to be Alfie Reynolds.'

'Of course!' Tom jumps off his chair, staring at me. 'The lad you said all along wasn't involved in the drugs raid.'

I nod. 'Yep. He's their son. Probably the one who told his mother about his dad's antics—at least that's what the police suspect, according to this,' I say, gesturing to the screen.

'Shit! Why didn't we think of that?' Dave looks really pissed off. Pity, I was going for impressed.

'We couldn't prove it anyway, with the young Reynolds boy having gone to ground and all,' I add.

'True.' Dave looks thoughtful. 'It's a good feeling that we're a step ahead of the cops though, eh?'

He smiles. He *actually* smiles. At *me*! Wow, this is a day for firsts.

'You did well putting all that together,' Tom says, coming over and giving me a pat on the back. 'Didn't she, Dave?'

I was expecting a non-committal reply from Dave but he actually gets up and rubs my shoulder. 'Yes. You did a great job there, Libby. Very well done. We'll make an investigative reporter out of you yet.'

I smile, though I'm not actually sure I want to be an investigative reporter anymore. I'm still hoping to join Siobhan in the fashion department of the women's news supplement.

'Something I should know about?' A man I don't recognise stands in the doorway.

'Phil. Yes, actually. Come and meet Libby Lawrence.'

I'm surprised to see the older man frown at me as he joins us. I'm used to people frowning at me—I know, it's hard to believe—but it's not usually perfect strangers.

'Libby, have you met Phil Peerless, our chief editor?'

Oh. That explains it. He looks to be in his sixties, hefty, with grey hair and a big nose, which is full of even more grey hair. *Yuk!*

'Not gone off half-cocked with another story, have you?' Phil sneers.

It seems my reputation has gone before me.

'Not this time. Not at all,' Dave interjects. 'She's actually pieced together three of our stories. Unfortunately, as Libby herself pointed out, we can't print anything without the evidence, but it certainly looks like she's hit the nail on the head.'

Phil stops frowning and raises his eyebrows. 'Three stories, eh?'

'Yep. She's found a common link and fixed the whole thing together like a jigsaw puzzle.' Dave actually looks impressed. Hallelujah!

'Really?' Phil looks stunned. Okay, I'll take that.

'That's what investigative journalism's all about, isn't it?' I say, feeling a little smug that the girls are all listening in.

'Absolutely,' Phil agrees. 'I think you'll go far in this department, young lady.'

Oh, no, please!

'Thank you.'

'Right, well. Keep up the good work.' Phil leaves to a chorus of thanks and goodbyes from everyone, including the girls.

'He didn't even acknowledge us,' I hear Bethany mutter.

Carol-Anne replies, but I don't bother to listen. I've got better things to do. I'm not sure what, to be honest, but anything's better than listening to them moaning.

'Any chance of looking into the Reynolds kid?' Dave suggests as he and Tom go back to their seats. 'Maybe we could prove your theory and write it up?'

I purse my lips. I can't exactly tell him I've already spoken to Alfie and I promised myself I wouldn't print anything he'd told me. He'd feel betrayed and with good reason. I didn't even try to come clean about who I was, and I'm sure he wouldn't have spoken to me if I had. No, the point of the exercise was to alleviate my own concerns about the boy and prove to Dave that I wasn't as stupid as he seemed to think. Mission accomplished on both counts. Time to move on.

'Actually, as the police are looking for him, I don't think we should interfere,' I say. 'But what about Alice McGurk? Is there any point in pressing her for details about Reynolds' business claims? Or rather, *false* business claims?'

Dave frowns. 'Probably not, to be honest. If she's already spoken to reporters, she's not likely to want to speak to us. And the cops will be looking into that anyhow, so we won't get anywhere until they've finished their investigations. Best to keep out of it, I reckon.'

'Hmm, I think you're right.' That was the answer I was hoping for.

My desk phone rings, which is unexpected.

'Hello. Liberty Lawrence, news desk.'

'I've got a Sergeant Harper on the line for you. Putting you through now.' The switchboard operator sounds very efficient.

'Thank you,' I reply, not sure if she can hear it or not.

'You need to switch your phone on,' a familiar voice tells me.

'Oh.' He's right. I turned it off last night so I wouldn't get his call and forgot to switch it back on again. 'Okay. I'll look into that.'

'Good. Are you all right?' James is nothing if not tenacious.

'Yes, thank you.' I'm aware of Dave glancing over at me. He knows how unusual it is for me to receive calls on the work phone, too. I'm not really well-known enough for business calls, and personal calls aren't allowed.

'Thank you for the information you supplied yesterday,' he goes on.

'I hope it was useful.'

'It was. Very.'

'Good.'

'Meet me for lunch.'

'I can't.'

'Tonight, then.'

'I'm sorry, I'm already booked up.'

'Libby, we need to talk.' He's pleading now, which makes me feel like crying. This wasn't supposed to happen.

'I'm really sorry, but I have to go.'

'Switch your phone on, then.'

'I will. Thanks for the reminder.' I place down the receiver.

God! That was awkward. I take a few deep breaths, reminding myself that I'm a strong, independent woman. That man was wrong to treat me the way he did on Saturday night and I'm not about to accept it. He should have stuck up for me, not his ex. And he shouldn't have spent the whole meal speaking to her, either. Even if she *was* seeing a con man. *Especially* as she was seeing a con man. Oh, gosh, I wonder if that's what they were talking about.

I excuse myself and go to the ladies'. Once inside the cubicle, I pull my phone from my handbag and switch it on. *Ding! Ding! Ding!* Straight away I switch it over to silent mode as loads of Facebook notifications mount up, as well as several text messages. Crikey, I've never been so popular!

I quickly hop onto Facebook. I've got a few hundred friends and relatives on there, but they're not usually this eager to contact me. I'm pleasantly surprised to see my Friend Request box has ten new requests. Clicking on them, I balk at some of the unfamiliar names: Cheryl Masterson, Bonny Bryony, Veronica Swann—hang on, Veronica's one of the women from the gala. So is Cheryl, Bryony, Aashi, Lydia—I can't believe all the girls want to 'friend' me on Facebook. Even Elizabeth Griffin wants to keep in touch. As well as Craig and Liam—I hadn't realised they all liked me that much. I'm so chuffed. I almost want to cry with happiness. Quickly, I accept them all, looking forward to messaging them later to thank them properly for their requests.

When I switch to messages, I want to cry for a completely differently reason. James must have rung several times last night, and as I scan quickly through his texts, I can tell he must have got quite worried that I didn't reply.

Libby, I'm so sorry about what happened at the gala. I didn't mean to look like I was defending Suzanne. I just wanted to end the whole debacle before it got out of hand. I wasn't quick enough. I'll pay for the damage to your dress. Please let me know you got home safely last night. Jx

I need to talk to you. Please call me. Jx

Please speak to me, Libby. This is all such a mess. We need to talk. Jx

Libby, thanks for the info you sent over via Cassie and the guys. Very useful. You're right about Suzanne being involved with Reynolds. She told me everything this evening. She's such an idiot. I need to explain it to you. Please call me, and thanks again for all your help. Jxx

When are you going to switch your damn phone back on? I've told you about this before. How can we sort this out if you won't speak to me? If you don't call me back within the next hour, I'm going to call you at work. Jx

Hmm. He's right. He did tell me before not to leave my phone switched off when I worked at the hotel. I didn't mean to leave it off so long that time, either, I just forget. He must realise I'm busy—wait a minute, two kisses? He's never given me two kisses before. I re-read the message and realise it's because I was right about Suzanne and Oliver Reynolds. I knew it. I hope Cassie and the guys explained to him that I couldn't tell him myself as he wouldn't have believed me. It's happened before that he thought I was wrong about something because it was just sour grapes. *I know it's hard to believe, isn't it? Me? How childish does he think I am?*

A door bangs and I realise I must've been in here ages.

'Libby? Are you in there? Are you okay?' It's Sophie.

'Yeah, I'm just coming.' I shove my phone back in my bag and pull the flush for good effect.

'Is it your tummy again?' she asks, a sympathetic expression on her face. 'I guessed it must be.'

'Yeah. Thanks for checking on me,' I say, washing my hands. I can't believe she's so gullible. *I know, I know, I'm a fine one to talk* .She's nice, though.

'That's all right. As soon as Dave started moaning about how long you'd been I said it was probably that.'

'Thanks,' I say, wondering just what Dave must have thought. 'Was he moaning a lot?' Damn. It's taken all this time to impress him and now it could all be undone by me spending too much time in the loo.

'You know,' she says, as I follow her out the door.

Frankly, I *don't* know, as I wasn't there, but I just nod anyway. I'd hate to confuse her. I've got the impression it wouldn't take much.

18

It's nice to go down to the canteen at lunchtime. I've never been here before and I wish I had. It's lovely. All bright and clean with vivid orange chairs and plastic tables. Vending machines line one wall with everything from drinks and confectionery to stationery equipment. There's a large hatch where ladies in white overalls and hairnets dish out the hot food, and chillers along the middle of the serving area with fresh baguettes, wraps, yoghurts, cream cakes, and a host of yummy desserts.

It certainly beats a boring old squashed sandwich from the bottom of my Marc Jacobs.

I choose a Chicken Caesar wrap and cup of tea. I'm planning to come back later for a dessert but pick up a KitKat from the display next to the till just in case.

'Eight pounds and twenty-three pence, please,' the plump lady says, ringing up my items.

How much? I stare at her. 'Are you sure?' It's only a two-finger KitKat as well.

I'm trying to keep calm but am aware of the man behind me clearing his throat loudly and there are a few tuts from the queue as the woman re-reads her screen.

'Yes.'

'Okay.' I try to sound light and casual as I open my purse. My credit card glares at me from the front pocket as I slide out my last tenner. That reminds me of my failed plan of taking the Jovani dress back for a refund. I'll have to find a way of paying that off somehow.

'Thank you,' says the cashier, who has to tug hard before I release the note. I give a nervous giggle.

She frowns at me as she hands me my change, mostly in coppers and five pence pieces, which she plonks right on top of the receipt. Great. Now I've got my handbag looped around my arm, my purse in one hand, the coins and receipt in the other and the tray of overpriced lunch to pick up and carry to a table. Furthermore, the man behind me could give The Flying Scotsman a run for its money with the amount of huffing he's doing.

In a fit of harassment, I throw the change onto the tray and plonk my purse right on top of my wrap—they just don't make the trays big enough for the huge crockery.

I hurry over to the side counter to fetch my cutlery. There's another queue, of course, and I have to wait while an older woman examines all the forks in the basket until she finds one that's clean enough/big enough/pretty enough or whatever for her liking. I grab a knife and teaspoon then look around for somewhere to sit.

When I came in there were plenty of seats, but now the place is full. I was hoping to sit at a table on my own, perhaps by the window, but no such luck. To make matters worse, I hardly know anyone. Goodness knows where Ben and Rob have their lunch, but they're clearly not here, Tom goes out for his meals and Dave thrives on protein bars and carbohydrate shakes to keep his strength up. I cast my mind back to the sight of him sitting in the café in Knightsbridge with that Cornish pasty, or whatever it was. I've never seen him eat anything like that before. Maybe he only has the healthy stuff when I'm about. *Sneaky git!*

Someone jostles me from behind, and the tea slops over the side of my cup, drenching the receipt. I quickly move out of the way. There are now a couple of seats empty on a nearby table, so I dive onto one of them. I immediately regret it.

'Hi, Libby.' It's Sophie.

'Oh, hello.' I like her, but she doesn't dine alone.

I immediately look at Carol-Anne, who's sitting next to her and force a smile. Well at least—oh, no, I thought too soon. Bethany bitch-face slides into the empty seat next to me.

'Hi,' I say as pleasantly as I can.

'Hello.' She looks disparagingly at my tray.

Glancing at their food, I note that they all have salads and fresh fruit. I'm glad now that I didn't pick up the sticky toffee pudding I had my eye on for dessert.

Carefully, I pick my purse—Kate Spade, bargain off eBay—from the now-squashed Chicken Caesar wrap. The lovely suede leather is covered in sauce and bits of carrot. Bethany gives a snort of laughter but pretends not to watch. *Damn!* I forgot to pick up a napkin, too, so I have to use the other hand to delve into my handbag, which is on my lap, to find a tissue.

I quickly wipe the gunk from the purse, though I'll never get the stain out, and pick up the soggy receipt and money from the tray. That's when I notice it's not all there. *Have I been short-changed?* I narrow my eyes at the cashier, who's not even looking my way. I'll have to take it up with her later, not that she'll believe me. I should have checked it at the time, like they always tell you to on those notices about 'mistakes cannot be rectified afterwards'. A hefty thud hits my stomach. And just when I need to hang on to every penny for that damned credit card bill, too.

'Everything all right?' Bethany asks, looking at my tray.

'Yes, of course.' I'm trying to sound bright and cheerful, though I'm seething inside.

I put what little change I can find on the tray into my purse, along with the unreadable receipt and tuck it back into my bag. After looping the chained handle around my chair, I take a deep breath and proceed to pour the milk into my cup.

While stirring my tea, I'm suddenly alarmed to hear a clanking sound as my spoon hits heavy resistance in the bottom of my cup. Amid sniggers from the girls at my table, I scoop up something and draw the spoon to the lip of the cup. My heart jolts when I recognise the pound coin.

Bethany lets out a very unladylike guffaw and points at the offending item, setting the other two off in hysterics. As the damage has already been done, I continue to fish more and more change from the bottom of my cup. Honestly, if I wasn't so worried about my finances right now I'd leave it there and pretend it had never happened, but I figure that now they've seen the first coin I might as well continue. However, when people from neighbouring tables look over and snigger at me, too, I suddenly wish I *had* abandoned the job after all.

I try to laugh it off, but my voice is shrill with nerves. I place the coins on my sauce-covered tissue, not sure what to do with them next. They need a good wipe before I can pop them into my purse. I think I've got another tissue in my bag, but it will be a bit of a palaver with everyone watching. On reflection, I decide it best to just ignore them and get on with my food. I'll sort them out once the girls have finished and left me alone, and everyone else has forgotten all about it. I cut my soggy wrap in half and pick up a small chunk. No way can I drink my tea now.

The girls are still sniggering next to me and I really wish—not for the first time—that I'd stuck with my home-made sandwich instead. Limp lettuce spills out of the squashed tortilla and the dressing oozes onto my fingers. The chunks of chicken are hard as rocks, and their bumpiness makes the whole thing very hard to handle. I try to smile in between nibbles but the girls look back at me incredulously.

Then it happens. I bite down hard on what I assume is a piece of chicken and my tooth breaks with a painful crunch.

'Oh, my God!' Bethany screeches and I realise that what I thought was Caesar dressing dripping from my mouth is actually blood.

Putting my hand to my mouth I retrieve the contents, much to the disgust of the other three who make their feelings crystal clear. Amid the blood and bits of lettuce I find part of my tooth and a twenty-pence piece. It must have rolled into my food when I put the change on my tray.

My mouth throbs, and everyone around me is pulling faces and making disparaging noises. Using my free hand, I root in my bag for another tissue—noticing that none of the girls have offered me a serviette—and roll the contents of my other hand onto it before leaving it on the tray. Then I quickly get up and leave.

I text Dave from the taxi on my way to the dentist to let him know what's happened and that I'll be back later. Probably a futile effort, as the girls will no doubt take great delight in telling him and everyone who'll listen what happened, but it's only polite. The agony I'm in is unbelievable and I'm glad not to have to wait too long to be seen, as it's an emergency.

The dentist injects some anaesthetic and removes the rest of the tooth, which luckily is at the back of my mouth so can't be seen. He tells me to take some painkillers once the numbness wears off and gives me some dense, cotton wool pads to bite on until the bleeding stops.

The last thing I want to do is go back to the office, but I'm going to the gym tonight with Cassie and I've left my other bag there. Besides, it's only a broken tooth. Plus, the girls will have probably blown it out of all proportion so I'd better get back there and set the record straight.

I check my phone as I head towards a taxi rank when movement in a nearby alleyway catches my eye. It's Dave. He's handing money to a guy whose face I can't see. I quickly take a picture as the guy gives him something that looks like a piece of paper, or maybe a small packet of something. They nod and turn to go their separate ways. Is it a drugs deal? Or is he buying information from one of his contacts? Whatever it is it's definitely shady. Why else would they conduct business in an alley? They could just as easily do it in a café or something if it's all above board. I wonder if that's what he was doing that day I saw him with the pasty—meeting up with someone?

I hurry past so they don't see me, before taking a taxi back to work. If Dave starts running now, he'll be back in the office before me, as he won't have all this traffic to deal with. Maybe I should tackle him about it when I get there, find out what he's up to? On second thoughts, he'll only clam up. I think I'll wait and see what transpires. Crikey, is he really an award-winning journalist, a nightclub bouncer, *and* a drug dealer? He's in a lot of trouble if he is.

***

I'm not entirely surprised to find Dave's desk empty when I return to the office.

'He had a tip-off about a story, so he's gone,' Tom explains.

Yeah, I'll bet he did. I hope that means he was paying for information when I saw him instead of buying drugs. I can't say anything, though.

The girls are all sniggering when I look over, but I ignore them. I'm certainly going to bring my own lunch in future, though. Having left the change on the tray in my hurry to get to the dentist, the whole meal actually cost me almost £10 plus taxi fares. James is right, it's much cheaper to bring home-made.

The thought of James brings a pang to my chest. I still haven't answered any of the messages he left me. I know it's cowardly, but I don't know what to say. He chose to stick up for his ex-wife instead of me, making me look like a fool. It shouldn't matter if she's in some kind of trouble, she's still his *ex*-wife and I'm his girlfriend. Or am I? He introduced me to Suzanne as a friend when we were at his flat. Maybe that's how he sees me? He's told me he likes me, cares about me and wants to be with me,but maybe he means as a mate, a pal? I know we've kissed a few times but that's about it. We've never... you know.

I check my phone again. That's one of the advantages of Dave not being in the office, no one else cares if I get my mobile out. They all do it.

Libby, I need to see you. For goodness' sake get in touch. J

Not even one kiss this time. I've obviously annoyed him. I sigh. But to be honest, I think, sitting up a bit straighter, he's annoyed me, too. I text back, if only to stop him ringing me on the desk phone again.

James, what do you want? I'm very busy with my important work and don't have time for this. L

There. See how he likes not getting kisses on his messages.

Straight away he texts back.

I know you're busy at work. I am, too. What do you not have time for? Me? I only want to arrange to see you. I need to explain a few things. Jx

Oh, the kiss is back, I see.

What sort of things? Like why you ignored me all through the meal on Saturday? Why you preferred to speak to your EX-WIFE instead of me? Why you didn't stick up for me when she was being a complete BITCH to me? Why you took HER side and told me I had to leave, not her? Libby.

I pressed the dot at the end really hard before sending it. Tears are welling up in my eyes just thinking about all these things, but I'm determined not to get upset. Not here. I blink hard and switch on my computer.

Look, Libby, I've explained all that to you. It was a misunderstanding. I'm sorry it looked that way. But did you really have to tell everyone that Suzanne and I had a son??? Jx

Oh, yes. I'd forgotten about that part. I got my wires a bit crossed there. Quite embarrassing, to be honest. But it wasn't my fault. Not *really.*

Is it surprising I thought that, when she was telling potential buyers that she had one of the bedrooms for her son? SHE lied! L

I quickly add another message as something else occurs to me.

And you did say you were paying maintenance. L

I put the phone back down and bring up eBay on my computer. Perhaps a bit of retail therapy might calm me down a bit. Because I am actually feeling quite irate. And hungry. I haven't even got a bar of chocolate in my bag as I didn't bring my own lunch. Plus, I left that KitKat on the tray. That reminds me, the numbness in my mouth is starting to wear off. I delve into my desk drawer and pull out a blister pack of paracetamol. Then go over to pour myself some coffee to take them with, remembering to add cold water so I don't scald my tongue.

Bethany bitch-face is whispering something to the girls and looking at me. She does that a lot. I ignore her. I do *that* a lot.

'Want one?' I offer Tom.

He looks up with a smile. 'Please.'

I pour them out, give him his and return to my desk, not looking over at the girls. It feels really good in my high heels and swishy dress, and I look much nicer than any of them. I still have to figure out why Bethany was so horrid to me the other day. And what I'm going to do about it. One thing's for sure, whatever it is it will be fun—for me anyway.

19

As soon as I finish work, I rush down to McDonald's for a Big Mac and fries. I'm so ravenous I devour it in minutes. The chocolate milkshake takes a bit longer, though, and I can't help thinking how much better it must taste than those healthy ones Dave has.

Talking of which, he didn't come back to the office at all this afternoon. I had an email from him saying that he'd been working on a story and had submitted it electronically to Phil Peerless. I was to see if I could dig up anything on Alfie Reynolds, in case we could actually print the story, but I didn't bother.

Instead, I've started 'watching' a few nice things on eBay. A pair of Christian Dior trousers that are actually a size too big for me, but if I got them at a good price, they'd be worth having altered. There are also several pairs of shoes and a Chanel handbag I've got my eye on. Oh, and a slow cooker. I've read all about it and thought it would be good for making stews and curries and stuff while Cassie and I are at work. You just put everything in before you go out and it cooks while you're not there. Magic. AND it'll save money. You can use cheaper cuts of meat as it tenderises it, and fill it up with veg, according to the blurb.

I'm on a strict budget now I've got to fork out an unexpected six hundred and forty-nine pounds ninety-nine for the Jovani dress—which is on my credit card so it's not really like spending money, is it?—so I have to think of ways to budget. Buying all my clothes from eBay will save me a fortune. And the good news is that I managed to get the stain out so I can use the dress for another occasion. That will automatically halve my cost per wear. If that's not saving money, I don't know what is.

I take the rest of my drink with me and trundle down to the gym. Cassie's already waiting for me outside, her face all flushed with excitement.

'This is going to be fun,' she says. I finish my drink and we go inside.

I'm not sure 'fun' is the word I would use, but I'm looking forward to the benefits of some gentle exercise—I could even race Dave to crime scenes.

We're in an old building that's been converted, and the changing room smells a bit damp. I'm wearing black cycling shorts and a white tank top—all Nike, to match my trainers. Cassie's wearing Nordstrom; Beyond Yoga ladder-back camisole with black and orange design, and matching black patch panel leggings. She looks great, as always. She also looks a lot fitter than I do, probably because she used to do yoga—she can still do the Lotus Position.

We go into the gym—which isn't as big or as well-equipped as I'd hoped—and join the others who are all huddled around the instructor. To be honest, I'm disappointed. I had hoped for a hunky Adonis to help show me how to use the buttons of the treadmill, but instead we've got a wrinkly old lady with knobbly knees.

'If we are all here, we can make a start,' she announces, looking over at Cassie and me.

I raise my eyebrows indignantly. I'm sure we weren't the last to get ready. All we did was get changed, go to the loo, touch up our make-up, tie our hair—oh, and have a little catch-up. No more than anyone else, surely? And we were only a *few* minutes late after I finished my milkshake. Well, how was I to know there'd be a huge sign on the door saying, 'only food and drinks bought on the premises may be consumed here'?

There's a vending machine selling bottles of water at two pounds each for a small one or four pounds for a normal one. Complete rip-off! You can't tell me people aren't going to smuggle their own in. And there's no chocolate or crisps, just some weird-looking cereal bars behind the counter. I'll definitely be bringing my own Yorkie next time, and probably one or two Mint Aeros as well.

The woman, who turns out to be called Peggy, warbles on about fire procedures and the rules and regulations of the premises before getting on to the interesting stuff about what we can actually do here.

'There are safety notices next to each piece of equipment,' she continues, 'outlining the correct measures of usage and cleaning. If you are unsure of anything, please ask me.'

My heart lightens. The instructions are all written down. So, we won't have to listen to her explaining everything. I quickly look around again and decide I might start with the cross-trainer. Arms and legs going at the same time. Getting all fit and slender. Yes. That's what I need. There are only two of them, so I surreptitiously point them out to Cassie who nods. She can understand what I'm telling her telepathically, which is that we'll start with them, but we'll have to be quick.

I sidle a little to the right, nearer my apparatus of choice. Peggy seems to have spotted me and is frowning. I smile at her and then look around at the others who are listening diligently to her spouting on about maintenance of equipment. I hadn't noticed before what a mixture we've got here. A few other women are wearing really smart outfits like Cassie and me, but there are some in baggy T-shirts and jogging bottoms. A guy with really hairy legs is wearing the shortest shorts imaginable, and I don't want to be anywhere near him when he moves his legs. Even from here, I can see a bit of flesh hanging precariously. I shudder and turn to look at something else. One woman's wearing a very tight bra top, which doesn't reach to her midriff. Her massive boobs are tucked under her chin and the Lycra is stretched so much that anything below her nipples is practically transparent.

Nudging Cassie, I take another sideways step towards the cross-trainers. I've become detached from the crowd now, standing alone. Peggy's giving me an odd look, but I just look away and nod, as though I'm absorbing all her information. To be honest, I'm not sure what she's talking about now. I've completely lost track. All I know is that if Cassie and I don't get to the cross-trainers soon, the man at the end of the front row is bound to nab one. Then what will we do? I quite fancy the treadmills, but everyone will want them. They're so easy.

'Are there any questions?' Peggy asks.

Great. She must be near the end.

I shake my head when she looks my way and am just about to whizz over to the equipment when a woman puts up her hand. *Are we in school?*

'Could you just confirm the correct procedure for locking the cross-trainer after use?' she asks.

I heat up from the inside. The cross-trainer? She wants the cross-trainer. And she's got someone with her. That means Cassie and I can't go on them.

'That's a very good question,' Peggy replies.

No, it's not. It's a horrid question. One she doesn't need answering as Cassie and I have got first dibs on the cross-trainers. And anyway, what's she on about with locking the equipment? I wonder if Peggy's mentioned it and I haven't heard. You don't have to lock every piece of apparatus after you've used it, do you? How would you unlock it when it's your go? Talk about a waste of time.

I take a larger stride towards the cross-trainer. Craning my neck, I try to see if there's some kind of locking mechanism on it somewhere. Or is it like a bicycle lock? Do you need a key?

Cassie gives me a funny look and I realise I'm standing on my own, while the rest of the crowd are all staring at me. I've strayed right into the empty floor space. An idea suddenly occurs to me and I quickly put my hands on my hips and bend my body from side to side. Then I try a few lunges.

'Just warming up,' I say, smiling at Peggy.

She doesn't smile back.

'Good idea,' Cassie says, taking a step back. She starts touching her toes and soon everyone else joins in, spreading out and doing star jumps and goodness-knows-what-else.

Peggy glares at me. 'Well, I think that concludes—'she starts.

'Bagsy the cross-trainers!' I yell and run over to them. I climb on. The metal's much colder than I expected and I'm glad I warmed up first. I should've worn leggings like Cassie, instead of shorts. I've got my arms and legs in place but am surprised that the room has gone silent.

'Isn't there any music?' As I raise my head, I see that no one else has moved. In fact, they've stopped exercising and are all staring at me again.

'What?' I frown. Cassie's blushing, and Peggy looks furious. Everyone else is just staring at me.

'Didn't you hear what I said about courtesy?' Peggy demands.

Nope. I didn't hear a word about that.

'Yes, of course,' I reply, a little taken aback. 'That's why I said bagsy.'

Her jaw drops, and I only hope her dentures are stuck in tightly. 'What did you say?'

She must be deaf. 'I said bagsy,' I shout over, enunciating my words in case she had to lip read.

'I heard what you said, young lady,' she snaps at me, her eyes flashing in anger. 'What on earth is that supposed to mean?'

Now it's my turn to look aghast.

'Bagsy,' I repeat. 'Don't you know the Law of Bagsy? You have to shout bagsy then whatever it is you're choosing and then no one else can have it.'

She just stares.

'Bagsy another cross-trainer,' Cassie shouts out, waving her hand in the air, and she runs over to the equipment next to me.

'Bagsy a treadmill,' the woman with the big boobs shouts.

'Bagsy the weights.'

Soon, everyone's bagsying the equipment and running over to it, and the room is full of shouts and giggles as everyone starts working out.

Peggy's still gawping at me.

'Don't we have music?' I ask again. 'They normally do in gyms'

'No,' she barks. 'We do *not* have music.'

I sigh. I was looking forward to a good singsong while I burn away the calories. 'We'll have to make our own, then,' I decide.

I look around the room. 'What shall we sing?'

'*Let's Get Physical*,' Cassie shouts from beside me.

Soon, we're all busy getting fit and doing our best Olivia Newton-John impersonations. Well, all except Peggy that is. She was last seen heading towards a dark corner with a hand on her head.

The singing gets a little less exuberant as time goes on and people run out of breath, but it's a great atmosphere. I think I might enjoy exercise, after all.

***

'Do you think we'll be allowed back at the gym next week?' Cassie asks the next morning, as I tuck my Nikes into my Marc Jacobs.

My body aches like fury.

'I'm not sure we'll need to,' I reply. 'I feel so much fitter already. I might not have to go and do it all again.' I do a few stretches just to prove my point.

Cassie giggles. 'Well, Peggy'll be relieved anyway.'

I'm wearing a flared skirt from Monsoon with a pretty top I picked up in Dorothy Perkins. My three-inch-heel Kurt Geigers look great with the outfit, and I've got a Chanel-style jacket to top it off.

I go through to the kitchen and pick up my lunchbox. I've also got a couple of packs of crisps and a four-pack of chunky KitKats to keep me going. All that exercise has made me quite hungry, and I don't want a repeat of yesterday. I grab another box of paracetamol, too, just in case my mouth starts hurting again. It's actually been okay today, thank goodness, although I don't think all that singing did it much good last night.

I've decided to use the Radley cross-over bag again today, too. It still looks nice with my outfit and I can fit more in it.

'Don't forget this.' Cassie picks up my phone from the coffee table.

'Thanks,' I say, stuffing it into my Radley.

James rang last night but I was too exhausted to speak to him, so he left a message asking me to call him again. I will, honestly. Just not right now.

'See you later.' I wave to Cassie and set off for the Tube station, James still weighing heavily on my mind.

I miss him. I miss his smile, his touch. I wonder what he's doing. Is he consoling Suzanne? How much money did she give to Oliver Reynolds? How much of *James'* money? I hope she's not depending on James now that she's on her own again—assuming that she *is* on her own. Last I heard, Reynolds was being questioned by the police, but I don't know if he's been locked away or not. He might still be there, trying to convince Suzanne that they've got it all wrong. I hope she doesn't believe him. James said she's an idiot, but I hope she's not *that* stupid. She must have been really hurt, though. He was living with her, for goodness' sake, so she must have had feelings for him.

By the time I reach the office, I'm feeling quite sorry for Suzanne. I never thought I'd say it, but I do hope she's okay. I have to admit I might not have felt so sympathetic towards her had the wine stain not come out of my Jovani dress, however.

As soon as I get to my desk, I fire up the computer, grab a coffee and type 'Oliver Reynolds' into the search engine. There's not that much information on him, unfortunately, although it does state that police suspect he's changed his name a few times to avoid detection. It seems most of his 'business' revolves around the selling of replica designer goods. That certainly explains Alfie's Rolex. It would seem everything about that man's fake.

My gaze lands on the row of Dave's trophies that proudly line the front of our desk. *His* desk, really, I'm just sharing it for a while. I smile. He's obviously been polishing them again as they're slightly askew. He's very particular about them being in exactly the right position. One of them has a shield that makes it wider than the rest, so that one goes in the centre, and there's another one that's quite tall so he stands that one at the end. One has a statue of a person on it, a bit like an Oscar. He's really proud of that one, although it's one of his oldest. I don't like it. The head seems too small for the body and it's all out of proportion. I'm just glad it points away from me as the face has no features, which makes it look a bit creepy. I'm staring at it now and it seems as if the head's moved slightly. Tilted to the left. I know I must be imagining it, but it still makes me shudder. When I was a kid, I always thought I could see my dolls move. It freaked me out, but I still watched them like a hawk.

'Penny for them?'

I look up to see Tom smiling at me. He really is good-looking.

'Nothing really,' I say with a sigh. 'I've just been looking into Oliver Reynolds again. Is he in jail, do you know?'

Tom frowns in thought. 'He was certainly taken in for questioning. I'm not sure if they had to let him go or not. We haven't heard if he's been charged with anything yet, but that woman, Alice McGurk, seemed to have quite a bit of evidence against him. If he's not in a cell now, he soon will be, I reckon.'

I nod. 'I hope so.'

I can't help feeling a little sorry for Alfie, with his dad going to prison, but it seems the best thing for everyone. At least the young lad will keep the roof over his head.

20

My phone flashes with a message from James.

Libby, please can I see you tonight? It's important. J xx

Two kisses? It must be crucial.

I'll come to yours after work if you like? L

I'm playing hard to get.

Great, I'll cook. Jxx

Another two kisses? He's trying, I'll give him that.

Okay. I'll be there around 6pm. L

Can't wait. Jxx

Play it cool, I don't need to reply to that one. I quickly get back to work to save being tempted to carry on the conversation. I really want to rabbit on about how it went last night at the gym, and ask him what's happening with Suzanne and Oliver Reynolds. I mustn't, though. I need to find out where I stand first.

Dave doesn't turn up until nearly half past ten, claiming he had a meeting to attend. I bite my lip, dying to ask about him doing some kind of deal in that alleyway yesterday. I daren't. I don't know enough facts to confront him. That's a lesson I learned from James. I need to play the long game.

There's a kerfuffle at the other end of the room, and I look over to see Bethany trying to ram some books into an already-full cupboard.

'It's no good,' Carol-Anne says loudly, 'we need to see if the others have got any space in theirs.'

'I suppose you're right.' Bethany bitch-face should be on the stage. As a prop.

She gives an exaggerated sigh and slowly walks over to our desk, still carrying the books. I narrow my eyes.

'Dave,' she says in a whiny tone.

He's on the phone. He holds up a finger to tell her to wait a minute. She huffs.

'These are heavy,' she moans, her arms sagging under the weight.

He continues his call.

'I'm going to drop them!' she shouts.

I shoot to my feet, arms outstretched.

'Here.' I take them from her.

Blimey, there must be a pile of bricks in here somewhere, these weigh a ton. I turn and plonk them on the desk at the same time Dave slams down his phone.

'What the—' he yells, just as the head rolls off his statuette trophy.

I gaze at it in horror.

'You clumsy bitch!' Red-faced, Dave reaches over and picks up the statue minus its head.

I'm stunned at his outburst.

'Oh, no. That was your favourite one, too, wasn't it, Dave?' Bethany bitch-face astounds me with her ham acting.

The other two girls come over and gasp, too.

'That's too bad, mate,' Tom says, joining us. 'But it was an accident.'

Dave scowls at me, his eyes flashing with anger. 'I knew you were jealous of my success,' he accuses me. 'But you didn't have to do this.'

'What?'

'Oh, no, Libby. I never thought you'd do something as mean as that,' Bethany sneers.

Just then Phil Peerless arrives.

'Bethany, I heard you wanted to see me.' He looks from her to Dave and then the trophy. 'Oh, no. Who did this?'

'She did!' Dave and Bethany say together.

'No, I didn't,' I protest. I don't believe this.

'Yes, you did. You slammed those books down on the table and it ricocheted and broke it,' Dave accuses me.

I stare at him, my jaw slackening.

'I was helping Bethany,' I say.

'Well, it looks like you've caused it,' Phil says, shaking his head at me. 'You really need to be more careful.'

'But Dave slammed the phone down at the same time. How do you know *he* didn't do it?' My voice is a few octaves higher than usual.

'I think a pile of books is a bit heavier than a telephone receiver, don't you?' Dave sounds really smarmy now.

'It depends how hard you slam them on the desk.' I'm fed up with taking the blame. It wasn't *my* fault.

'Oh, give me strength.' Dave looks at me as though I'm a two-year-old.

I put my hands on my hips, standing tall. I'm sick of being made to look stupid. First Suzanne, then James, and now Dave. I've had it up to here. *That's above my head, by the way.*

'How do you know the trophy wasn't faulty?' I snap.

Dave rolls his eyes. 'I've had it for years. It's never broken before.'

'Maybe it's because it's old, then? It's not as strong as it was. Wear and tear and all that.' I'm not letting this go.

Dave tuts. I hate that.

'Look, I think we need to face facts, Libby,' Phil interjects. 'You've accidentally ruined the trophy. Now, don't you think you should apologise?'

'Yeah,' Bethany bitch-face echoes.

It's not just my blood that's boiling. My whole body feels like one of those thermostats you see on cartoons where the mercury rises to the top and the whole thing bursts into flames.

This is so unjust. And something tells me it's no coincidence that Phil Peerless came to visit Bethany bitch-face at such an opportune moment. What can I do though? I *did* dump the books on the table causing the head to fall off that stupid trophy. How thick could I be? I still smell a rat that it only happened because I was helping Bethany, but there's nothing I can do about it now.

Everyone's glowering at me expectantly. Only Tom has actually pointed out that it was a complete accident.

'I'm sorry for what happened,' I say slowly. 'It wasn't done on purpose; I would never do a thing like that. I'm happy to pay for a replacement or to get it mended or whatever.'

Dave still doesn't look happy. What does he want—blood? 'I'll have it checked out,' he mumbles, tucking it into his desk drawer.

'Thank you, Libby.' Phil Peerless sounds just like my dad. I'm glad Dad doesn't have his nose hair problem, though.

'Just be more careful in future,' Dave snarls.

I stare at him. Has he actually accepted my apology or not? And why's everyone *still* making me feel bad about it?

Bethany gives me a smug look and takes Phil off to one side, muttering quietly. Everyone else goes back to work. I stare at the pile of books that's still on our desk, blocking my computer.

'Where should I put these?' I ask Dave.

'I think you've done enough for one day,' he replies and removes them himself.

I slump into my chair. This has all gone so horribly wrong. I actually thought I'd impressed everyone yesterday and now this. My face is still hot but as the anger has dissipated, I feel more and more like I'm going to cry. Not here. I get up and head for the ladies', wondering how long it'll be before Sophie comes to find me.

I actually allow the floodgates to open once I'm locked in a cubicle. Suddenly, I feel tired. The effort of trying to keep going as though nothing has happened is finally taking its toll. The business with James and Suzanne has hurt me much more than I'd care to admit. I haven't even spoken to Cassie about it, although she's tried on several occasions. Somehow, I feel if I don't say it, then it won't be true. James and I won't have split up. Which I think we have. He made his choice who to back and he chose his ex-wife. It will be good to draw a line under the whole thing tonight. I'm dreading it, but in a way, looking forward to getting it over and done with.

I blow my nose, flush the tissue down the loo and go to the vanity to touch up my face. Now all I need to do is get through the rest of the day.

The cavalry that is Sophie comes in as I finish my make-up. It's taken a lot of concealer to hide the redness, but I don't look too bad and I'm glad I'm wearing heels and smart clothes. It makes me feel better, somehow.

'Are you okay?'

I look at her reflection in the mirror. It's good of her to be concerned.

'Yeah. I just don't know why everyone hates me here.' It's true. I've never worked in a place where I felt such animosity.

'We don't,' she says, taking a step closer. 'It's just Beth.'

'But why? What have I done to her?'

'It's not you.' She shakes her head, then looks towards the door. 'It's Dave,' she whispers.

My jaw drops just as the door opens and Bethany bitch-face glares at us.

'I came to see if she was all right.' Sophie sounds flustered. It's then that I realise she hasn't been sent, as I'd assumed, she's actually come out of concern. Sophie cares about me.

I narrow my eyes at Bethany.

She raises one eyebrow in a patronising fashion, her arms folded across her chest. This reminds me of the bullies in the school playground. The teachers seemed to believe all their lies without question. My whole life seems to have been a struggle against people who thought they were superior to me when they actually weren't. Then, one day I read a motto in a magazine: 'No one can make you feel inferior without your consent'. I'd printed it out and pinned it up beside my bed at my parents' house. I often think about those words.

'I don't know why you've got it in for me, but you won't get away with it,' I tell her, staring her straight in the eye.

Did she just flinch?

'I've no idea what you're talking about,' she says with a deep swallow.

I tuck my make-up into my Radley, still watching her expression.

'Tell your face that,' I say as I walk past her on my way out the door.

I return to the office feeling strangely empowered. The atmosphere is cold and unfriendly, but I can deal with it. I somehow feel vindicated, not about the trophy, but about Bethany. Sophie's confirmed there's a problem. It's not all in my imagination. I just need to get her on her own again and find out what's gone on between the bitch and Dave Chandler. Why does she dislike him so much? And how did I get caught in the crossfire?

When Rob and Ben come in to spend their morning break with me a bit later, Dave doesn't make any comment. I can't tell them what's gone on here, but I'll certainly fill them in later.

'How is everything?' Rob asks, perching on the edge of the desk, as usual.

By 'everything' he clearly means with James, but I can hardly discuss that now. Besides, I don't know for sure how things are yet.

'I'm having dinner with James tonight,' I say.

'Right.'

'How are you getting on with your 'House and Home' features?'

'Really well,' Ben replies. 'We were talking to Siobhan about it and she's come up with a piece on packing your moving clothes. You know, what you should wear for the actual move and things to pack in a separate bag for your arrival at the new house. A sort of 'capsule wardrobe for moving' type thing.'

'What a great idea. I'd love to work on something like that,' I say. It'd be much more interesting than potholes and knife-wielding women hiding behind cars.

'We're all meeting up tonight,' Rob pipes up. 'Siobhan and Tammy as well. Why don't you and James come along? It'll be a great laugh.'

There's a thud of regret in my stomach. I'd love to go with them more than anything. Siobhan and Tammy work for the women's supplement of the *Chronicle*, discussing beauty and fashion. Exactly what *I* want to work on. But apparently, I need to experience different departments. It's company rules. Then they tell you which area they think suits you best. Although I already know where I'd be best placed, and I was hoping Siobhan might put in a good word for me. Tonight would have been great for networking. But I've been putting off seeing James for days and we badly need to talk. Alone. In private.

'Count me in next time?' I plead. 'I'm really sorry we can't do tonight.'

'Of course,' Rob replies, grinning.

After they've gone, I get stuck back into my work to avoid having to speak to Dave. He's not much of a talker anyway, but today he's hardly said two words since the debacle with the trophy. At least one good thing about it is that he hasn't objected to me chatting with the guys. I'm entitled to a coffee break like them, but Dave expects me to work right through because it's what he does. So, when the guys come to join me, Dave usually huffs and puffs to make it clear he doesn't approve of me stopping for a chat. Today's different, though.

I'm following up a story on the proposed distribution of the council's budget for next year. I don't normally deal with financial issues, but this is to tie in with the piece on potholes I did last week. The idea is to ascertain whether they are planning to put any measures in place to avoid the same situation next year if we get similar conditions. Of course, no one at the council is available for comment, so much of it is speculation, but I'm comparing what they've done in previous years to establish the likelihood of them implementing preventative measures in future.

It's all very boring and I'd much rather be putting together capsule wardrobes for moving house—or anything else, for that matter. Obviously, I'd want flat shoes and comfy clothes for the actual move, especially if I was loading the van myself—or, at least, helping. But when I arrived at the new place, I'd want to make a good impression with the neighbours, so I'd need to wear something stylish but practical. I've got some really nice cropped jeans from Dorothy Perkins that suit either heels or flats. If I wore them with my red Jimmy Choos—that I'm going to buy as soon as I can afford them—and put a nice, floaty top on that would be ideal for meeting the new neighbours. Then, after they'd invited me in for tea I could change to my flat, nude Vivienne Westwoods— that I'm going to get to replace the Kurt Geigers that are absolutely ruined thanks to this job—in case I need to help unload the last of the things off the removal van.

I'm already having second thoughts about that floaty top. It's ideal for tea with the Montgomerys, or whoever lives next door, but not so practical if I *do* have to shift stuff off the van. It might float in the way and get ruined. I'll have to think of something else.

That reminds me. I meant to ask about company compensation for my Kurt Geigers, seeing as how they were wrecked doing my job. I could put it towards the Vivienne Westwoods, which are £100. I won't be wearing them for running around in, of course. I might leave it a while, though. Dave's not in the mood to discuss it, and if it has to be referred through Phil Peerless, it might be wise to leave it a day or two. Still, there's no hurry. I'm not moving yet. Or at all, actually, come to think of it.

It's a relief when lunchtime comes around and everyone piles out of the office. I half hoped that I could spend it with Sophie, finding out more about this grudge Bethany bitch-face seems to be holding against Dave, but she's gone off with the others, as usual.

I tuck into my ham sandwich, but I don't really taste it. I'm not in the mood for eating—which is very unusual for me—as my stomach's grumbling with everything that's going on, making me feel sick.

I'm disappointed to be missing out on seeing Siobhan and Tammy tonight, so I decide to take a stroll down to their office to see if they're around for a chat.

'Hey, look at you!' Siobhan beams when she sees me peer around the doorway of their large room. I'm glad I dressed up a bit today and wore heels.

'Hi, I just thought I'd come and see you,' I say, instantly touched by the warm welcome.

I've only met the girls once before, on a night out with Ben and Rob and a few others, including Cassie, of course. I took to Siobhan straight away, she's lovely. I'm not sure how Tammy feels about me, though. She has her own unique sense of fashion, too. I can't quite make her out, but I'd really love to get to know her. She's not here at the moment but there's another girl who seems to be working with Siobhan. She smiles when she sees me. Her hair's a mass of wild, red curls and she's a little plump, which makes her look even prettier. She's wearing an ankle-length boho dress in black with bright pink flowers. Lots of necklaces and chains hang around her neck in varying lengths and she's got black ankle boots—I've no idea what make. She looks great. Very individual.

'Come on in,' Siobhan urges. 'You can give Francesca here a second opinion.'

She's dressed a mannequin in a pair of Victoria Beckham jeans and holds up two tops.

'Which one?' she asks.

One is a Vivienne Westwood T-shirt, all bright colours and swirls. The other is a tailored shirt in pale blue and white stripes with rolled-up sleeves. I think it might be a Chloe.

'It's for moving house,' Siobhan explains glancing up from her computer.

'So... chic but practical,' I say, getting closer and studying the clothes.

'The shirt's lovely but might get dirty,' I suggest. 'Maybe go for the T-shirt.'

'That's what I thought,' Siobhan shouts over. She's beautiful, with a stylish, black bob, wearing a stunning, fitted blue and orange dress by Diane von Furstenberg, which accentuates her slim figure.

Francesca screws up her nose. 'Okay,' she says after a few seconds' thought. 'But I really like the shirt, too.'

'You could change into that when you get there. You'd need to freshen up and it would be easy to slip on over the jeans to go and meet the neighbours.' The scenario from earlier is playing out in my head and I think that shirt would be ideal, much better than the floaty top, which might look a bit frivolous apart from anything else. I'd want the neighbours to take me seriously, after all.

'Great idea.' Francesca throws her arms around me in a sudden pique of excitement, taking me by surprise.

Siobhan nods, giggling. 'Yep. That'll work.'

'So, we can use both.' Francesca beams.

Siobhan comes over to join us at the mannequin. 'We often get given discounts or the actual items we feature,' she explains. 'Fran wanted the shirt, but I thought the T-shirt was more practical for the article.'

I nod, even more determined to get a job in this department.

'Vivienne Westwood's great for moving house,' I agree. 'I've seen some fantastic little shoes that would finish off the outfit, if you're interested.'

Siobhan grins and leads me over to her desk, where I quickly tap in the website for the nude flats I saw earlier.

'Perfect!' Her eyes light up. 'We need you in this office. How much longer have you got with 'the running man'?'

I shrug, suddenly feeling gloomy at the thought of going back to my corner of Dave's desk. 'I'm not sure,' I say.

'Aren't you enjoying it, then?' Siobhan studies my face.

I shake my head. 'I'd rather be with you guys doing all this.' I wave my hand at the displays of textiles and mood boards that adorn the office. There are a couple of friendly-looking girls at the other end of the room, and everyone seems to get on great.

'Well, Melanie's about to go off on maternity leave so we could use an extra pair of hands,' she replies. 'Want me to suggest you?'

My heart leaps. 'Yes, please. I'd love that!'

'Yay, that'll be fun,' Francesca says, clapping.

'Well, you obviously know your stuff,' Siobhan acknowledges. 'Leave it with me; I'll see what I can do.'

'Thank you so much.' I want to hug her but she's not quite as tactile as Fran and I'd hate to crease her dress. Instead, I clench my hands.

'Are you coming tonight?' Siobhan asks.

'I wish I could.' My thoughts immediately turn to James and my stomach roils. 'Prior commitments, I'm afraid. Definitely next time, though.'

I glance up at the George Nelson Vitra Ball Clock on the wall and gasp.

'I've got to get back, I'm afraid.' I curl my lip.

'Not for much longer,' Siobhan replies with a wink.

'Thanks, girls. You've made my day.' I kiss my hand and wave to them as I dive out the door and rush back to the newsroom.

Maybe, just maybe things are going to be okay...

21

After a long afternoon in an extremely hostile atmosphere, I finally switch off the computer and pick up my jacket. I had hoped to go out and report on a story, just to get out of the office, but nothing came up—well, not for me and Dave, at least. It's been a pretty quiet couple of days.

Bethany bitch-face snubs me on her way out the door, but Sophie gives me a little wave. I wave back. I like Sophie. It's just a shame she likes Bethany.

'Bye,' I say to the guys.

Tom replies, but Dave just grunts.

I've never been so glad to leave the building. I texted Cassie earlier and told her I was going to James' tonight and didn't know what time I'd be back. I wish now that I was going out with her and the gang instead. It occurred to me that maybe I could put James off until another night, but he's probably already bought food, and besides, we need to get this over with.

I take the Tube to Fulham and walk the short distance to his flat. His battered Ford Focus stands in the little, residents' parking bay. No Merc next to it this time, thank goodness. If I'd realised it was Suzanne's last time, I might have been tempted to deflate her tyres.

I head up to his flat and press the buzzer.

'Hi,' he says, smiling as he opens the door.

God, he looks edible. He's got his suit trousers on with his shirt open at the neck and his sleeves rolled up. I love his arms. There's something about the muscles, the tan, and the perfect amount of hair.

'Hi.' I go in, and he takes my bags and jacket. I watch quietly as he hangs them in the hall.

'How are you?' He's still smiling, but I can sense his uneasiness.

'I'm fine, thanks. How about you?'

He grimaces. 'I've been better. Ever since Saturday night I've wanted to talk to you, but you seem to keep blocking me. You don't answer my calls and—' He runs a hand through his hair. 'Anyway, let's get a drink. Dinner will only be a few more minutes.'

The smells emanating from his small kitchen make my mouth water. Looks like we're having steak tonight with all the trimmings. Mmm, one of my favourites.

'Can I do anything to help?' I ask, as he hands me a glass of Cabernet Sauvignon.

'Nope. Just take a seat. I'm about to dish up.'

There's a little table with two chairs at one end of his living room and he lights the candle as I sit.

'This is lovely,' I say with a smile.

I get a whiff of his alluring scent as he leans over and my stomach roils. Is this goodbye? Are we really going to sit down to a nice meal while he tells me he's decided to get back with his ex? I take a large gulp of my wine—which is also lovely.

'I think we should start from the beginning,' James says, placing our food on the table, then taking the chair opposite me.

I suck in a deep breath, glancing briefly around his neat little flat. It's as organised as the man himself.

'I didn't know that Suzanne was coming to the gala and I've no idea how she ended up sitting next to us,' he says.

'She'll have messed with the place names.'

He nods. 'Very probably.'

'Why did she want to see you?'

There's a pause and a pained expression passes over his face. 'To ask for more money.'

I stare at him, a chip still on my fork.

'I told her no,' he says before I speak.

'Was it for her boyfriend?'

He wipes a hand over his mouth. 'I didn't know about him at the time. I assumed it was for the house. Anyway, she pestered me all through the meal as I'm sure you noticed.'

I feel sorry for him. He was put in an impossible situation with his superiors sitting at the table.

'This is delicious, by the way,' I say, cutting another piece of my steak. He's cooked it perfectly. Not raw and not like charcoal. Exactly how I like it.

He nods. 'Glad you're enjoying it.'

I feel hot. I don't know what to say. I've no idea what *he's* about to say. Did they make up after I'd gone? God, I hate this. Why can't he just get on with it?

'We had a nice time on the dance floor,' I remind him.

He smiles. 'Yes, it was lovely. I haven't enjoyed myself so much in ages. And you seemed to make lots of friends.'

'I did.'

There's a silence as we both eat our meals, the air thickening around us. When I've finished, I put my cutlery down, take a long swig of my drink and sigh.

'Why didn't you stick up for me when Suzanne was yelling at me in the corridor?' I had to ask. It was just hanging there in the ether, about to drop on our heads.

He runs a finger up the stem of his glass. 'I thought I was,' he says. 'As soon as I heard there was trouble, I dashed down with your jacket. I thought if we just left straight away it would avoid—'

'What? A scene? That ship had already sailed. Suzanne was screaming like a banshee in the middle of the hotel. Everyone was staring. She humiliated me, James. Having tried to make me look a fool for wearing the same style dress as her—which was probably something else she'd planned—she then informed everyone I got mine in the sale. I didn't deserve that.'

'I can't believe you paid that much for the dress in the first place. And I thought you said it was Cassie's anyway?' He's frowning.

Shit. I'd forgotten that.

'Okay. The truth is I bought it on my credit card. I wanted something special to impress your boss. I wanted to portray a good image, being with a sergeant.'

His face clouds over. 'There was no need for that.'

'There was as far as I was concerned. Anyway, I know the dress was expensive, but I thought I could take it back the next day for a refund. Say it wasn't suitable or something.' I don't look at him. I can feel his disapproving expression already. 'But you pulled the label off. Then your ex threw wine all down me so I couldn't return it anyway. I'll just have to pay it off.'

'I'll pay.'

'No.'

He huffs. I think it's safer not to mention the Louboutins.

'But when you came and found her berating me at full blast in front of everyone, you didn't defend me. Even after she threw wine at me.' Tears prick my eyes.

'Libby, I just wanted to defuse the situation. I thought if I just took you away from there then she'd have no one to shout at.'

'But you should have said something. I needed you to defend me in front of everyone. To prove that she was wrong to treat me like that.'

'But why did you carry it on? Why say all that stuff about me maintaining her—and our *son*?' He looks bewildered. 'How could you possibly think I'd have a child and not tell you?'

'You know how.' I sniffle. 'She told Ben and Rob she had a bedroom for her son. And you told me you were paying her maintenance. It just sort of... added up.' Huge tears stream down my face. I can't see any way of us getting over this one. He's hardly touched me since I arrived.

'I also told you it was maintenance for the house. It costs a lot to run a four-bed detached in Richmond. She couldn't afford it on just her wage. You knew all that. Why didn't you believe me? Why not just ask if you thought I had a secret baby stashed away?' He looks hurt, his face blank and confused.

'I was going to. I wasn't going to say anything until I'd asked you all about it. But then she started saying all that stuff about me and you didn't defend me. James, I *needed* you to stick up for me.' I sob heavily into my napkin. 'You ch-chose to support h-her instead.'

'No, I didn't. You just walked out.' He looks incredulous.

'Th-that was b-because you d-didn't d-defend me,' I wail between sobs.

'I didn't mean it like that, Libby. You caught me off guard with all that stuff about Suzanne's boyfriend and me having a son. I was shocked.' He's pleading me to understand but it doesn't make any difference. He let me down.

I get up to go. This isn't working. It can't work.

James shoots to his feet. 'What, so you're leaving now?' he demands.

'I think it's best.'

'Best for whom? You? You've made all those accusations about me in front of everyone—my colleagues, bosses, their wives—and now you're just going to walk out, is that it?'

I gape at him. How dare he be angry?

'You chose your ex-wife over me,' I manage, fury surpassing upset for a second. I turn towards the door.

'I didn't *choose* anyone. You walked out on me, just like you're about to do now.'

I spin back around to face him. 'How can you say that? You took her side! You were supposed to be with *me,* but you supported *her.*'

'Don't you yell at me. You got it wrong, Libby. Big time. Just admit it.' His teeth are clenched as he speaks.

'Yeah, like I always do, don't I? Well, I certainly got *you* wrong, James Harper. I thought you were a *real* man. Instead, you've been taken for a mug by your ex-wife, given her loads of money to pass on to her fancy man and his family, and now you're blaming me. Well, I've had enough. You ruined everything. Even my job. So, just stay away from me from now on!'

I almost reach the front door before he grabs my arm and pulls me around to face him. He looks dumbfounded.

'Your job? What the hell has your job got to do with me?'

'You know damn well,' I snap. 'You heard me say *in confidence* that Dave had a contact at the police station, and you went right off and arrested him. He told me he spent nearly all day being questioned about it. I trusted you, James. I spoke to you as my boyfriend, not a copper. And you *used* me. You took my information and ran with it. How *could* you?'

He shakes his head. 'I didn't.'

'Don't,' I say, before turning around and leaving.

***

It's a cold, lonely night. I eventually cry myself to sleep. Even in my dream, the events of the evening play on a continual loop, the ending never getting any better.

I wake up early and can't get back to sleep. Or don't want to. I take a long, warm shower using my Estee Lauder gel. It smells heavenly.

I dry my hair and tie it in a chignon. I spend a little longer than usual on my make-up and then put on my bright red dress from L.K. Bennett, which matches my lipstick perfectly. I also wear my red Stella McCartneys that I was actually saving for a special occasion, but I need to look really good today. I top it all with a black jacket that matches my Radley.

Cassie's jaw drops when I walk into the kitchen.

'Wow! You look gorgeous.'

'Thanks.'

She's still in her bathrobe, her hair wet. She grins. 'Aren't you going to work today?'

I nod, reaching behind her for the kettle. 'Yep.'

She gives me a knowing look. 'But I take it you're meeting James for lunch? It must have gone well last night. I told you it'd be fine.' Her face falls as she studies mine. 'Libby? Is everything all right?'

I will not cry. I will not cry. 'Yes.' I force myself to smile. 'But we've split up, I'm afraid. It didn't work out.' I shrug.

'Oh, no!' She looks horrified and goes to put an arm around me, but I take a step back. If she's nice to me, I swear I'll break down and never get back together again.

Our telepathic powers seem to be working, as she gives me an understanding look and shoves her hands in her pockets.

'It's for the best,' I tell her—and myself. 'We just couldn't settle our differences.'

She frowns at me. 'Oh. Exactly what differences?'

She pulls up a seat at our little table and I reluctantly put my cup of tea down, joining her.

'He didn't stick up for me at the ball.'

'I told you, policemen don't have balls,' she says with a snigger.

I grimace. 'That's the trouble.'

She puts a hand to her mouth. 'Oh, I'm so sorry. I didn't mean... I was only joking.'

I sit forward, my hands around my warm cup. 'I know. But it really seems to be true in James' case. Rather than stick up for me, he stood back and did nothing, while his wife screamed at me and threw wine down my dress in front of everyone.' The lump in my throat just got bigger.

Cassie stares at me in horror. 'I can't believe James would do that.'

'Well, he did.'

She frowns. 'What about his wife seeing that con man? And whose son is it? Did you ask him about all that?'

I nod, biting my lip. 'That's the other problem,' I admit. 'I brought it up at the time. When she was yelling at me. It just sort of slipped out.'

She looks stunned. 'Oh, no.'

'The kid belongs to Reynolds, the con man.' I shrug.

She nods. 'Well that's okay, then.'

I sigh. 'It would have been if I hadn't accused James of being the father and maintaining him.'

Her expression changes from horror to disbelief and then pity. I preferred the first two.

'I've got to get going.' I stand, take my sandwich box from the fridge, stuff it into my Marc Jacobs along with a packet of Hula Hoops, and head for the door.

I breathe in the cold air. It would be easy to think that today's going to be one of those awful days that go on forever, while I mope about all day being ignored by my colleagues and missing James. But I hold a strong belief that life's what you make it, and I'm determined to make today a good day. I look absolutely stunning—even if I do say so myself—and I've got a good chance of getting the job I want in the women's supplement. All I've got to do is keep my head up and stay positive.

***

Okay, so it's much easier said than done, especially when hardly anyone's talking to me in the office, and there's absolutely nothing interesting going on—at least, nothing Dave and I are sent to investigate.

I'm delighted by an email part way through the morning. It's from Francesca.

Hey, Libby,

Which would you say looks better for a housewarming party? x

She attaches a picture of a Jasper Conran floral, midi-length chiffon dress, and a calf-length, Karen Millen cold-shoulder dress with a cinched-in waist.

Hi, Fran,

The Karen Millen. Definitely.x

I guess the house-moving features are going well. It's nice to be partially involved, and I begin to wonder what it would be like to work in that lovely office with all the inspiring décor and lovely clothes to choose from.

My phone jerks me back to the present and I frown as I lift the receiver.

'Liberty Lawrence. Newsroom.'

'Sergeant Harper on the line for you,' comes the efficient voice of the operator.

'Thank you.' Now what? I'm suddenly hot and trembling.

'You've turned your phone off again.'

I'd forgotten. I didn't want any calls last night after—well, you know—so I switched it off and forgot to flick it back on when I popped it in my bag this morning.

'Okay. Is that a problem?' I wasn't really expecting to hear from him, anyway.

'No. It's just the reason I've used this phone instead.' He sounds very business-like but not as curt as me.

'What for?'

My heart leaps, and for a wonderful second I actually think he's going to say he wants to apologise.

He doesn't.

'I looked into the business of who reported your colleague as having a contact in the station,' he says quietly.

I swallow hard. 'Oh?'

'Apparently, a woman came in and offered the information at the front desk. When asked for her name she said it was Liberty Lawrence.'

Silence.

My heart's hammering. This can't be true. For a start, I was certain it was him and for a finish...

'It wasn't,' I say at last.

'I gathered that.'

'But I can't prove it.' This is so unfair.

'Maybe, you can. We have CCTV in the reception area. If you're free at lunchtime, I could arrange to view it?'

I gulp. 'You could? Yes, please. I'd like to see that.' I'm not so sure about seeing him, though, but what choice do I have? It's the only way to get to the bottom of it and clear my name—and his, though I know I should have believed him in the first place.

'Shall we say about one o'clock?'

'Yes that would be fine. Thank you.'

'You're welcome. I'll see you then. Just ask for me at the desk if I'm not down there.'

'I will. Th-thanks again.'

There's a click as he puts down his receiver, but I'm still holding mine, paralysed. My mind's whirring.

How could I have been so certain it was him without checking first? I just assumed...

'Are you all right?' Dave's frowning at me. That's the most words he's said to me since the head fell off his trophy.

'Er... yes. Of course.' I quickly replace the receiver and get back to my screen.

Francesca emailed her thanks and added a cute emoji. I didn't even know we had emojis on these computers.

I try to immerse myself in the borough council's budget proposals for the past three years. I wish I'd had these to read last night when I was trying to get to sleep. My eyelids are heavy after the first five minutes.

After a while I sneak off to the ladies'. I don't really need to go, but I have to get out of the office for a few minutes. Even Tom's hardly spoken to me today, though I have to admit he's been in and out all morning. Bethany bitch-face has been whispering with Carol-Anne and Sophie as usual. I take my time touching up my lippy, admiring my business-like look. Power-dressing always makes me feel a bit better and I certainly needed this today.

When the door opens, I'm secretly hoping it's Sophie so I can get more info on Bethany, but I'm sorely disappointed.

'Thought I'd find you skiving in here.' Bethany bitch-face scowls at me.

'I'm entitled to toilet breaks,' I inform her. She's not my boss.

'You know, Dave doesn't like you? No one does.'

Ouch! Too much like the playground bullies.

I smack my lips together, still looking in the mirror, lippy in hand.

'That's fine,' I say. 'I'm not too keen on him, either. Or you.'

She sniggers. 'Yeah, right.'

I raise my eyebrows, turning to face her.

'No, it's true. I think you're horrid.'

'I didn't mean *me*,' she sneers. 'You like Dave, don't you? But I'm telling you now, he's not interested.'

I stare at her, my mind in a whirl. '*You* like Dave Chandler?'

'That's not what I said. I said *you* do. It's obvious. Well, he doesn't like you one bit. He thinks you're stupid.'

I narrow my eyes, tucking my lipstick back in my Radley on my way past her. 'Well, maybe I'm not quite as stupid as you all seem to think.'

22

For a change, I'm the first one to leave the office at lunchtime. My heart's pumping and I'm not sure if it's the thought of checking the tape or seeing James. I really like him. Love him, I think. And I miss him like mad. I keep reliving the fun we had on the dance floor on Saturday night. Despite having spent the previous couple of hours talking to his ex, I actually felt that everything was going great.

Visions of his smile cross my mind as I jump on the Tube. He looked so relaxed, laughing. And he seemed much younger when we sat at the table with Veronica and the gang. My heart misses a beat. How did I mess this up so royally?

He's waiting for me in the foyer of the police station when I arrive. He's wearing a suit with a starched white shirt. No tie, as usual, and a few hairs poke through enticingly from his open buttons. I swallow hard.

'Hi,' he says. 'I've already signed you in. Come on up. I think I've found the part we need.'

'Great.' Although he seems very pragmatic, he's still incredibly handsome and I'm impressed he's already checked the tape.

'You look nice,' he says. He leads me over to the lift and I stand next to him, breathing in his heady cologne as we travel upwards.

There are several other people with us, some in uniform, and I chew my lip, a little disappointed that we can't make light conversation. I hate the tense atmosphere that surrounds us, especially knowing that in this aspect, at least, I was wrong.

He puts a hand in the small of my back, ushering me out of the lift, and the man in front of me politely steps back to let us pass. Warmth spreads up my body, and I'm delighted that he doesn't remove his hand, as he guides me down the corridor and into a large office with huge glass windows and desks partitioned by low screens.

A few people look up and nod at James as we pass, and I feel a sense of pride at being with him. Then a thought occurs to me.

'They don't think I'm a criminal, do they?' I turn back slightly to ask and am rewarded with a beautiful smile.

'No. Although I could always use handcuffs if that's your thing?'

The sudden surprise of his amusing comment makes me laugh out loud and I quickly cover my mouth, blushing as a few more people look up from their desks.

'We're in here.' James shows me into a small room off the main office and closes the door.

A large desk almost fills the space and a computer screen faces us. James holds out one of the chairs for me and then sits on the other. He punches in his password, presses a few keys, and soon we're looking at the footage of people coming and going in the station's reception area.

'I checked on the log when the allegations were made so it was an easy job to scroll to the right day and time on here,' he says.

'It's really good of you.'

I'm enjoying his nearness a lot more than I should. I need to keep reminding myself that he didn't stick up for me and if that's what he's going to be like in the future, we can't be together. No matter how much I want to. It's something that will always come between us. I once went out with a boy called Jonathan Parker and he wouldn't stand up for me either, and it was disastrous. 'Nuff said.

'I had to clear my name somehow,' he replies, his mouth twitching at the corners.

I roll my eyes. 'I'm sorry. I shouldn't have accused you.'

'You should always be sure of your facts before making allegations,' he says, a little more seriously. 'You haven't got a case without proof.'

'I know.'

'Do you recognise her?' He points to the screen before enlarging the image.

A young girl with sandy-coloured hair and a smart suit is approaching the front desk. She speaks to the policeman on duty, looking around surreptitiously. He scribbles something on a pad of paper and then looks back up at her. She shakes her head and quickly leaves.

'I knew it.'

'You know her?'

'Her name's Bethany Thomas. She's taken an instant dislike to me,' I admit. 'She's been trying to get me into trouble at work, but I can't prove anything.' The thought makes me feel sick. 'I can't wait to move departments.'

He frowns at me. 'You shouldn't feel like that. I thought you liked your job?'

'I like writing about interesting stuff. And some of the investigations have been really enlightening. But she just makes me look stupid. And now no one's speaking to me.' Tears suddenly gush down my face.

'Hey.' He puts an arm around me and offers me a handkerchief. 'It can't be that bad, surely?'

I nod. 'I only tried to help her and now it looks like I've broken this important trophy, and everyone hates me. She even told me today that no one likes me there.'

'You broke a trophy?'

I sniff and go on to explain the whole debacle.

'What's it made of?' he asks. 'The trophy.'

I shrug, wiping my face. 'I've no idea.'

'It must be pretty flimsy to fall apart that easily. Has it ever broken before?'

I grimace. 'I wouldn't think so. Not with the amount of fuss he made about it.'

'I just wondered.' He raises his eyebrows.

He's got a good point. Whenever you see people get awarded trophies on the telly, they always seem quite substantial. You wouldn't expect them to fall to bits just because someone put a pile of books next to them. I mean, it's not like it fell on the floor or anything.

'It must have been a cheap one,' I surmise.

He narrows his eyes. 'Well, just make sure you're not taking the blame for something that wasn't your fault.'

I smile. It's really good of him to be so concerned.

'I'm really sorry I accused you of betraying me.'

'I'd never do that, Libby. You mean far too much to me.'

My heart skips.

'And I hope I didn't ruin everything for you here with my big mouth,' I go on. 'I should never have suggested that Alfie was your son.'

'Alfie?' He frowns.

'Oliver Reynolds' son's called Alfie,' I explain with a nod. 'He's the guy you got them to set free when he wasn't involved in the Withywood Way drugs raid. Thanks again for that, by the way.'

He shakes his head. 'I don't have the authority to get people freed,' he says. 'I told you. I just asked one officer why he was being detained. That's all.'

'Well, it worked.'

'Good.'

'And he definitely wasn't involved. I checked.'

He frowns again. 'I don't think you should go into detail about that here,' he says, his voice quiet. 'If anyone gets the idea you've been getting involved in a police issue—'

'Okay.' I hadn't thought of it like that. Perhaps this isn't the place to discuss it. But I'm still glad I was right about Alfie.

'And don't worry about my colleagues thinking I was a father,' he says, with a wink. 'Most of them were too drunk by then to take any notice, and those who weren't were more impressed than shocked. You know how men are.' He gives a self-deprecating smile that just makes him look even more delectable.

I inch closer wanting to kiss him, but something stops me.

As if reading my mind, James gives a gentle sigh.

'What time do you need to be back?'

I stare at him, then check my watch. 'Oh, no, in about ten minutes.'

'I'll drive you.' He quickly logs out of the computer, gets up and opens the door for me. He locks it once we're out and we hurry over to the lift.

'How come you've got this car when Suzanne gets a Mercedes?' I ask as he drives out of the station compound.

'I like this car. It's comfy. Besides, it's great for undercover operations.'

I hadn't even thought of that. How stupid am I?

'Do you do lots of undercover stuff?'

He nods. 'Quite a bit.'

I don't ask any more. I know he can't tell me much about his job, so I tell him about mine instead.

'Siobhan's going to put in a word for me in the women's supplement office,' I say, excitedly. It feels so natural chatting to James about my work. 'She's got a really nice girl called Francesca working with her at the moment. I think we're going to be good friends. I've already helped a little on a couple of things they're working on.'

'Good for you.' He smiles.

'I can't wait to get out of the newsroom. And the work's so much more interesting with Siobhan. Did you know they actually get discounts or vouchers or whatever for recommending certain items of clothing? And they're not the manky ones? It's top-quality stuff. Though I'd never let that cloud my judgement,' I add quickly.

'Good.'

'Especially if my name's going on the article. Imagine everyone thinking I'd actually put together a horrid outfit? I'd never live it down. And what if Mum saw it?'

He chuckles. 'Do they get the *Daily Chronicle* down in Kent?'

'No. But, still. Someone might show it to her. Especially if my article's in it.'

He nods. 'Someone like who?'

I balk. 'Well, like me, for instance. Though not if it said I liked horrid clothes.'

'Of course.' His lips are twitching again, and I'm sure he's laughing at me inside. I don't mind, though. He looks more scrumptious than ever, and things seem much better between us.

I'm not certain everything's actually okay now, but I feel a lot more hopeful when he drops me off outside my office building.

'How about a drink tonight?' he offers. 'You can tell me more about this Alfie Reynolds guy. Off the record, of course.'

'I'd love to.'

'Switch your phone on then, so I can text you the time. I'm not sure when I'll be finished yet.'

'I will.'

My stomach feels all gooey and I'm reluctant to leave him. I reach in my bag and immediately switch my mobile back on before heading back to the office.

Dave glances up at the wall clock as soon as I walk into the room. It's one of those boring old bog-standard office clocks with bold numbers and a grey rim.

Nothing like the one in Siobhan's department. One more reason why I want to move.

'Wow. I'm SO glad I made it on time,' I say pointedly. 'And with one minute to spare, too. I'd hate to have been back late.'

Dave grunts but says nothing. I'm appalled at his attitude, to be honest. I never leave the office at lunchtime—apart from yesterday, of course, and the other day when I went to the canteen, but I think we should forget about that. Anyway, it's not like I'm always late back or anything. Okay, so I *did* have to go to the dentist after breaking my tooth and didn't get back for a couple of hours, but I'm allowed time off for appointments, even emergency ones. In fact, *especially* emergency ones. After all, that's the whole point of emergencies, isn't it? You can't schedule them into your diary.

Anyway, Dave Chandler isn't going to upset me today. Nor Bethany bitch-face. Something told me she'd be the one impersonating me at the station. I just need to figure out why. Apart from the fact that she hates me, of course. And I can't believe she thinks I fancy Dave. Ugh! Doesn't she think I have *any* taste? She obviously likes him herself. They'd make a good pair. Gormless and Grumpy. I snigger at the thought, causing Dave to glance up and scowl at me.

I try to concentrate on the budget reports I'm studying, determined not to let the tense atmosphere get to me. It does, though. A bit. Well, maybe a bit more than a bit. To be honest, I've had enough of being ignored for something that probably wasn't even my fault in the first place. In fact, that reminds me...

'Dave. You know that trophy. Can I have a look at it, please?' I ask, innocently. I've already fired up my computer, so he can't say I'm not doing any work.

He eyes me suspiciously. 'What for?'

'I just want to look at it.'

'Why?'

'Because as I'm getting the blame for breaking it, I should at least see what it is I'm supposed to have done.'

He huffs, opening his drawer. 'It can't be mended. It's ruined.'

'And you did say nothing like this has happened before?' I ask, going around to his side of the desk.

'Of course, not.'

Reluctantly, he hands it over. It's not as heavy as I expected. I'm sure the Oscars are much better made than this. I examine both halves. Looking closely at the area around the break, I notice it's not quite as clean as I expected.

'You're not *still* going on about that, are you?' Bethany bitch-face calls over. 'I can see you don't have enough work to do, unlike the rest of us.'

'You just get back to work if you're so busy,' I say coolly. 'In the meantime, I'll just investigate who broke this trophy and stuck the head back on. Hmm, looks like a recent mend, too. The glue's still a bit tacky.'

Her face turns bright red.

'Let me see,' Dave demands and grabs both pieces from me.

'Careful, it might break,' I tell him. 'Oh, look, it already did. Twice. At least.'

'Is that so?' Tom strides over excitedly and studies the pieces in Dave's hands.

Dave holds up the body, showing the neck area with blobs of dried-in superglue. He nods. 'She's right.'

'But who would do something like that?' Tom looks straight at Bethany, who I can't help thinking looks as guilty as sin.

'Well, it's funny how Libby knew to check for the break isn't it? No one else would have guessed it had been damaged before. I reckon she must have snapped it in the first place and stuck it back together hoping no one would notice.' She gives me a really sneery look.

Yesterday, I might have burst into tears at such a ludicrous allegation but not today. Knowing that the bitch has already tried to use my name in vain, I'm not about to let her get away with it again.

'Prove it.'

'What?' Bethany scoffs.

'If you think I broke the trophy and then stuck it back together again, then prove it was me. You haven't got a case without proof.'

I learn a lot from James.

'But how? There's no way of proving who did it. Why don't you just admit it was you and we'll all get on?' Bethany bitch-face seems to enjoy trying to belittle me.

I hope she makes the most of it. I'm determined to make sure it doesn't last long...

23

'CCTV,' I say. 'Check the footage. It shouldn't take long.'

'They don't work,' Bethany sneers. 'They've been broken for ages.'

I look questioningly at Tom, who seems to cotton on immediately. Perhaps he's telepathic like me and Cassie.

'Yes, they do,' he says, a grin starting to appear on his lips. 'The guy came and mended them the day before yesterday. Didn't you see him?'

Bethany looks stunned, her face paling.

'Good. Well I want the tapes checked.'

'You've got no right to give orders.' Bethany can't keep the tremble from her voice.

'Actually, I have every right. I've been accused of something in front of witnesses—and on tape.' I nod towards the nearest camera. 'Now, I've got a right to see the proof. You can't make accusations without evidence.'

'You can if it's just in the office,' Carol-Anne butts in. 'We're not in a court or anything.'

Bethany bitch-face's supercilious grin is the last straw. I take a deep breath.

'If I don't see the evidence that I committed the act that I've been accused of, then I will demand that the police are called in right now.'

'But it's not a criminal act,' Bethany blusters, walking over to us.

'Whether slander is regarded as a criminal act or a civil act is a case for the law to decide,' I state. 'Either way, slander and defamation need to be proven and I will demand that the footage from those cameras is used to support my case.'

'What case? You broke a flaming trophy—why don't you just admit it?' Bethany's really riled.

'The case of slander and defamation of character that I will bring against this company unless you can prove that I broke that statuette and stuck it back together again. The proof will be on the tape. All you have to do is check it.' I rub my hands together.

'Well said, Miss Lawrence.'

I spin around and stare at James, who's standing in the doorway. My heart thumps and I feel hot all over. That gooey feeling returns to my tummy and my mouth goes dry. What on earth is he doing here? I thought he drove away as soon as he dropped me off—clearly not.

He flashes his badge. 'Sergeant James Harper. Who's in charge here?'

Dave slowly rises to his feet. 'I'm the senior member of staff. Dave Chandler. Editor.'

James does well to hide his smirk at the row of trophies lined up across the front of the desk. 'I take it it's your trophy that got damaged?' he asks.

Dave actually looks quite embarrassed as he admits that it was. He gives it to James to examine.

'Who called the police?' Bethany's voice is trembling again.

'And you are...?' James asks, looking up.

'Bethany Thomas.'

James narrows his eyes. 'Funny, you look vaguely familiar. Not been in any trouble with the police have you, Miss Thomas?'

Her eyes widen in horror. 'No.'

'No matter,' James says flippantly. 'I can always check at the station. For your information, any accusation that might lead to a defamation lawsuit should be investigated thoroughly. As Miss Lawrence stated, if she has been falsely accused of something that might ruin her reputation in any way, shape or form, she has every right to demand proof. If there is substantial evidence to support her claim that the accusation is false, she will have no problem in suing the company. She might also make any personal claims against individuals, too.'

Bethany takes a step back, her jaw dropping open. She eyes the CCTV camera.

James gives the broken trophy back to Dave.

'Whoever tried to stick it back together did an awful job,' he says, rolling his eyes. 'Are you in a position to authorise the scrutiny of the security tapes?'

'Yes,' Dave replies.

James turns back to me, a twinkle in his eye. 'Miss Lawrence, are you happy for Mr Chandler to organise for you to examine the tapes? If not, I can—'

'Yes. That will be fine, thank you, Sergeant,' I reply.

'Good.' He nods. 'In that case, I'll get on. I'll check with your management later, see if any charges need to be brought.'

'Thank you.'

He gives a smile of satisfaction and leaves the room, while everyone stares at me.

'Did *you* call the cops?' Carol-Anne asks, wide-eyed. 'I know you threatened to.'

I frown at her. 'When exactly do you think I'd have done that?'

She shrugs.

'More likely that management would have brought them in after Phil Peerless reported what had happened yesterday,' I say, pursing my lips. I'm not lying, exactly.

'Why would he do that? I thought it was all sorted.' Dave frowns.

'Sorted? I apologised for slamming the books on the desk,' I reply, 'but that doesn't mean I was guilty of breaking your trophy. As it's turned out, I'm clearly not guilty, am I? But you've all treated me as though I was. Surely, you didn't think I was going to take the blame without any proof? How stupid do you think I am?' I look pointedly at Bethany, who seethes.

Trying not to smirk, I lean over and switch off my computer. 'Now, I'm sure you're as eager as I am to know who *really* broke your trophy,' I say to Dave. 'After all, it's your favourite one, according to Bethany, isn't it?'

Dave calls security while Bethany bitch-face slinks back to her desk.

Tom sniggers. 'Can I come, too?' His eyes flash with mirth.

'No,' Dave says, standing up. He looks over at me. 'We can go up now. They're just pulling the tapes for us. They're also calling Phil Peerless, who'll no doubt want to join us.'

'Great.'

***

According to the tape, it was 5.34pm on Monday 17 October when Bethany bitch-face returned to the office to collect the copy of *Heat* magazine from her desk drawer. As she'd swept past our desk on her way out, her bag—an oversized, fake Louis Vuitton—had swiped a couple of Dave's trophies onto the floor. The one depicting an open book was unscathed, but the head fell off the statuette. After some unrepeatable profanities, she hastily replaced the book one, then took the two halves of the broken item and shoved them in her bag.

She arrived in the empty office at 7.43am on Tuesday 18 October and placed the mended trophy back on the desk.

Phil starts to apologise to me, but I cut him off.

'Mr Peerless, I think that, as the accusations were made in front of everyone, the apology should be, too, don't you?'

His eyes widen at my audacity, but I stand my ground. I won't be walked all over. And it's only fair that if I have to suffer the humiliation of being accused with everyone watching, then he can endure the embarrassment of admitting he was wrong and apologising with the same people watching. He's had a face like thunder ever since he walked into the security office, and this clearly isn't making him any happier.

We return to the news office, which is in silence for a change. I wonder if it's always this quiet when I'm not here. The atmosphere could be cut with a knife, as it cloaks the whole room in a thick shadow of recrimination and apprehension.

Everyone looks up except Bethany bitch-face, who seems unable to meet my eye.

'We've examined the tape and it would appear that I... er... *we*... were wrong to accuse Miss Lawrence of breaking the trophy.' Phil stands just inside the doorway, and I wonder if he's hoping to make a quick getaway. I'm right next to him.

'Who was it, then?' Tom asks.

Phil and I look over at Bethany bitch-face, who's taken a sudden interest in the floor.

'Bethany Thomas,' Phil says.

She looks up slowly. 'It was an accident,' she wails, tears suddenly streaming down her cheeks.

'We know that,' Phil replies. 'So, why didn't you just come clean in the first place?'

'I-I thought Dave would be angry.' She can hardly get the words out through her sobs.

'You're right there,' Dave says. 'But not as angry as I am now that you've tried to blame someone else for it.' He turns to me. 'Libby, I'm so sorry.'

I want to reply *and so you should be,* but I don't. I accept his apology graciously, as with that of Phil, Tom, and Bethany. Even Carol-Anne and Sophie admit to knowing about it, although neither of them actually took part in the act.

When Phil takes Bethany to his office, the whole atmosphere lightens. Dave even makes me a coffee.

'You seem to know a lot about the law,' he says, placing the cup in front of me. He's even added a couple of biscuits.

'Well, you know,' I say with a shrug. I don't want to tell him that the hunky copper who actually came to back me up was my boyfriend. Or, at least, I *hope* he still is.

'You're certainly keen on getting your facts right,' Tom remarks.

'I am,' I agree. 'I'd hate to think I'd falsely accused anyone of anything.' My stomach roils with regret as a reminder of Saturday night flashes in my mind. And last night. How could I have accused James like that?

'Usually, anyway,' Dave says with a knowing grin.

I stare at him. 'What's that supposed to mean?' I don't like the way he said that at all.

'Well, there was that story about the potholes, wasn't there? You could have got the whole paper shut down if that accusation against the council had been printed.'

I flush.

'Oh, yeah, but that wasn't her fault,' Sophie pipes up.

We all turn to stare at her.

'What?' Dave frowns.

'Bethany told her that story to make her look bad in front of you,' she says with a shrug.

'Yeah, she was jealous that you seemed impressed by Libby,' Carol-Anne adds.

Dave stares at me. 'Bethany told you that piece of fake news? Why didn't you tell me?'

I glow hot. 'I didn't want to get her into trouble.'

'But that's exactly what she did to you,' Dave points out.

'I know. Maybe she's just like that. I'm not,' I reply.

'We can see that,' Tom says, smiling at me.

I get even hotter and concentrate on my work to try to hide my blushes.

'You really are something else,' Dave says, just as Bethany bitch-face returns, glowering.

'Yeah, you can say that again,' she sneers, walking back to her desk.

'What the hell's that supposed to mean?' Dave demands, scowling at her.

She looks shocked.

'Yeah, don't be so nasty,' Sophie tells her.

'She tried to save your bacon,' Carol-Anne says.

'Oh, so you're all on her side now, are you?' Bethany clenches her jaw as she glares at her colleagues.

'Well, you could be nicer to her,' Sophie protests.

'I think we all could,' Dave interjects. 'It seems we've been blaming Libby for stuff that was entirely *someone else's* fault.' He looks purposely at Bethany.

Oh, no! It was bad enough when they were all being horrid to me, but this is downright embarrassing.

'How about going for a drink tonight at The Lamb and Bell?' Tom suggests. 'Office outing.'

'I can't tonight,' I say, shaking my head. I've suddenly remembered I'm going out with James later.

I quickly check my phone.

Hi, Libby. Hope I didn't embarrass you earlier. You were right. I should stick up for you more. I'm so sorry.

Meet me at Ricardo's at 6pm? I'll get off early.

Btw—did I tell you how beautiful you look today?

Can't wait to see you. Jxx

I glance over at Dave in case he's cross with me using my mobile, but he's busy making arrangements to meet up with Tom later.

You were my knight in shining armour. Thank you.

See you at 6. Looking forward to it.

Libby xx

PS—Glad you like the outfit. :)

The last time he told me I was beautiful was on Saturday night when I wore the Jovani. I'm glad I managed to get the stain out, as I felt amazing in it and would love to wear it again. And the Louboutins, of course.

My credit card bill isn't due for at least another week, so I've got plenty of time to figure out how to make the payment. Even then, I could just pay the minimum and give myself time to figure out the rest later. And they don't always add stuff on straight away, do they? I'm sure it'll be fine. Everything will be. I can feel it. I knew I was right to stay positive today.

***

It's not long before I'm switching off my computer and putting on my jacket. Bethany bitch-face glowers as she passes our desk. I'm sorry I accepted her apology now. She obviously didn't mean it. Well, in that case, I didn't mean my acceptance, either.

'See you tomorrow,' Sophie says, smiling at me.

'Come on,' Bethany practically hauls her out of the office, while Carol-Anne just grins.

'Sure you can't join us?' Tom says, as I follow him and Dave to the door.

'Sorry, I've already made plans.' I smile apologetically.

'Another time, maybe,' Tom says.

He and Dave take the stairs while I wait for the lift. I know I could use the exercise but I daren't wear out my Stella McCartneys on their first outing. Besides, I exerted enough energy at the gym on Monday to last me at least a month. Luckily, we didn't have to pay membership as it was just a taster session, and I'm not sure about going back. Peggy wasn't all that friendly, and there was hardly enough equipment to go round. I might think about it again when all the excitement dies down, with it just opening and everything. And they might let me just pay to go every three months or something, just to top up my fitness. Or maybe, they'll do a pay-as-you-go deal like they do with phones. Either way, it's a great way I can save money—which has got to be a good thing, right? I'll have that credit card bill paid off in no time at this rate.

I take the Tube up to Notting Hill Gate and from there it's a short walk to Ricardo's. Notting Hill is one of my favourite parts of London, with its quaint Victorian terraces and cosmopolitan atmosphere. I keep hoping to spy Hugh Grant popping out of one of the little shops, like in the film. There are several people around but sadly he's not one of them.

I'm not far from Ricardo's when I stop short, noticing Dave Chandler walking along the street towards me. What on earth's he doing here? He's got a woman with him who looks familiar.

She's wearing a really nice Karen Millen black coat with black Kurt Geigers with a sort of fancy fret work across the front. I've seen them before. Probably on her. *Think. Think.* I hate forgetting names. And I never forget shoes. Bryony! That's it. Bryony, the pregnant lady from the gala. These must be her best going-out shoes. They are lovely. I feel a thrill of excitement. She's one of the girls who befriended me on Facebook after we had all that fun dancing.

They're only a few feet away from me through the crowd when I catch Dave's eye. I know he sees me, but he pretends not to recognise me. In fact, he totally blanks me. Flaming cheek! After everything that's happened today, too. He steers Bryony down a side street, and they disappear from view. I'm stunned. Not to mention hurt. And angry.

'Hey, gorgeous.' James suddenly comes up behind me, smiling.

I stare at him for a moment, gathering my thoughts.

'Are you okay?' he asks.

'Um... yeah.' I'm not sure that I am, to be honest. I gaze up at his handsome face and manage to smile back. 'Hi, how are you?'

'Great. Let's get a drink.' He puts a hand in the small of my back again and leads me into the restaurant. 'Are you hungry? I thought we could eat here, unless you'd prefer somewhere else?' He's so suave I can't resist reaching up and kissing him on the cheek.

'That would be lovely.' I suddenly feel much better. And who cares about Dave Chandler anyway?

'Thank you so much for coming to support me today,' I say as we tuck into our meal. We're both having the lamb. It's a bit of a treat because when I used to work in a hotel, the chef wasn't allowed to put it on the menu because it was too expensive.

'As I said, you were right. I'm so sorry, Libby, I should have done more to defend you at the gala. I was so shocked to hear that Suzanne had a boyfriend after she'd told me she was struggling all on her own. I felt such a fool.'

'It couldn't have helped when I accused you of having a son.' My stomach churns with regret for opening my big mouth. He didn't deserve that. What annoys me even more is that I'd promised myself I wouldn't mention any of it until I was sure of my facts. It just all came out in the heat of the moment.

'I was rather surprised,' he admits with a grin.

'I'm sorry.'

He holds my hand across the table and I suddenly feel that we're all right again at last. My stomach goes all warm and fuzzy at the thought.

'And I'm sorry for not stopping Suzanne from ruining your lovely dress. I meant what I said; I'll pay for the damage.'

'There's no need. I managed to remove the stain and it's fine.'

He raises his eyebrows. It's good to see that he's impressed with my efforts, but I won't tell him just how adept I am at removing wine stains from my clothes. I should be after all the practice I've had, but I have to admit it's usually because I've managed to spill my own drink in a pub, not had one thrown over me in a Mayfair hotel.

'I went after you, but you were already in a taxi when I got to the door,' he says with a grimace.

'Did you speak to Suzanne?' I don't really want to talk about his ex tonight, but I suppose there are still things that need to be ironed out.

'Yes. Reynolds had been putting pressure on her to give him money,' James says, ruefully. 'She didn't know about his reputation as a womaniser, or about him being a con man, of course. She said she felt so stupid when I told her who he was. I also told her she'd been a complete idiot.'

I expected him to be sympathetic, but he seems more annoyed. I can't really blame him—it was *his* money she was giving to the bastard.

'Is he locked up now?' I ask.

'Yes. Alice McGurk pressed charges, and I've told Suzanne to do the same. The longer he's off the streets the better.'

I have to agree. Alfie and his mum will be relieved, too.

'Anyway, enough about all that, did the CCTV footage confirm your suspicions this afternoon?' He brightens immediately.

I grin. 'Yep. Bethany bitch-face Thomas broke it and tried to mend it. She staged the whole thing with the books to frame me. Phil Peerless, our chief editor, didn't look at all happy about it.'

'I can imagine. She kept her job, though?'

'Yes. It was only a stupid trophy, not the crown jewels.'

The thought reminds me of something. 'I think she likes Dave,' I add. 'She must be annoyed that I'm working with him and keeps trying to make me look stupid in front of him.'

'That would make sense.' He takes a sip of his wine.

'But I saw him tonight with another woman. Bryony from the gala. Do you know her?'

He frowns. 'Bryony Peterson? She's one of our WPCs. You're sure it was her?'

'Positive. They didn't speak to me, though. Probably because they weren't supposed to be here. Dave had arranged to go to The Lamb and Bell near work with Tom, but I saw him with Bryony just down the road from here. Looks like he had a better offer.'

James frowns. 'I'll bet no one at the station realises she's seeing a journalist.'

'Oh.' I gasp. 'You don't think she's his golden snitch, do you? The one who's been leaking information about drugs busts and stuff?'

I can see from James' expression that that's *exactly* what he thinks, though he seems a little distracted.

'I wonder if that's who he was with at the café that day.' I muse. 'When all that ri… er, kerfuffle was going on about the potholes in Knightsbridge. Dave said he was going to do some networking, but I assumed he meant with his contacts. He was having coffee in the window of a café near Harrods.'

'You think he might have been meeting Bryony?'

I shrug. 'I didn't actually see him. I was reporting on the potholes and took some random snaps. It was only afterwards that I noticed Dave in the background of one of them. I'd been too busy with... other stuff to notice at the time.' I'm still trying to forget that whole event, but it seems determined to haunt me.

'That's interesting,' James replies, pursing his lips. 'Do you still have the picture?'

'It's on my iPad,' I tell him. 'I'm keeping it as evidence.'

He gives me a warning look. 'Evidence of what, exactly? It' not against the law to drink coffee, you know?'

I shake my head. 'It wasn't just the coffee. By the looks of it, he was eating a huge Cornish pasty. After all the times he's preached about the virtues of protein shakes and grotty cereal bars. It might come in handy next time he tries to make me feel guilty about eating a Mint Aero.'

'Have you got it with you? Your iPad?'

I shake my head. 'I left my stuff in my Marc Jacobs at the office to save carting it here,' I admit. The iPad doesn't fit in my Radley. 'I've got this, though.'

I root in my bag and pull out my phone. 'I saw him acting suspiciously in an alley when I went to the dentist on Monday. I didn't know if it'd be useful.'

Scrolling down, I find the photo I want. 'It's not all that good. It was pretty dark under there, but it's definitely him, isn't it?'

James takes it from me. 'It certainly looks that way,' he says, examining it. 'Could I have a copy?'

I'd forgotten James isn't all that familiar with modern technology. Last time I mentioned Bluetooth, he thought I was talking about some ancient king of Norway or somewhere. Tragic, really! He honestly has no idea. Anyway, I think it's safer to just take the phone from him and send the pic to his messenger account.

'I'll send you over the one from my iPad in the morning,' I promise.

'Thanks. You didn't recognise who he was with in this one, I don't suppose?' He's studying the photo on his own phone now.

'No, sorry.'

'It doesn't matter. I might be able to get it blown up and see if it's anyone we know.'

'You don't think it's a drugs deal, do you?' I lower my voice. 'They often take place in dark alleyways, don't they? Could Dave be a junkie? He's got lots of energy, maybe it's those antibiotic steroids or something?'

'Anabolic,' he corrects me.

'Who?'

'Never mind.' He shakes his head. 'And no, I think it's highly unlikely that he's into drugs, but we'll take a look anyway.'

'Right.' All the same, it's quite exciting to think I *might* be working alongside a drugs baron.

'He gets awful mood swings.' I suddenly remember him yelling at me about the broken trophy— totally unjustified, of course.

'Probably just bad-tempered,' James says calmly, getting back to his meal.

I narrow my eyes at him, wondering if he's just trying to put me off the scent. I've probably hit the nail right on the head and he doesn't want to admit it. Of course, he'll have to prove it before we can say anything.

We continue eating quietly for a few minutes.

'You look lovely today,' James says, at last.

I blush. 'Thank you. I've been taking my trainers to work to change into if I need to run anywhere since I joined the gym,' I tell him. Well, I *did* go for one night—that means I *temporarily* joined, doesn't it?

He looks astonished. 'Really?'

I'm not sure what he's alluding to, so I just carry on. 'But funnily enough, ever since I started doing that Dave hasn't wanted to take me running off all over London.'

James frowns. 'Has he said why?'

'No. The girls seem to have interesting stories to report on, but we've been stuck in the office writing follow-up articles and researching stuff. It's a bit boring, to tell the truth.'

James finishes his dinner and puts down his cutlery.

'So, this has been since we brought Dave in for questioning? Ever since then he hasn't had any urgent tip-offs about stories?' His voice is quiet.

I stare at him.

'Yes.'

He takes a slow swig of his wine.

'Interesting,' he says with a frown.

'So, whoever his informant is has realised you're onto them and has stopped feeding him information.' I feel like a detective myself. Maybe I should consider a career change?

'Let's not jump to conclusions,' James says. He gives me another warning look. I don't know why, but he just seems to think I'll go off half-cocked or something. Which I wouldn't. Well, not again, anyway.

'I'm not,' I say. 'Just... considering the possibilities.' I raise my eyebrows innocently.

'Hmm.' James doesn't look convinced.

I finish my food, which was scrumptious, by the way.

The waiter comes to clear our plates, and I sneak a glance over at the sweet trolley. It looks scrummy. When I look back at James, he's grinning at me. My face goes hot.

'We'd like dessert as soon as you're ready,' James tells the waiter.

It's almost as if he can read minds or something.

I opt for a slice of strawberry pavlova that comes with lashings of cream. I think the waiter must like me, too, as I'm sure I've got extra strawberries. James has a crème brûlée, which I think looks a bit burnt but he insists is delicious.

The sweetness of the meringue is delightful, and I moan as it mingles with the strawberries and cream.

'This is gorgeous,' I say, closing my eyes for a second to savour the flavours.

'So are you,' James says, reaching out and taking my hand in his.

I open my eyes and gaze into his handsome face. His eyes are twinkling and he's smiling.

'Thank you.'

'Libby, I really am sorry about the other night.'

'It's okay,' I reply. 'I get that you were being supportive. I just would have preferred it to have been towards me instead of Suzanne. I get it, though; she was your wife, after all.' I'm surprised how adult I suddenly feel. I'm still not sure I'm all that happy about it, though.

'I don't feel any allegiance to *her*,' he assures me, raising his eyebrows. 'Especially not now that I know she's been seeing this Reynolds guy. I can't believe how stupid she is—or how stupid *I* was not to know.'

'It's not your fault. You believed her. Why wouldn't you?'

'I'm afraid I took a little too long to absorb the information, though. I can see how that must have looked to you, particularly after she'd thrown wine all over you. I can't apologise enough.'

His contrite expression tugs at my heart. I shouldn't have blamed him, he was doing enough of that himself.

'It's all right,' I assure him.

His smile makes my insides go all gooey. He seems to have that effect on me a lot.

We take our coffees into the lounge area and sit by the window looking out at the twinkling lights in the trees just outside. It's not really like being in London here. It's a little, quiet back street with no traffic.

I'm actually sad when the night ends and we have to part company. I feel so happy and peaceful in his arms. Safe. And I'm excited at the prospect of seeing him in action tomorrow when he comes to arrest Dave Chandler. Excited and nervous.

***

Cassie's up and ready when I wander into the kitchen the next morning.

'Happy Thursday,' she says, offering me a cup of tea.

'There's nothing happy about a Thursday,' I tell her. 'It's the worst day of the week.'

'Not today. Not for me, anyway.' She looks all flushed with excitement.

I grab a piece of toast from her plate and raise my eyebrows.

'I'm going buying,' she informs me. 'I get to help pick the colours for the new collection.'

I beam at her, the toast halfway to my mouth. 'Oh, gosh that's wonderful!'

'I know, right?' She gets up and does a little happy dance around the kitchen. 'Of course, I'm not actually designing the whole thing, I'm just giving input. But Meredith Harrington-Fforbes said I've got a real eye for colour, so she wants me on the buying team today.'

They've all got posh names at Crystal, the fashion designer's where Cassie works. Perdita Huckabee is the other newish girl there, then there's Allegra Myerscough, Chantelle Rutherford and Sarah-Jayne Sherwood who all work in the same office.

Meredith is the main boss of their department and there are loads of others, too. It's a massive building, all glass and concrete with huge windows, blonde wood floors and rooms so big they echo. Some of the girls insist on calling Cassie 'Cassandra', which she normally hates but she doesn't seem to mind so much from them.

'What're you going to get?' I ask, wishing my job was as exciting as hers.

She screws up her nose in thought. 'I don't know yet. Allegra said I have to choose whatever sings to me at the time. Maybe I'll get something light and frothy. It's for the summer collection, after all.'

'Ooh, all those lovely colours.' I can just imagine it. 'Pastel or bright, do you think?'

'We have to have a mixture of both but at the same time they have to blend well for the collection to maintain its cohesive look,' she says, frowning.

'Well, good luck with that. Personally, I like things like pink and black or yellow with navy.'

'Yes!' she sounds like she's just won the lottery. 'Meredith loves pink.'

She scoops up her enormous bag, gives me a quick hug, and makes for the door.

'Have fun,' I call after her.

I'm really happy thatshe's enjoying her new job so much. She's always been creative, apparently, and this role is perfect for her. It makes me even more determined to work on our women's supplement with

Siobhan, Fran, and Tammy. Today, though, is going to be a whole different kettle of fish.

I was hoping to fill Cassie in on the business with Dave being a drug dealer—possibly—and his girlfriend being the vole in the police station. I really like Bryony; I hope she's not in trouble. A horrid thought occurs to me. What if Bryony and Dave go to prison? It'll be my fault. Did I do the right thing in informing James? Does that make *me* a vole, or whatever it is, too? I didn't mean to be. I was just... sort of... well... *telling* him, I suppose.

I gasp, dropping my toast and put my hand to my mouth. 'Oh, no! I've just turned into a golden snitch!'

It's quite nerve-wracking working alongside a criminal. Well, a possible one, anyway. Make that probable. Dave's up to something, I know it. I glance at his trophies. He's spaced them all out to make up for the missing statuette. They don't hold the same appeal that they did. In fact, I'm not at all impressed.

I've put on my knee-high boots today, which have eyelets all up the back. They make my legs look really slim. I got them from Deichmann, they're part of the Ellie Goulding Star Collection—only forty quid, but they look much more expensive. Cassie said so, too. I've teamed them with my Nora Gardner fit and flare dress, which is a lovely deep wine colour, a bit more demure than yesterday's bright red, which I thought was more befitting, seeing as I'm about to witness my mentor being arrested. I've never had to dress for this sort of occasion before, so it was hard to pick an outfit, but I think this is more appropriate than something bright or frivolous.

I take my iPad from my Marc Jacobs and send James the picture of Dave at the café. At the forefront of the photo are some of the people rioting. I hope James doesn't ask what that was all about.

Dave's looking quite calm, tapping away on his keyboard. I've got to hand it to him, he's a cool dude.

'Did you have a nice time at The Lamb and Bell last night?' I ask, studying his and Tom's reactions.

I'm waiting for Dave to come up with some lame excuse as to why he couldn't make it in the end, so I'm really shocked when he replies, 'Yes, thanks,' without even looking up.

I nod slowly, trying to hide my surprise. I'm watching Tom for a response, but he's just sifting through some photos on his own desk.

'Was it busy?' I ask.

'Not especially.' Again, Dave doesn't even look at me.

'Did you stay late?' I ask, waiting for Tom to point out that Dave actually stood him up.

'No, we were there 'til about...' Dave actually looks over to Tom. 'Tennish, would you say, Tom? Maybe a bit later?'

Tom nods, looking over. 'Yeah. Nearer half past, I'd say.'

Dave glances at me. 'I take it you're hoping we're going to enquire about *your* evening, are you?'

Does he honestly think that's why I asked? And why's Tom sticking up for him? Giving him an alibi? Surely, he's not in on this, too?

'No,' I say, an octave higher than usual. This has got me more riled than I thought. 'Though it was very nice, thank you.'

'Good.'

Dave's irritated. Have I rattled him? He knows I know where he was last night, so why keep up the pretence? Is he hoping I didn't recognise him in Notting Hill? Perhaps he thinks if he denies it, I'll think I must have been mistaken and assume it was someone else. But it wasn't. I mean, how many bald-headed, seven-foot giants are there in this borough? He's got to think I'm stupid.

There's a snort from the other end of the room, and I look up to see Bethany bitch-face giving me a dirty look. Nothing new there. What *is* new, however, is the warning look Dave gives her after he spins around in his seat to glare at her. I wonder if he still feels bad about the trophy incident. *Pity Bethany doesn't.*

I get back to writing the report on the likelihood of the council taking measures to avoid the pothole situation in the future, while Dave answers his mobile, leaving the room quickly.

I use the opportunity to send a quick text to James.

Hi, James, Dave maintains he was at The Lamb and Bell with Tom until 10.30pm last night. Tom's backing him up! Lxx

I stuff my phone inside my jacket pocket as Dave hurries back into the office.

'I hope you can run in those boots,' he says. 'We've got a story.'

'What?'

I gape at him. I was sure he wouldn't get a tip-off again today. In fact, I depended on it when I put these boots on.

'You need to hurry,' he says, quickly logging off his computer.

I left my trainers here in my Marc Jacobs last night, so I quickly unzip my boots and step into them. It's a good job I didn't wear a straight dress. Grabbing my Radley, I follow him out the door, my feet feeling very strange but unexpectedly comfy in flat running shoes.

Mercifully, we take the lift. We're the only ones in it. I take the opportunity to do a few stretches, bending my left knee and holding my foot behind me. Dave gives me a weird look. For the first time, I actually feel a bit nervous being in such a confined space with him. I mean, what if he's taken some drugs this morning? Come to think of it, his eyes do look a bit bloodshot. I continue with a few warm-ups. I'll be ready for him if he does anything.

'What *are* you doing?'

See? He's worried. I've got him on the back foot. Ha!

'Just limbering up,' I reply. 'If we're going to run halfway around London, I don't want to cause myself an injury, do I?'

I'm waiting for him to point out that it's never bothered me before, but the lift pings so he doesn't get the time. Good. I don't want to forewarn him about how much fitter I am now.

'It's this way.' He starts to sprint up the road.

'What is?' I'm actually keeping up with him—for now.

'Withywood Way,' he says, not even panting. Unlike me.

My jaw drops. 'That's miles away.'

'Hurry up, then.'

I'm surprised how agile I feel as I run along behind him—though not as far behind as I usually am—however, I get some really strange looks from passers-by. I suppose if I were wearing a tracksuit like Dave, I might not look quite so strange, but my nice dress and jacket doesn't really go with my stark, white Nikes.

I'm pegging Dave—so to speak—all the way through back streets and narrow alleys, puffing like a steam engine, but determined to keep up.

We get to Withywood Way, and he leads me to the house of the drugs bust. My heart's pounding—not just because of the exercise. All the windows have been boarded up and the grass badly needs mowing. It looks like it's been empty for years, not just a week.

'Stay back.' Dave pulls me behind a car just down the street.

'What is it? What's happened?' I whisper, craning my neck to see around him.

'I'm not sure,' Dave mutters.

Nothing. Nothing seems to have happened. Whatever he's been told is rubbish. We're still crouched behind that car fifteen minutes' later when an old man comes to drive it away.

Dave looks flummoxed, but I improvise by bending down and pretending to pick something up off the ground.

'I've found it!' I say, holding my hand up, fist clenched.

The old man frowns at me.

'It's okay, I dropped my earring.' I show him my clenched hand.

'Really?' He sounds most disinterested.

'Yes. Well, I'll just put it in. Thank you.' I'm trying to stay all bright and cheerful, but he's still scowling at me.

'Where?'

'What?'

'Where are you going to put it? You've already got two earrings in.' He's eyeing me suspiciously now.

'Oh... er... yes, yes, I know. I... erm... lost it the other day when I was here. When I said I was going to put it in I... er... meant... my bag. I'll put it in my bag.' I hold up the Radley, which is crossing my body.

His eyes are still narrowed, so I quickly go to unzip it. The sooner I get this over with the better. Unfortunately, the zip gets stuck on a piece of the lining material and I have to use two hands to undo it.

'Got it,' I say with relief when I finally get it open.

That's when it occurs to me that I was supposed to be holding an earring in one of the hands I've just used to unzip the bag. There's only one thing for it—bluff it.

'Good job it's only tiny,' I say, pretending to pop the invisible item into my bag.

He doesn't look convinced for a second. Damn! I smile anyway, sidling off the road to join Dave on the pavement.

'Play along,' I mutter through gritted teeth.

To my horror, he takes my arm. 'Come on, let's get you back to the home,' he says in a soothing tone. Then he turns to the bewildered man standing next to his open car door. 'She's only allowed out for the day,' he explains, and then—just to make matters worse—he taps the side of his head, indicating that I'm mental or something! Can you believe it?

The man gives an understanding nod, looks sympathetically at me, and then climbs into his car. Dave leads me up the street a little way.

'What do you think you're doing?' I demand, wrenching my arm from his grip as soon as the man drives off.

'Playing along. You were acting like a madwoman, so I thought—'

'I was not,' I snap at him. 'I was just... improvising.'

'How was I to know?' Dave raises his eyebrows. 'All I saw was—hang on.'

He urges me towards a tree—the kind that appear to sprout from the pavement—and we watch the drugs house. A young lad with sandy-coloured hair is skulking around by the side door. He's got something in his hand and is using it to pick the lock. I gasp. What on earth's Alfie doing here?

He sneaks inside just as a couple of police cars pull up next to us. Dave and I try to look casual, like two normal people leaning against a silver birch in the middle of the street.

'He must have gone inside,' one of the uniformed officers mutters to another two as they pass us. They give us funny looks but head towards the side of the house. A few minutes later, two of them reappear, holding onto Alfie. He's got what looks like a gift in his hand, loosely wrapped in the paper they use for flowers at the supermarket. Either Quality Street or Roses I'd say, judging by the shape.

The other cop emerges and begins to secure the side door.

'I haven't done anything,' Alfie protests as they near us. 'I'd just hidden my mum's present in the attic. It's her birthday today, so I had to get it and wrap it up.'

I look away, hoping he doesn't recognise me.

'Then you've got nothing to worry about, son,' one of the cops says to him in a calm tone. 'We'll just take your statement, check there's nothing in that package that shouldn't be there, and you'll be back in time for your mum's birthday tea.'

Dave and I make our way back up the street, trying not to look suspicious while curtains twitch from a couple of the neighbours' windows. If it was one of those who called the police, it begs the question who called Dave. And how come he knew something was going to happen so long before it did? Just how many people has he got feeding him information?

I feel a bit wary of my mentor as we head back to the office. Had I not worn my Nikes today and been so fit I might not have realised he'd got to the scene so early. By my reckoning, I would have been at least ten minutes behind him, maybe more. It might have saved me all the embarrassment of the 'earring' incident, but I certainly couldn't have known what I know now. I decide to tackle him about it while we're in a busy street. It feels safer, somehow.

'How did your informant know this was going to happen before it did?' I ask as casually as I can.

'It was just a hunch.' He shrugs.

'That the lad would have to fetch his mum's birthday present from that house?' That's incredible in anyone's view.

He shrugs again. 'Come on, we'd best get back and write this up.'

'It's hardly much of a story.'

'Youth breaks into drugs baron's house? I think we could do something with that, don't you? Did the guy know they were all in prison? What else might he have gone back for? Did he get interrupted by the cops? Is he actually connected with the dealers and did *they* send him back for something?'

'Hardly,' I say, rolling my eyes. 'He's an innocent young lad who was squatting in the wrong place at the wrong time. He left his mum's gift there when the cops carted him off with the rest of them and now, he's come back to get it. Hardly a front-page story.'

'How do you know he's innocent? He's Oliver Reynolds' son, for Christ's sake. Like father like son. And anyway, why didn't the cops find the present when they searched the house after the arrests?'

'It's a box of chocolates, for goodness' sake. They might well have found them, they probably even checked them over, but I doubt they'd think them important enough to confiscate, do you?'

He shakes his head. 'Okay, out of the two stories, whose do you think would be more print worthy?'

'Well, yours obviously. But it's full of speculation. You're not sticking to the facts.'

'What facts? He broke in, didn't he? It's the house that was raided recently and some drug dealers were arrested. How is that not factual?'

I huff. 'You're suggesting things you know aren't true. Alfie isn't a criminal. And he's certainly not working for those dealers.'

'You seem very sure of that.'

'The police let him go, didn't they?'

'Doesn't mean a thing. Cops can be wrong.'

I shake my head to save me from throttling him. How dare he suggest that the police don't know their stuff? And Alfie's a bit rough but he's a good kid. Unfortunately, I can't tell him that, though, so I stay quiet.

Dave takes the stairs when we get back to our office block, so I jump in the lift and quickly text James to tell him where we've been. Hopefully, he'll be here soon to arrest Dave. I know he'll be really worried that I had to go off with him, now we know he could be dangerous. I mean, if he *is* taking drugs anything could have happened. I wonder if I'll get compensation when this is all sorted. After all, unbeknownst to me, I've been put in danger right from the start. As soon as I started working with Dave Chandler. I've been very lucky up until now, but he was certainly angry when he thought I'd broken his trophy. Perhaps it was the drugs heightening his emotions. Or perhaps all those trophies are hiding drugs? Cocaine or heroin or something. That would explain why he was so furious about the head falling off one—he was afraid we'd all see the white powder come pouring out and his game'd be up. I quickly send James another text.

Hey, James, I think the drugs might be hidden in Dave's trophies. L xx

Straight away I get a reply.

What drugs? Jx

Hmm. He could have put *two* kisses like I did. Doesn't he know how this works? You always check what the first person puts and then copy it. It's the Law of Kisses. He should know that, being a policeman. I wonder if he never put kisses on Suzanne's messages. A smile creeps over my face. Maybe he likes me more than he liked her.

You know. We talked about it last night. Lxx

Two kisses. Ha! Now he'll realise that I like him more than she did.

We didn't ascertain he was involved with drugs. Don't worry. I'm working on something pivotal. Jx

I'll ignore the fact he's only put one kiss again. He's obviously busy with the case. He'll probably be here at any moment. I get out of the lift and wander into the office. Dave's already there, sitting at his desk.

'You took your time.'

'It was the lift. Bit busy today.'

Actually, I was the only one in there, and I *might* have pressed the button for the top floor and then the bottom and then our floor. It was a nice, safe place to text James without being missed.

I sit down, remove my bag and jacket and fire up my computer. Dave's already tapping away at his, and I can only guess what work of fiction he's dreaming up.

My mind's on his trophies. Hiding the drugs in plain sight. Clever. No one would suspect that, especially as he's so highly thought of. Though not by me. Or Sophie or Carol-Anne I wouldn't think, they hardly speak to him. And Tom's quieter when Dave's in the office. And I know Bethany fancies him, but I'm not so sure she actually *likes* him all that much. She tends to stay down her end of the room and rarely holds a conversation with him. But she *is* jealous of me being so close to him. She can have him.

I pick up the book-shaped award and examine it. It's not very heavy. I wonder if they do light drugs. You know, like they do with everything else. Light mayonnaise, light butter or light yoghurt, that sort of thing. I don't mean as a healthy alternative for overweight junkies, I mean actual *carrying* weight. So they can hide it easier. Or so it costs less if they send it by post.

'What're you doing?' Dave asks.

'I was just... admiring it,' I reply. 'And checking it in case it got damaged when Bethany knocked it onto the floor the other night.'

'Why?'

'Just in case... um... in case it needed to go to the menders like the other one. You haven't had the statuette fixed yet, have you?' I smile at him, but he doesn't smile back. I'm used to that.

'No.'

'Can I just see it a minute? The broken one?'

He frowns. 'What for?'

'I just want to see how much work it'll take. I know someone who mends things. I could ask him to do it for you, if you like? In fact, why don't I send him a photo of the damage? Then he can tell me if he'd be able to fix it.'

Dave doesn't look convinced but opens his drawer and hands over the two parts of the trophy.

'I doubt anyone can mend it,' he says sighing.

'I know what you're trying to do.' Bethany bitch-face approaches our desk.

Oh, no. I suddenly get very hot. She can't have sussed my plan. How on earth…?

'You're just trying to make me feel bad, aren't you?' she hisses at me.

'No.'

I quickly take the photos while I've got the chance. On closer examination—surreptitiously, of course—I notice that the whole thing seems to be made of solid plastic. Even where the head's broken off it's still sealed on both parts. He couldn't have put anything inside it, after all. I give it a little shake just to be sure.

'You're going to break it! Don't you try blaming me if you do any more damage,' Bethany yells at me.

I can't hear anything shushing about inside.

'Give it here.' Dave stretches out for it and I place it in his hands—which aren't even shaking or anything. He's doing a sterling job of hiding the effects of whatever it is he's taking. He won't be able to fool James, though. In fact, he should be here by now...

26

It's now three in the afternoon, and James and his squad still haven't arrived to arrest Dave Chandler. I'm a bit miffed, to be honest. Doesn't he care how much danger I'm in every minute I have to spend in the company of this criminal? Isn't he worried about me at all? He's supposed to be my boyfriend. He's meant to have feelings for me. All he seems to be feeling right now is too busy to come and rescue me. I mean, anything could happen, couldn't it? Anything at all in this large office with four other people and a really good CCTV system that catches every last corner of the room with pinpoint accuracy. It's amazing I'm not having a panic attack right now, with all this pressure.

James did say he was working on something, but that was hours ago. And I did assume it was something to do with the case, although he didn't actually *say* that. Maybe he meant he was working on something else? Something more important than saving me from the clutches of a drugged-up madman. He didn't seem convinced by my theory about the trophies containing heroin or whatever. I'll have the last laugh, though, when Dave needs his next fix and disappears to the gents' clutching that feather-shaped award. I'll bet the inkpot at the base of the quill contains a different kind of 'pot' altogether.

Sophie just disappeared to the loo, and I really want to go and join her for a chat. I'm dying for some gossip on Bethany bitch-face, who's spent the whole day sneering at me, as usual.

I can't believe she actually fancies Dave Chandler. I mean, I wouldn't describe him as ugly exactly but... ugh! I suppose he's quite muscular, but his head seems to go to a sort of point at the top. And he does have pale blue eyes but one's a bit droopy, which makes him look patronising all the time. Or maybe he *is* being patronising. Perhaps that look's just for me.

I'm suddenly aware that he's staring back at me. *Oh, no*. He thinks I'm admiring him. He actually thinks *I* fancy him now. I can see it in his smug expression. Ew!

Dragging my gaze away from him, I force myself to concentrate on my computer. But I can feel him watching me. And he gives a satisfied sigh as though he knows I want him, but he's too professional to have a relationship with a work colleague. Now, I feel really stupid. *Damn!*

But I could never go for a criminal. Especially not one who takes drugs. Or gets awards and trophies by underhand means. How to tell him that, though? I'd have to let him down gently. Explain that I've got morals. But in a nice way. I don't want him getting angry. Or violent. Oh, crikey, what if he goes mad when I tell him I don't fancy him? He might threaten to do something rash or—hang on, I could be getting a bit ahead of myself here. After all, I haven't actually *told* him I've got feelings for him, have I? Because I don't. Of course, I don't. I mean he's... he's... oh, God, I wish James would just hurry up and arrest him. That would solve everything.

I check my phone. Nothing. What's he playing at? I'm beginning to think James Harper doesn't care about me at all. I mean, fancy leaving a girl in danger all day and not even explaining what the holdup is.

Suddenly, Dave's desk phone rings and he gives a grunt before he answers it. He always does that. I used to think it was because he didn't like being interrupted, but I'm wondering if it's not just to draw attention to how important he is. He puts on his telephone voice to answer. Just like my mum. She always picks up the phone and says, in a really posh voice, 'The Lawrence residence, how may I help you?' Then I say, 'Hi, Mum', and she says, 'Libby', in her real voice and then we chat normally.

Dave's face has turned pale. Even through his tan I can see it. It must be James ringing him to tell him he's under arrest. Do they read criminals their rights over the phone? I suppose in this day and age anything's possible; it's all about saving time and resources, but I'd be surprised if they're telling Dave to make his own way down to the station so they can lock him up.

He slowly replaces the receiver, a grave expression on his face.

'I've got to go out,' he says slowly.

He switches off his computer as though on automatic pilot.

'Is it a story?' I ask. 'Can I come?'

'No.'

'Are you okay, mate? Has something happened?' Tom frowns at Dave's shocked expression and comes over to our desk.

Dave looks up and nods. 'Yeah. I have to go to the police station.'

I knew it! I still can't believe he has to take himself there, though. I mean, hasn't it occurred to anyone that he might make a run for it instead? Am I the only one who can see the flaw in this plan?

'Shall I come with you?' Tom offers.

Damn! Why didn't I think of that? I could go along to make sure he gets there and then they might let me stay for the questioning. Or *do* the questioning. I'd be really good at that. I'd ask some brilliant questions, in fact, like:

'I notice you favour the Nike Air Zoom Pegasus 34 trainers. Would you ever consider something like the Asics Gel Nimbus 19?'

The Asics are cheaper so he might be tempted to save his money for buying drugs or paying contacts, but they're also much heavier trainers and would slow him down. Thus, he might not get to scenes of crime so quickly—and he might arrive *after* the crime instead of before it.

'And on the subject of footwear, where would you say the best place to buy Kurt Geiger ladies' shoes is?'

Bryony Peterson wore Kurt Geigers to the gala *and* on her date with him the other night. This suggests they are her favourite and probably most expensive shoes. If she *is* his informant in the police station, which seems likely, then he must be rewarding her in some way, especially if she's his girlfriend. Every woman knows that the best gift anyone can buy you is a pair of shoes. If Kurt Geigers are her preferred brand, it makes sense that he would buy her those. And he'd be a fool to buy them from the most expensive outlet.

'What food product do you buy most often?'

Bear with me on this one. Food products aren't just for eating—though that's my preferred use, if I'm honest. But they're also invaluable for household jobs like cleaning. If he's taking drugs, he'll be dealing with stains like vomit, blood, urine, and possibly sweat. Vinegar might be the obvious choice as it's very effective for cleaning away all those things. However, heroin smells like vinegar, so if he's taking that he won't want to advertise the fact by risking the smell of it on his clothes. Therefore, the better choice of stain removal would be bicarbonate of soda. This is not only a powerful cleaning agent, but it also neutralises odours. If he's got a store cupboard full of the stuff, there's a good chance he's taking drugs—or he's just very messy, of course, but I know which one my money's on.

I'll bet no one at the station will think of asking anything like that, but it would save them a lot of time if they did. Actually, I think I'll just check with James if I'm allowed to come and help. He might appreciate that.

***

Hi, James, Dave's just got the call to come to the station. Shall I accompany him and help out with the interrogations? I've got some great questions ready. L x

He's only getting one kiss as I'm really peeved it's taken him all day to consider my safety, and even now he hasn't so much as sent anyone to pick Dave up. Besides, he only gave me one kiss earlier.

Dave's already left before I get a reply from James. I stare at it, disappointed.

No. Jx

Humph. That's gratitude for you! It'll be his own fault if Dave decides to abscond instead of going to the station. I noticed he didn't want Tom to go with him. I consider following him but I've no idea which way he'd go. Knowing Dave, he'll be running along the railway track or across football fields to get there. He never takes the sensible route. Like the road.

'I wonder what that's all about,' I say, breaking the silence that's fallen since he left.

Bethany bitch-face is looking suspiciously smug, and I wonder if she thinks her interference the other day is responsible for the arrest. *As if!* She's obviously

320

hoping I'll get the blame for it all. Well, I've got news for her.

'I've no idea,' she says, raising her eyebrows in innocence.

Yeah, right.

'He certainly looked worried,' Tom says, having returned to his desk.

'Do you think he's in trouble?' Sophie asks, wide-eyed.

Well, duh!

'Not Dave,' Tom says with surety. 'He's as straight as a die.'

I gape at him, unaware at first that my mouth has dropped open. Tom notices.

'What?'

'N-nothing,' I reply.

Bethany narrows her eyes at me. 'You don't believe it, do you? You think Dave's done something wrong. Or you *wish* he had. You're just jealous because he's so successful.'

'Well, it wasn't *me* who broke his trophy and then tried to blame it on someone else,' I remind her.

'Oh, change the record,' she snaps back. 'That's old news and it's got nothing to do with this. If Dave's in some kind of trouble, it's got nothing to do with me.' Bethany sneers. 'I've always been a good friend to Dave.'

'It wasn't very friendly of you to break his favourite award,' I mutter.

'Just you take that back!' She's on her feet now, marching towards me.

'Why? Does the truth hurt?' I stand up, too, glad that I've changed back into my boots. I place my hands on my hips, squaring up to her. This has been a long time coming.

'You haven't been here five minutes. You don't even *know* him,' she snarls.

'Well, not as well as you, obviously.' The innuendo is thick in my remark and I wonder if she'll take the bait. She doesn't disappoint.

'What's that supposed to mean? Are you making insinuations about me and Dave?' She does a good impression of being appalled by the suggestion.

'Why? Should I? Is there something I could be implying?' I'm enjoying this.

Bethany opens her mouth to speak then closes it again. She scowls at me then blurts out, 'You bitch!'

'Is there something going on between you and Dave? Or is it all in your imagination?' I ask calmly, ignoring her outburst.

Her face heats up and her eyes flash at me.

'That's none of your bloody business,' she shouts.

'It is when you try to involve me in your petty vendettas,' I reply.

There are gasps all around the room and Bethany just glares at me.

'What? Are you going to deny it?' I taunt her. 'The invention of CCTV is a wonderful thing, you know, and it's not just in this office.'

She gulps, taken aback.

'I told you. That business with the trophies is irrelevant.'

'Framing me isn't.'

'I apologised. You should be adult enough to accept that and move on. That's what any civil person would do. Anyone with an ounce of decency.' She sticks her nose in the air.

'Oh, p-lease! I've got heels higher than your standards,' I tell her.

She glares at me.

'Besides,' I go on, 'you only apologised for trying to frame me in the office. What about the other time? Or have you forgotten that already?'

'What *are* you talking about?' She folds her arms, her lip curling into a sneer.

'The police station, of course. When you told the desk sergeant that you were me and made allegations about Dave having an informant in the force. Don't tell me you're about to deny it?'

'Is this true, Bethany?'

Phil Peerless suddenly appears in the doorway.

She jumps. 'Oh, hi, Phil. What brings you down here?' She's trying to sound all bright and innocent but is fooling no one.

'All the shouting, of course! I could hear it right up the corridor. Now, what's this about you accusing Dave Chandler of having illegal contacts?'

'I don't know,' she quips.

'Well, we can always go down to the station and you can see your picture on the CCTV,' I say. 'You might like to see it, too, Phil.' I turn to him. 'And the log report that states that she made the claim using my name.'

Bethany's face puffs up and turns beetroot.

'Yes, I think I might,' Phil says, his face almost matching hers.

'Great. We can visit Dave while we're there,' I say, grabbing my jacket from the back of my chair.

'Oh, no. He's got enough to worry about with that brother of his,' Phil says, frowning. He puts up a hand to stop me. 'Let's wait and see what happens before we add to his worries.'

I gape at him. 'His *brother*? What brother?' Come to think of it, this kind of rings a bell. Didn't he say he had a brother in Fulham?

'Reuben, of course. The only one he has. His *twin* brother.'

I grab the edge of the desk to stop myself falling over. It feels like someone's just socked me in the stomach and winded me.

'That wouldn't be an *identical* twin, by any chance?' I mutter.

'Yes,' Phil replies.

'Is he okay?' Tom comes over. 'Reuben hasn't been hurt again or anything has he?'

'No, nothing like that. The police just wanted to talk to him that's all. And Reuben asked for his brother to join them.' Phil shakes his head. 'I don't know what it's about.'

I do.

One scenario after another flashes in front of my eyes. Each time I thought I saw Dave outside work, was I really looking at his brother?

'We'll resume this later, ladies,' Phil says abruptly. 'When Dave's here to defend himself.'

I don't watch him leave. I just sit down before I fall. My legs feel really wobbly. My heart's thumping painfully. Bethany says something sarcastic to me but I'm not listening. My brain's gone to mush.

When I finally gather my thoughts, I reach for my mobile and text James. I have to warn him.

Hey, James, Dave's got an identical twin brother! Lx

I'm surprised to get a reply almost straight away.

I know. Jx

What? Why didn't he tell me? Here was me worried he was about to arrest the wrong guy and he knew all along! Or did he? How did he find out? And more importantly, when?

27

James is waiting for me when I finish work. He's leaning against his Ford Focus, his sleeves casually rolled up despite the cold breeze. He's not even wearing a jacket. I'm amazed at how relaxed he looks given the day he must have had.

'Hi,' I say, walking over to him and reaching up for a kiss.

He kisses me back, his soft mouth encasing mine, sending jitters through my stomach.

'Hi, yourself,' he says when he finally frees our lips.

Shrouded in his familiar scent, I can't help feeling the stress ease from my body. I'm so full of questions, but I know we can't talk here.

He opens the car door and I climb inside. The comforting smell of worn leather and polish greet me, and I sit back into the cosiness of the seat. I like this car, I've decided. It reminds me of its owner with its slightly maverick appearance on the outside but sumptuous warmth inside.

'My place?' he asks, getting in and shutting his door.

'Yes, please.' I'm desperate for him to start telling me what on earth's going on. I'm being patient, though. Waiting. But he doesn't say anything. At all. It's as though he loves taunting me.

'So.' We both speak at the same time. Typical.

Silence. I'm determined not to go first.

'Did you have a good day?' he says at last.

How frustrating is that? He *knows* what I want to talk about, and he just comes out with something as lame as that.

I raise my eyebrows at him.

'Did *you*?'

'Yes, it was fine.'

Is that it? That's all I'm getting after being so patient and understanding? I've given him all that important—no, *crucial*—information and that's all I get? I huff.

'Did you arrest Dave Chandler?' There. I've said it.

'No.' He looks surprised.

Give me strength!

'Are you going to tell me what happened?' I know my voice sounds curt, but I'm trying *really hard* not to explode. And he knows it. That's what makes it even worse. And that's why I'm not going to give him the satisfaction.

'We can talk when we get home,' he says.

I love how he refers to his place as home. Not that it is *my* home, of course. Although I do feel very comfortable there. But I've never even spent a night there. Not yet, anyway. I've got high hopes, one of these days... or nights...

'If that's all right with you?'

His question pulls me up short.

'Of course.'

'I mean, if you'd rather go for a drink or something…?'

'No. Let's go back and relax.'

I know what his game is. If we go to a pub or whatever he'll say that we can't discuss the case there, as it's too public. I've fallen for that one before.

'Okay. If you're sure?'

'Quite sure.'

I stare out the window for most of the journey, turning back for the odd ogle at his bare arms on the steering wheel. Eventually, we pull up outside his flat.

'Looks like it's going to rain,' he says, putting an arm around me as he leads me inside the main door.

I can't believe he's talking about the damn weather.

He chuckles. He's doing that mind-reading thing again. I just know it.

'Tea or something stronger?' he offers.

'Wine, if you have any.'

I need it after the day I've had.

He grins and opens a bottle of Merlot. He purposely takes his time coming to sit next to me on the sofa with the two glasses and slowly pours the drinks.

'Thanks,' I say.

'Cheers.' He chinks his glass against mine.

I sit back waiting for him to begin. He's driving me mad, stringing this out so long.

'How did you know Dave Chandler had a twin?' he asks, after taking a long gulp of his wine.

I wanted to ask him that!

'It came up in conversation,' I reply. 'How about you?'

'Those photos you sent me,' he says.

I stare at him agog. 'But they're identical twins.'

'Yep.' He reaches into his case and pulls out an envelope. Inside are some blown-up photographs. He shows me the one I took in the café in Knightsbridge.

'Notice anything?'

I study it closely. It's a bit grainy where it's been enlarged, but it shows a familiar-looking man eating what is clearly a double-decker, triangular sandwich—not a Cornish pasty, after all. He's talking with a man opposite him whose face is partially obscured by his black hoodie.

'Here.' James taps at the sandwich.

I frown.

'It's in his left hand,' he says. 'And look, his teacup's on his right.'

My mouth gapes open as the penny drops. 'He's right-handed!'

James smiles. 'And I noticed in this one...' he switches to the picture taken in the alleyway, 'he's taking something off this guy in his right hand. It doesn't prove anything, but it was enough to arouse my suspicions.'

'It's a good job,' I mutter, envisaging how awkward it would have been if he'd listened to me and arrested the wrong person—again.

'It's what I'm paid for,' he says with a grin. 'Besides, we were interested in the guys he was with, too.'

'You know them?' I look closely at the one in the alley. I can't even see him properly, let alone recognise him.

'This one's known to us,' he says, pointing to the one in the café. 'Beeston. Nasty piece of work. And we suspected this guy was involved with him because of where the photo was taken.'

'Really?'

He nods. 'Near Beeston's office.'

'Is it drugs?' I ask, squinting at the picture in the alleyway.

'Could be. Beeston has been known to dabble in that world. Among other things.'

'So, what's he doing with Dave's brother?'

'Giving him information. Reuben Chandler has some 'friends' in very low places,' James explains, using his fingers for quotation marks. 'He meets them where he works, at a couple of seedy nightclubs in the town.'

I stare at him. 'He's a doorman?'

'Yep.'

'Shit!'

'What?'

I feel so stupid. Why didn't it occur to me before?

'Alfie Reynolds had seen me with Dave and thought it was Reuben. He assumed I was his girlfriend for some reason.'

'Bryony has long, blonde hair,' James says. 'She's Reuben's girlfriend.'

I nod. She's also pregnant, I remember. I suddenly don't feel so flattered about being mistaken for her.

'When did you speak to Alfie Reynolds?' James frowns at me.

'Oh, um. Just the other day. I happened to bump into him that's all.' I shrug, hoping he'll drop the subject. I know I shouldn't really have approached Alfie, but it didn't do any harm, did it?

James gives me a look that tells me he doesn't believe me, but he carries on anyway.

'Beeston's got a lot of underground contacts,' he says. 'He finds out from them when something's planned to go down—a deal or theft or whatever—and arranges his own sordid undertakings to coincide. Then he tips off Reuben about the other gang's ventures, Reuben informs Bryony who alerts the cops to go there, and his brother who gets the story, taking the heat right off Beeston's own operations.'

'Oh, my God!' I put my hand to my mouth.

'The Chandlers are still down at the station, but it looks like they didn't realise what was going on.

Although Reuben knew Beeston had a reputation, he didn't have a clue the guy was using him to set up a diversion. He thought he was just paying the guy for information he'd heard on the grapevine. Dave was quite happy to compensate his brother for the tips that got him farther up the promotional ladder—and won him all those awards, of course.'

'And all because Dave's left–handed.' I can't believe something so simple has turned out to be so crucial.

James nods. 'Remember the other day when I asked to take a look at the broken statuette in your office? You might have noticed that Dave handed both the body and head to me separately. But when I gave them back to him, I held them in one hand. He used his left hand to retrieve them from me. I noticed it felt a little awkward at the time as I'm right-handed. It didn't occur to me why until all this came to light.'

He takes a swig of his wine.

'Amazing,' I say, shaking my head.

'There's something else, too. Dave had an alibi for when he was supposed to be at the café in Knightsbridge. I checked our records. That was when he was at the station answering questions about Bethany's allegations. And when you thought he was at Notting Hill last night he was definitely at the pub with Tom. We checked their cameras.'

'Good old CCTV,' I mutter.

'It's invaluable,' he says with a nod. 'As are photographs that are date and time-stamped.'

I sit a little straighter, proud that I've helped in a way.

'So, what happens now?' I ask. 'Have they managed to catch that Beeston guy?'

James sighs. 'Not yet. Unfortunately, we've got nothing concrete on him. Chief Inspector Hinchley's gunning for Bryony, not only for acting on unofficial tip-offs but also for passing police information on to her boyfriend. It seems Reuben's been feeding information to his brother from her, too. Her job is on the line for this.'

'But that's not fair. I like Bryony. I'm sure she didn't do any of it on purpose. And you did manage to get some arrests from it.'

'Not the arrests the chief inspector would have liked, though. While she had officers chasing the small fry, the big fish, i.e. Beeston, was getting away with murder, so to speak. Which was Beeston's intention, of course.'

'Oh, no. She wasn't to know, though, was she? It's not her fault.'

'No, but if she'd told someone that Reuben was getting information from the likes of Beeston, they might have been able to use that information to flush out Beeston himself. It would at least tell them when Beeston had something going down. All they'd have to do was find out where.'

'I hadn't thought of that,' I confess.

'Neither did Bryony.'

***

By the time I get back to Chelsea, Cassie's in her dressing gown. She quickly clicks off the TV and grabs me a glass.

'What're we celebrating?' I ask, eyeing the bottle of Prosecco on the coffee table.

'Meredith was so pleased with the colours I picked out today that she's told Allegra to include me in the design team for the summer collection.' Her face is pink and beaming.

'That's terrific!' I give her a massive hug before she pours the drinks.

'I went for pink and black, like you said. And navy. Allegra and Chantelle picked out all pastel colours. When we added mine to theirs, the colours just popped. They're going to look gorgeous!'

She takes a sip of wine.

'Brilliant! So did Meredith know who chose what?'

She nods. 'Oh, yeah. She was over the moon that I'd 'been insightful enough to embrace the bold colours' and she was dead chuffed that I'd put pink in there, too.' She uses the fingers of one hand for the quotation marks as the other one's clutching her glass.

'So, will you get promoted?' I ask, taking off my boots and snuggling on the sofa next to her.

'It's the first step, I think.'

'Good. You deserve it.'

'Dad'll be pleased I'm actually using that degree,' she says with a nod.

'Of course, he will. And I imagine you'll be sticking at this job for a while, too. That'll make him happy.'

She nods, taking another gulp of her wine. In her last job, Cassie got paid thousands of pounds by her dad as a reward for lasting there a whole year. She hadn't really decided what she wanted to do before, so she'd been taking odd jobs but never actually stuck at any for long. It was mostly in fashion retail, though, as she knew she wanted to do something with clothes, so her current job is perfect.

'How was your day?' she asks, once we've polished off the whole bottle and started on a cheeky little Sauvignon Blanc.

'You'll never believe it.'

I go on to describe everything that had happened. Needless to say, the birds are singing before we get to bed.

***

Neither of us relishes getting up when our alarms go off, but at least it's Friday. And I've got a plan.

As I was talking to Cassie last night—or earlier this morning, actually—I mentioned Bryony and her Kurt Geigers. While I was describing them, I remembered that there would be pictures of her in them on Facebook, where the girls uploaded several photos of the gala. There are a few brilliant ones on there of some of the guys who got drunk, too, as well as... never mind. Anyway, practically everyone I met that night has befriended me on there, including Elizabeth, Andy's wife. That's when it hit me. I sent her a message asking if I could meet up with her this morning and she actually replied straight away and said yes. I was amazed—it was after 2am but she was obviously still awake. She said she'd love to see me, so we're having a breakfast meeting in about... ooh, less than an hour.

I quickly get into my black, knitted Karen Millen dress that has eyelets running down the sides of the centre panels and I've borrowed Cassie's Louboutin ankle boots, Gena 85s, which are also black. I'm wearing a red jacket and taking my black Radley, of course, and the outfit looks great. I shove my hair up in a messy bun and hit the road. Well, the pavement.

Elizabeth's already waiting for me at Starbucks, near the Tube station, and she offers me a warm smile and a hug. She's really bright and cheerful, considering it's not even eight o'clock yet, and offers me a drink.

'I'll get it,' I insist, seeing that she's already got herself a herbal tea.

I order the same—as well as some croissants—and take the seat opposite her on the little corner table she's chosen.

'Have you heard about Bryony?' I ask her in a soft voice as we tuck into the flaky croissants.

'Yes. Andrew told me last night. Dreadful business.' She brushes a pastry crumb off her Chanel suit jacket, shaking her head. Elizabeth really suits powder blue, which complements her silver hair.

'James said she might lose her job,' I go on. 'Which I think is really unfair, considering she actually helped the police catch some criminals that they might not otherwise have known about.'

'You're right,' Elizabeth says, putting down her cup with a frown. 'Andrew said that Hinchley fellow was cross that they'd missed out on catching the big boys because they were going after the small fry, but actually you've got a point. If it wasn't for Bryony, they wouldn't have caught either.'

'Exactly!' I'm so glad we're both on the same wavelength.

I take a sip of my tea while the thought sinks in.

'And now they know that Reuben's got connections with Beeston, they've got a good chance of catching him anyway,' I continue.

She picks up her cup again. 'Hmm. That'll be a tricky business.'

'Well, anyway, the thing is... with Bryony being pregnant and all... we need to help her. I mean, she didn't really do anything wrong, did she?'

Elizabeth looks doubtful.

'What I mean is... she didn't tell Reuben anything really *significant* did she? Otherwise, Dave and I would have been following much more interesting stories than potholes.' I wave my hand to emphasise how tedious the subject is, and she nods.

Great. I've got her back on side.

I take another mouthful of tea, still trying to make my mind up if I like it or not. I mean, I *want* to like it. It's healthy, after all, and it's what posh people like Elizabeth drink, so I feel I ought to drink it, too. I just can't help thinking it smells a bit like a stinky sock. Would Elizabeth notice if I held my nose while I drank it? I wonder.

'You've got a point there,' Elizabeth says, just as I put my hand to my face.

'Really?' I quickly move my hand to my lap. I'm trying to remember what I said. 'I-I mean, I'm glad you agree.'

'Yes.' She looks thoughtful.

'So... did Andy, er, your husband say anything about what would happen next?'

'No. He's not really part of the enquiry,' she says, pursing her lips.

'But he's the boss. Surely, he has a say in it?' Oh, no. This can't all be down to Hinchley—he'll sack her on the spot, I know he will. And then what will she do? And that poor baby? They'll be out on the streets with no food or anything. How will they cope? And Hinchley won't give a mouldy fig!

28

'Let's have another cup of tea and think about this properly,' Elizabeth says, standing up.

What does she mean 'think about it properly'? What does she think we've been up until now? There was nothing half-hearted about *my* thinking. I certainly think Bryony needs our help—and I definitely think that the superintendent's just the man to come to her rescue.

I stand up, but Elizabeth's already got the drinks and is coming back to the table. I reach for my purse.

'No, no, on me,' she insists, waving me off. 'My treat. I got us large ones. We deserve it.' She giggles.

My heart sags. What on earth have I done to deserve this? We haven't even got any croissants left to soak up the flavour.

'Oh... thank you.' What else can I say?

'Right, well, let's go through all the facts, shall we?' She rummages in her bag, pulls out a notepad and pen and starts jotting everything down.

Why didn't she just do that in the first place?

I have to jog her memory on a few points, but she gets it all written down in the end.

'There's quite a lot there,' she says afterwards, studying the notes.

'Yes. And it all points to the fact that Bryony shouldn't be sacked,' I say. 'In fact, think of that little baby. Bryony must be really stressed over all this, which can't be good for either of them.'

'You're right, dear.' She scribbles something else at the end of the list.

'Do you have children? Or grandchildren?' I ask.

Her face lights up. 'Yes, we've got two daughters and three beautiful grandchildren. Two boys and a girl.'

'I'll bet you and your husband spoil them rotten,' I say. And talking of rotten, I take a tiny sip of my tea. It's all I can stomach. I've decided I really don't like it, after all.

'Of course, dear. That's what grandchildren are for, isn't it?' She looks all dreamy just thinking about them.

'And does your husband feel the same way?' I ask, as casually as I can. It's really odd referring to Andy as 'your husband' but I'm not really sure if I should refer to him by his first name to her. Especially as *she* doesn't even call him Andy.

'Oh, yes,' she says, raising her eyebrows. 'He's a big softie where they're concerned.'

Just what I wanted to hear. I say nothing for a short while, hoping she'll get the message. She doesn't seem as receptive as Cassie—we're actually a bit telepathic, I think—but I concentrate hard saying 'get your husband to help Bryony' over and over again in my head. Even in my head, I can't call him Andy in case she actually gets the message and is offended by it.

'Do you know something, dear?' she says, after drinking about a gallon of her tea.

I haven't touched mine since that sip. I'm actually considering knocking it over by accident, so I don't upset her by not drinking it. Where's a pot plant when you need one?

'Yes?' My heart's thudding loudly.

'I think we should show this list to my husband.'

Hallelujah!

'Would it help, do you think?'

'I'm sure *he'd* help,' she replies triumphantly. 'I know he comes across as strict and super-efficient, but he's a big teddy bear really.' She winks at me.

I smile at her, refraining from telling her I couldn't imagine him being anything *but* a big teddy bear—he was a real hoot at the gala and I'm sure he was a bit tipsy before we even started dinner. But then, I've never seen him at work, have I? In his natural habitat, as it were.

'Come on, we'll go now.' She stands and picks up her handbag.

'Now?' I've got work to go to. But then, this is more important. I mean, this is Bryony's job on the line. Not to mention that poor baby's welfare.

'No time like the present, dear. And Andrew will be in the office by now. Come on.' She ties an exquisite lilac silk scarf around her neck, and I follow her out the door.

***

Twenty minutes later, we arrive in the foyer of the police station. The desk sergeant recognises Elizabeth straight away and smiles.

'Is he in the office?' she calls over.

'Yes, ma'am.'

'Thank you, Sergeant.'

We take the lift and arrive on the top floor. The building's all glass and chrome. I just hope it's toughened glass, what with all the criminals they must get in here. Imagine, one chair through the window and all hell would break loose. They probably don't get near the offices, though, come to think of it. I let out a sigh of relief.

Andy looks up in surprise as we march into his office. Well, Elizabeth marches, I sort of skulk in behind her. I didn't expect him to have company.

'Andrew, we need a word.'

Immediately, the three men sitting opposite him get up and leave the room.

'Well, this is a surprise,' Andy says. 'And it's Suzanne, isn't it? I remember you from the other night.' He frowns. 'Was everything all right in the end?'

'Oh, yes, thank you. And it's Libby, by the way.' I'm gutted that he'd heard about the fracas with James' ex.

'Of course,' he says. 'Shall I order coffee?'

'No time for that,' Elizabeth insists. 'We need to sort this out now.'

'Oh, right. Go on.'

So, she goes on... and on... and on. And at the end of it, I wish I'd had that coffee to keep me awake. For someone as forthright as she appears, she takes ages to get to the point.

'So, we need you to do something,' she finishes.

He stares at her. Then at me.

'Well, yes, of course. I hadn't looked at it that way.' He puts his finger on his phone and tells his secretary, 'Get Hinchley up here, will you, Anna? Toute suite.'

'He's seeing her this morning, not sure what time,' Andy says, looking up at the wall clock.

I turn to look at it too. Oh, no! It's almost ten fifteen.

'I have to go,' I say. 'Do you have everything you need from me?'

There's a knock at the door.

'Yes,' Andy says, though I'm not sure if it's to me or not.

Chief Inspector Hinchley opens the door and walks in. He takes one look at Elizabeth and me and scowls. I'm not sure at which one of us he's directing his look, but I've got a horrible feeling it's me.

'Well, thank you,' I say, standing up. 'Both of you.'

Andy nods.

'I'll be in touch, dear,' Elizabeth promises before I dive out the office.

***

I arrive at work just before eleven, my mind racing with possible excuses for being so late. Could I say I broke my leg and had to go to hospital? No. I've got no cast on. Besides, it would stop me doing my job, and that might be a problem if Dave's not in this morning. I wonder what's happening with him? I consider claiming I missed the Tube, but there's one every few minutes so that won't work. Maybe everyone'll be so busy speculating about Dave they won't even notice I'm not there? Yes. That's it. I'll just pretend I've been in the loo or something if they say anything and they'll assume I've been there all morning. Perfect.

'Where have you been?' Carol-Anne demands as soon as I walk in the door.

'What?' I raise my eyes in innocence as I attempt to sneak my Marc Jacobs under my chair. 'I was only in the... er...'

'Phil Peerless has been after you all morning. And Kevin Stratton's with him.'

My stomach lurches. That's the owner of the newspaper. I hadn't expected him to be involved. This is serious.

'Do they need to see me?' I ask, telepathically pleading her to say no.

'Yes. You're to go up there right away. They've had Bethany with them for hours. She was in bits when she arrived.' Carol-Anne shakes her head.

'Really?' Somehow, I can't imagine Bethany Thomas being upset about anything. She's a conniving, lying little—

'She really likes Dave,' Sophie says. 'She was just jealous because you got to work so closely with him.'

'That's no excuse,' I reply, but inside I can sort of see that it *is* an excuse. It was a crime of passion. I huff, looking at their miserable faces. They're her friends and they care about her. They're worried. 'Right, I'll go up.'

My hand shakes as I knock on the door of Phil Peerless' office. I've never even been on this floor before, let alone in his office. The corridor has a thick, plush carpet and the paintwork is a muted peach colour, nothing like the stark white of downstairs. Soft music is playing through hidden speakers, and there's an aura of calmness. I just wish it would rub off on me—I'm literally quaking in my Louboutins.

'Come in.'

I'm not sure I want to. I hesitate. Is there time to turn and run away? After all, I've got away with not being here all morning, haven't I?

The door suddenly swings open and I'm facing a man I've never seen before.

'Oh... um... hello.'

'Come in,' he says.

'Thank you.'

Phil Peerless is sitting at an enormous walnut desk with shelves of files lining the wall behind him. Bethany's sitting crying in front of him, and this man's narrowing his eyes at me.

'Liberty. There you are!' Phil doesn't look happy to see me. Perhaps he didn't want me to come up, after all.

'Good morning.' I try to sound confident. 'I heard you wanted me, but if it's a bad time I can always...'

'So, you're Liberty Lawrence.' The man who I assume is Kevin Stratton butts in.

I look up at him. 'Yes.'

'This is Mr Stratton, the owner and executive director of the *Daily Chronicle*. Come and sit down. Where have you been?' Phil snaps.

'You've caused all this chaos and then disappeared,' Mr Stratton accuses me. 'What exactly do you think you're doing?' He takes a seat at the end of Phil's desk.

'I was...' My heart's pounding. Why is everyone mad at *me*? And how have *I* caused this mess, anyway? 'I was at the police station,' I admit. I want to add 'so there.'

Everyone gawps at me, even Bethany. The men exchange a wary look.

'What on earth were you doing there?' Mr Stratton asks, frowning hard.

'I was asked to attend a meeting with the superintendent,' I reply, which is true, in a way.

They both stare at me.

'It was a confidential matter regarding the leaking of police business. I'm not allowed to discuss it yet.'

I want to laugh at their indignant expressions, so I look at Bethany instead. She looks like she's been crying for ages, her face is all red and puffy, and mascara is smeared down her cheeks. The rest of her make-up—which I assume she was wearing—has been cried off. My heart sinks and I can't help feeling sorry for her. I offer her a faint smile and she stares at me.

'We'll get on to the subject of Dave Chandler later,' Mr Stratton says, 'when we have more information.'

I nod, wondering if he means more information from me or the police.

'In the meantime, we've been discussing the business with Bethany Thomas here.'

No shit, Sherlock!

'Right,' I say.

'We have all the evidence we need from the security cameras,' Phil informs, me shuffling some papers on his desk. 'Although we don't actually have photographic evidence in some cases, your colleagues have divulged on tape what actually happened.'

I nod. What am I supposed to say to that?

'So, as we now know, Bethany Thomas fed you false news that you nearly had printed in the *Chronicle* because Tom Pinder tampered with your computer and sent it to the editorial department.'

'Yes.' I hope Tom's not in trouble now as well.

'Bethany then broke one of Dave Chandler's trophies, tried to mend it and then framed you for the damage.'

I nod again. Bethany gives a loud sniff, and I look over at her, swallowing hard.

'Then it transpired that Bethany had impersonated you at the police station where she alleged that Dave had been getting information illegally through an unofficial police source.' Phil glares at Bethany, who cowers in her seat. 'Is there anything else you want to add to the list?' He's looking at me now.

'Um...' This is horrid.

'I think that's enough to warrant her immediate dismissal,' Mr Stratton says, closing a file on the desk.

Phil nods.

'Actually,' I say, my heart racing. 'I don't think it is.'

I become hot as their eyes bore into me.

'I mean... Bethany was right in her report to the police, wasn't she? Dave *was* getting information illegally.'

Mr Stratton flips open the file again. 'Well, yes,' he admits.

'So, she did nothing wrong there.'

'She used your name,' Phil points out.

'What does it matter who reported it? The fact is the police were told. Isn't that what counts? And you have to remember that Bethany's been working with Dave for a long time and must have felt awful going behind his back like that. She probably gave my name in case he ever found out, so it wouldn't ruin their friendship.'

Mr Stratton looks over at Bethany, whose mouth has dropped open as she gawps at me.

I nod, encouraging her to do the same.

'I'm sure it was the same with the trophy. Bethany was afraid of ruining her affiliation with Dave if he knew she'd broken something of value to him. She only blamed me because she knew it wouldn't really matter what he thought of me. It was an attempt to maintain a good working relationship, which is for the benefit of everyone in the department. It would be difficult working in a frosty atmosphere. She knew I was only there temporarily before I changed sections so it didn't really matter if he was annoyed with me.'

Phil raises his eyebrows. 'Well, I see what you mean but... um...'

'It was still wrong,' Mr Stratton protests. 'You can't blame other people for your actions.'

'That's why she apologised afterwards,' I point out. 'Didn't you, Bethany? You said sorry to all of us, and we just drew a line under the incident like any decent person would.' I smile at her.

Bethany looks confused. I think she's a bit suspicious of me. Heaven knows why. She nods though.

'Yes,' she manages with great effort, and sniffs again.

'So, what about the fake news story?' Mr Stratton asks sharply. 'How do you explain that one?'

I raise my eyebrows at him. 'Anyone can make a mistake, Mr Stratton. Bethany had obviously heard the rumour somewhere and believed it to be true. I was in the middle of checking the facts when I got called away. Unfortunately, Tom thought he was doing me a favour by sending in my report, so we'd meet the deadline. He didn't realise I hadn't finished—how could he?' My mind's whirling.

'Well,' Mr Stratton says with a sigh. 'That's certainly shone a different light on everything.' He looks bemused as he glances at Phil. 'I think maybe we'll talk about this a little more before we make a decision.'

'Yes,' Phil says. 'We don't want to do anything hasty.'

'I agree,' I say. 'Especially as Bethany has been here for a while now and has a good record with the company. She's an asset. It would be a shame to lose her just because of a few simple misunderstandings.' I really don't know what her record is like, or whether she's actually considered a valuable member of the team or not, but I do think it'd be a shame to lose her job just because she was trying to impress a guy.

'You two go back to your office and we'll speak again later,' Mr Stratton says, flicking through the file again.

'Thank you.'

I'm the first out the door. Gosh, it was tense in there. Bethany follows me down the corridor, still sniffing.

'Are you okay?' I ask, once we're in the privacy of the lift.

'I don't get it,' she says in a croaky voice. 'Why did you just do that? I thought I'd lost my job for definite.'

I shrug. I don't really understand it myself, to be honest. Bethany bitch-face tried to make my life hell in that office. Why on earth am I helping her now? Guilt? Sympathy? I'm really not sure. Whatever it is, it just feels right.

'Thanks, though. I really mean it.'

She smiles, and I believe her.

'That's okay.'

For a second, I think she's going to give me a hug but then the lift door opens, and we just get out as though nothing's happened.

Carol-Anne and Sophie welcome Bethany back with open arms. It's good to see such a good friendship. It reminds me of how I am with Cassie. And how I want to be with Siobhan, Tammy, and Fran. But maybe without the hugging part. Siobhan's not really into that. I wonder if I'll ever get a job in the women's supplement section.

I grab a coffee while the others chatter about everything that's gone on. Mr Stratton certainly sounded annoyed with me. He said I'd caused all the chaos! *Me?* What had I done? I sit at my desk. I'm afraid he's just taken a dislike to me, which isn't good when I want him to help me further my career. I need him to sanction me taking over from Melanie in Siobhan's team. And now I've thrown a spanner in the works by defending Bethany. He'll hate me even more now. Oh, God, what have I done?

29

I'm thrilled a while later when I receive a message from Elizabeth.

Hi, Libby. It's all sorted. Andrew insisted that Ch Insp Hinchley didn't sack Bryony. Instead, she's agreed to take her maternity leave early (paid, of course) and she's confided in me that she doesn't intend to return to her job afterwards anyway. Hinchley's not happy but Bryony's over the moon! Chat later, Elizabeth.

Yes! That's what I call a result! I quickly reply.

Thanks so much, Elizabeth, that's brilliant news! Well done speaking to your husband about the situation. Sincere thanks to both of you. Will call you tonight. Libby x

I'm so thrilled for Bryony. I'll call her later, too, to see how she is. She must be relieved.

***

It's really hard to concentrate on work today, with everything that's happened. Bethany and the girls are chatting away merrily—they even included me in their conversation a couple of times. It wasn't very interesting, though. They were on about horse riding, which I don't do. Then they started talking about netball. I mentioned that I work out—well, I went to the gym this week, didn't I?—but Carol-Anne said it's not the same thing. After that, I sort of ducked out of the discussion.

Tom's out on a shoot, apparently, but the girls aren't sure what it's for. We had a message from Phil saying he wants a word with him when he returns. I can guess what that's about.

It's almost lunchtime when Dave appears, looking tired and rough. The girls all crowd around him as soon as he walks in the door. I fetch him a coffee.

'Thanks,' he says as he sits down. 'I need that.'

'What's happened?' the girls have been chorusing since he got here.

'I've been let off with a warning,' he says with a sigh, 'from the cops anyway. I've got to go up and meet with the boss shortly to see if I've still got a job.'

'What can they sack you for?' I ask. 'You were only using your contacts like any other journalist. You weren't to know your brother was getting information from the police.'

He raises his eyebrows. 'I hadn't thought of it like that. Reuben was in a lot of trouble, and it looks like Bryony's going to lose her job.'

'She's not.'

'What?'

'How do you know?' Bethany asks.

'I can't reveal my sources,' I say, and wink.

There are gasps all round.

'You've got contacts, too!' Sophie accuses.

I shrug.

'Have they let Reuben go?' I ask Dave when he's swallowed a good glug of coffee.

'Not yet. But they will. They just want to talk to him some more about something, but he's not being charged. He got a warning, though, too.'

I sigh with relief. It actually looks like everyone's going to be okay. Except me. I stare at my coffee cup. I could do with something stronger.

'Hey, why don't we all go for a lunchtime drink?' I suggest. 'It is Friday, after all.'

'Great idea!' Sophie says straight away.

'God, yeah. I could use a stiff one,' Dave says, standing up.

'Me, too,' Bethany says, winking at him.

The innuendo's not lost on any of us, and I'm pleased they've all got a sense of humour. There were times I'd honestly doubted it.

We're all crowding towards the door when Tom arrives.

'Come on, mate, we're going down the pub,' Dave tells him.

Tom doesn't need telling twice. 'I'll just dump my stuff.'

***

We actually have a good laugh in the bar of The Lamb and Bell. It's a very modern building with polished wood floors and high-back chairs. Bethany and Dave are far more relaxed now that they've both had a couple of brandies—for the shock, apparently—and the rest of us are drinking lager in really swish tall glasses.

'Hey, maybe I should have one of those,' Tom says as Dave gives Bethany yet another cognac. 'I've got to see Phil later.'

'You'll be fiiine,' Bethany assures him, sounding like she's had more than enough to drink. 'Libby's shorted it. She's shorted all of it.' She points at the gaming machine behind us, but I think it was meant to be me she was indicating.

We all laugh. She's certainly enjoying herself. And I can't help thinking she and Dave seem to have bonded quite well since suffering their ordeals. It's a good job he's not aware that it was her who reported him for his police contacts, though.

'What've you said?' Tom narrows his eyes at me.

'I just told them you had the best intentions when you sent the story to editing,' I said. 'I really don't know why they had to bring it up again.'

'Thanks.' He chinks his glass against mine.

'You're welcome.'

'Was anything said about us?' Sophie asks, and I get the impression she and Carol-Anne are feeling a bit left out.

'Luckily, no,' I tell her. 'You two must be relieved your jobs have been safe all along.'

I wish I could say the same about mine.

'We're the best,' Carol-Anne says, giving Sophie a hug.

I glance at the time and wince.

'We'd best get back if we don't all want to get sacked for skiving off.'

Amid groans and the quick knocking back of drinks we all slope towards the door.

'Whoa!' The cold air hits me as soon as Tom opens it. I didn't think I'd drunk that much, but my head suddenly feels like cotton wool.

Bethany staggers, as Dave supports her.

'We'd best get you some coffee,' he tells her.

'I'm fiiine,' she replies. Then 'Ooh!' as she grips his arm.

I've certainly seen a different side to my colleagues today, I'm pleased to say. They're actually quite a fun bunch when you get to know them—and when Bethany's drunk.

****

We all sit around Dave's desk drinking strong, black coffee after we return to the office. No one's in the mood to work, and I just study the Christian Louboutin website while we all chat. Suddenly, my phone pings, making me jump.

Hi, Libby, I hear you've had a busy morning. Are you okay? Jx

I gulp. What does he mean by that? Who's he been talking to? I quickly text back:

I'm fine, thanks. You? Lx

Good. Andy was very impressed by you! I'm fine—great, actually. We've had an offer on the house. Full asking price. We've accepted. Suzanne's looking for somewhere to live. Jx

Oh, my God! That's just the greatest news! Apart from Bryony not getting sacked, of course. Or Bethany. Or Dave getting arrested. Or... actually it's a pretty good day all round, I'd say.

Fantastic! How long will it take to go through? Lx

Not long. Cash buyers. Jx

Oh, James, I'm so happy for you. Lxx

I'm happy for all of us. Jxx

Yes, he's got it! He actually understands the Law of Kisses. I put two so he puts two. I'm so chuffed!

Tom's desk phone rings and we all stare at it. He rolls his eyes and picks up the receiver.

'Yes, sir.'

He turns to us as he replaces the handset. 'Here goes...'

'You'll be fine,' we all tell him as he leaves the office.

'It'll be me next,' Dave says with a scowl. 'I'd better have more of that coffee. I don't want to go in there smelling of booze.'

Bethany immediately jumps up and goes to fetch him a refill. At least she can walk in a straight line now. And she and Dave seem to have really hit it off.

My phone pings again.

Hey, Libby, I've had an idea. Are you free tonight? Jxx

I raise my eyebrows wondering what he means.

Hi, James. What about? Yes, I'm free tonight.Lxx

Brilliant. I'll tell you later. Can you come after work? And bring your toothbrush. Jxxx

Oh, my God. Suddenly my stomach's churning with excitement, my heart's palpitating, and I can hardly breathe. This is it! He wants me to stay overnight. Our first time. How do I respond to that? What do you usually say to something like that? Okay, keep cool, Libby. Don't get your hopes up too much. After all, knowing my luck it might not mean what I think it means. What I *hope* it means. A whole night. With James. Oh, God. What else *could* it mean? I take a deep breath.

Okay. Lxxx

There. Cool. To the point. No room for ambiguity. I tuck the phone back into my jacket pocket. Job done.

***

Tom returns after a while, frowning. Oh, no!

'What happened, mate?' Dave asks, as soon as he sees him. 'Is everything okay?'

Tom nods. 'Yeah. Well... for me it is. They said it was completely understandable and agreed I had good intentions but best not to do it again just in case. You know, the usual thing. I wasn't in any trouble, though.'

'Well that's good.' Dave nods.

'So, it was just about you sending my story in that time?' I ask, relieved but not really surprised. He hadn't done anything wrong.

'Mostly.'

I look back up at him, without even looking at the price of the new Louis Junior Strass pumps I'm considering might go with my outfits as well as enabling me to run around London with style. 'What does that mean?'

'Well.' He looks discomfited. Not a good sign.

'Spit it out,' Dave urges.

'Okay, they both asked lots of questions about Libby.'

'Both?'

'Yeah, Kevin Stratton was there with Phil.'

'What sort of questions?' I ask.

'Things like whether you were a troublemaker, did you make it difficult to do my job, did you hold any grudges against anyone. That sort of thing.' He purses his lips. 'Of course, I said no,' he adds quickly.

My heart's racing for a totally different reason now. They think this is all my fault.

Dave's phone rings, interrupting my inner rant.

'On my way.' He drops the receiver into the cradle with a frown. 'My turn.'

I want to tell him to make sure he says something nice about me, but he's out the door too fast. This is so unfair. I'm getting the blame for everything.

'Don't worry about it,' Tom says. 'They were probably just asking in passing. You know, how's the new girl working out? It's natural.'

'They didn't ask *me* that,' Bethany pipes up, sounding a lot more sober than earlier.

She and the girls get up and move back to their own desk. My phone pings.

Any idea why Ch Insp Hinchley has demanded to see me urgently? Jx

Oh, no! This doesn't look good. I text back.

Not really. Good luck. Lxx

He must be worried to have only put one kiss. And to be so abrupt following his last message. I hope he's not in trouble. Surely, it can't be anything to do with me. I mean, I know Hinchley gave me a dirty look this morning but... no. That look might have been for Elizabeth. He probably didn't approve of Andy having his wife there. That'll be it. Maybe Hinchley's wife was sorry to have missed us at the gala and wants us to go round for dinner. He's going to invite James and me now. That's why he was demanding—his wife's really eager to meet us. That'll be it. I hope.

Dave seems to be gone ages, and we're all speculating about what's going on. Bethany's really rooting for him and keeps saying how wonderful he is, and with all those awards he's won they'd be fools to sack him. I'm not saying too much. After all, I thought he was a drug dealer yesterday, I can hardly admit that. I'm glad he's not, though. I wonder if his brother Reuben is. He seems to have a lot of friends in low places. Maybe he's one of them. That could be why he's still down at the station. Dave said they wanted to talk to him about something. Maybe they want him to be a double agent. Wow—that would be a dangerous job. I'll bet it pays well, though. And on that subject, I glance back at my computer screen and check the price of those pumps.

'One thousand, six hundred and twenty-five pounds!' I didn't mean to say it aloud.

'What is?' Sophie asks.

'Oh, nothing.'

I can't tell them I'm looking at Louboutins. They think I'm working. Or at least, I hope that's what they think. Then if Phil Peerless asks them about me, they can say how diligent I am, always working, never stops. He can't fire me then, can he?

Dave eventually returns, looking quite shell-shocked. 'Boy that was close. I've kept my job, though,' he informs us.

'Are you okay?' Bethany immediately gets him a cup of coffee.

He sits at his desk, frowning at me.

'They're giving me another chance,' he says with a sigh.

'Good.' *What about me? Did they ask about me?*

'I'm not so sure they're planning to do the same for you, I'm afraid,' he says, as though he's heard me. Not another mind reader!

A massive boulder hits my stomach. 'Why?'

Before he can answer, my phone rings and I grab the receiver.

'Yes. On my way.'

'Good luck,' Dave says, and I've got a feeling I'll need it.

My heart's almost beating out of my body as I take the lift up to the top floor. Apart from feeling scared stiff I'm about to lose everything, I also feel angry because I haven't deserved any of this. I'm not going down without a fight. I just hope James is faring better in his meeting with Chief Inspector Hinchley.

This time, I open the door as soon as Phil shouts 'come in.' He looks a little surprised when I close it with a little more force than is strictly necessary.

'Sit down,' he says.

I don't even thank him, and his expression suggests he's noticed. He and Kevin Stratton exchange glances.

'Libby, your work in the newsroom seems to be quite acceptable, and you certainly seem to have a nose for a good story.' I'd have preferred Phil to have sounded more complimentary than patronising as he says this.

'Unfortunately,' Kevin Stratton continues for him, 'you also seem to have a nose for trouble.'

'In what way?' *Keep calm, Libby.*

'Well.' Stratton clears his throat, shuffling some papers about on the desk. 'You seemed to be in a prime position when all that rioting went on in Knightsbridge,' I hear.

I nod. 'That's right. I was following up the story Dave Chandler asked me to, regarding the potholes.'

'And there have been several incidences here at the office with various members of staff,' he goes on.

'Do you mean those that were resolved earlier?' I check, leaning forward slightly.

'Well, yes.' Stratton looks over at Phil a little doubtfully.

'Are you suggesting any of that was my fault?' I query, raising my eyebrows. 'Being falsely accused and so forth?'

'Well, no one's saying that, exactly,' Phil blusters.

'So, what are you saying *exactly*?' I narrow my eyes, trying to hide my nerves. This could all go horribly wrong.

'Just that you seem to be *involved* in a lot of the trouble,' Phil replies, carefully.

What the heck's that supposed to mean?

I nod. 'Yes. As the *victim*.'

Stratton sighs. 'It just seems to be a little distracting.'

'I agree, Mr Stratton. I don't know how I'm supposed to work in that office with everything that's been going on. I feel so victimised and ostracised and...' I'm trying to think of another 'cised' but the words elude me.

'Yes, quite.' Phil takes the opportunity of jumping in before I finish. I hate that.

'So, you feel unpopular in the newsroom?' Stratton clarifies.

'Um...' Oh, damn! If I say yes, he'll say it's my fault and it might be best if I resigned. But if I say no he'll ask what the heck all the fuss has been about. 'Um... it's hard to say,' I manage. 'I mean, I thought they all hated me when Bethany was framing me for everything and making everyone dislike me, but now they've all apologised, so hopefully it's okay.' Great save! *I think.*

Both men look confused. I'm not sure if that's good or bad.

Then I get a brainwave, so I dive in before they can gather their thoughts.

'I'd hate to think I was the cause of any embarrassment of my colleagues,' I go on. 'I mean, having them all eat humble pie has been a bit disconcerting for me to say the least. I know they all feel guilty for the way they were with me, and it'll be hard to convince them to just forget about it and treat me as a normal person.'

'Quite.' Stratton's eyeing me suspiciously.

I take a deep breath, gearing up for the punchline, but he butts in.

'So, we wondered if you might be happier not working here anymore,' he says, 'I mean, we don't want you to work anywhere you're not happy, and if you feel uncomfortable then maybe you should just—'

'Leave the department, you mean?' I jump in. 'Go and work in another section altogether? Well, that's an idea. I could still support the *Chronicle*, just another part of it. With colleagues who won't feel ashamed every time they see me. Maybe somewhere like the women's supplement? Mr Stratton, you're an absolute genius, if you don't mind me saying. Who would have thought of such a perfect solution to a very difficult problem?' I smile sweetly at him and he looks totally thrown.

Phil clears his throat, frowning.

'I know Dave and the others have their flaws,' I go on, 'but it was such a relief that none of them got fired, even though everything they did was evidenced. I mean, they're good people really, and they were truly sorry for what they did. I know some people will say you couldn't sack anyone because the *Chronicle* would lose face, but I'm sure you did it for the right reasons.'

'Lose face?' Phil looks appalled.

'Yes. You know, if it came out in public that, say, Dave had been using illegal contacts, especially when he's won all those awards. Or that Bethany lied to the police about being me—that would give the paper and its staff such a bad reputation. I know that's not why you did it, of course. I'm just saying I'm glad I work for such an upright and transparent company.'

'Yes... well...' Stratton's frowning again, and I hope he's being thoughtful rather than annoyed.

I look at him expectantly, my eyebrows raised and a pleasant smile on my face.

'The thing is,' he says, 'that there aren't really any vacancies in any of the other departments. So, you see—'

'Apart from the women's supplement, you mean? I know Melanie's going on maternity leave very soon, isn't she? If that's all there is, I'd be happy to go there—just for the sake of harmony, of course.' My heart's hammering as I telepathically tell him to agree with me.

The men look at each other, their expressions worried.

'I'd need to have a word with their chief editor down there,' Stratton says, fiddling with his pen. 'See how the ground lies.'

'That'll be wonderful,' I say, trying not to smile too brightly. 'Thank you.'

Both men look as shell-shocked as Dave did earlier.

I uncross my legs and jerk forward as if to get up, then look questioningly at them.

'Yes. I think that's everything, don't you?' Stratton still looks bewildered as he asks Phil, who just nods, with a similar expression.

'Have a great weekend, gentlemen,' I say, standing up and shaking their hands before leaving the room.

That went well, *I think.*

I'm on a real high as I make my way home. My day went much better than I could ever have hoped, and I can't wait to see James tonight. I haven't heard yet how his meeting went with Chief Inspector Hinchley, but I hope it was as good as mine.

'I'm staying at James' tonight,' I tell Cassie as soon as I get in. 'I just need to grab a few things.'

'At last!' Cassie comes over and gives me a big hug. 'I'm so happy for you.'

'Thanks, I'm really excited but nervous at the same time,' I admit, as she follows me into my bedroom. 'It's been ages since I've... you know.'

'You'll be fine,' she assures me. 'It's like riding a bike.'

I turn and gape at her. 'I'm not planning on doing any of that kinky stuff!'

She bursts out laughing. 'You know what I mean, you just never forget.'

'I'd like to forget one or two times,' I say, thinking back. 'In fact, most of the times, if I'm honest.'

She rolls her eyes as she helps me get my things together.

'What're you and Rob up to?' I shout from the bathroom as I grab my toothbrush.

'Wow, we're getting a bit personal now, aren't we?' she giggles.

'Ha-ha,' I say sarcastically. 'You know what I mean. Are you going out tonight?'

'Yeah, we're going for a meal and then meeting the gang for drinks later.' She smiles. 'Siobhan's coming, I think.'

'That reminds me,' I say, my heart thumping. 'I had a meeting today about my job.'

She stares at me. 'Oh, Libby, is everything all right? They haven't sacked you or anything, have they?'

'No... at least... I'm not quite sure. They're going to consider letting me work on the women's supplement, I believe.' Now that I think back, I can't help worrying that it might not have been such a positive meeting after all.

'That's great! Isn't that just what you wanted?' She's frowning at me in confusion. 'Libby? What happened, exactly?'

'Well, I think they might have been planning to sack me,' I admit, recalling the looks on the men's faces when I walked in.

I go on to explain how I pointed out that it would look bad for the paper if they sacked anyone—not mentioning me, of course.

'Oh, God, Libby. You threatened your bosses with adverse publicity?'

Did I?

'Not exactly. I was just pointing out how it would reflect on the *Chronicle* when it got out that Dave was using illegal sources and Bethany could have been in trouble with the police. I didn't say I was going to blab about it or anything.'

'No, but you implied it.'

'Did I?'

I hadn't really thought of it that way. I mean, I suppose it *could* have been construed like that. Is that what I meant? I'm not sure, now, to be honest. I thought I was just... sort of... warning them. *Oh, no!* She's right.

'Looks like you've got the job with Siobhan,' she says with a giggle. 'They wouldn't dare not give it to you after all that.'

Actually, I'm not convinced I've still got a job at all, to be honest.

'I hope so. It would be great to work with the girls and I'd love to do all the beauty and fashion stuff instead of running around after stupid stories. Especially now I know how Dave makes them all sound so interesting and exciting. He lies.'

'I think he'd call it something like 'embellishing the truth',' she says, laughing.

'I just couldn't do that,' I say. 'Well, not for a newspaper story, anyway.'

My stomach feels a bit jittery for some reason. I quickly stuff the rest of my things into my Ted Baker overnight bag.

'I'll speak to Siobhan, make sure she put that recommendation in for you,' Cassie promises.

'Thanks, babe. Right, I'm off.'

We have a quick hug and I head for the Tube, feeling like a kid on my first day of school.

***

James welcomes me with a glass of Muscadet and a broad smile, and I suddenly feel even more nervous than ever.

'I've ordered Chinese, I hope that's okay?' He kisses me softly and I immediately feel more relaxed.

'Perfect.' *I wasn't just talking about the Chinese when I said that.*

'Great. We're getting a selection as I wasn't sure what you'd prefer.'

'Even better.' I smile and follow him through to the bedroom where I dump my overnight bag. His room's a fresh shade of pale green and he's got white furniture coupled with green bedding and curtains with tiny daisies on. It all looks fresh and cool. *A bit like him—not that I'm saying he's green, of course, not even when he's angry, lol!*

'Is everything okay?' I ask, sensing a little uneasiness as we return to the living room. 'What did Chief Inspector Hinchley want?'

James rolls his eyes, and we both sit on the sofa with our drinks. He looks incredible, having earlier changed into a pair of tight-fitting jeans and a Ralph Lauren shirt rolled to just above the elbows.

'Suzanne's been talking to him. She doesn't think I'm being very sympathetic about her 'situation'.' He uses one-handed finger quotes. 'Apparently, some of her belongings have gone missing,' he continues, an annoyed edge to his voice.

'Missing or stolen?'

He huffs. 'I assumed stolen by Reynolds, but we can't prove anything.'

'He's the obvious choice,' I reply. 'Who else could it be?'

He sighs. 'She's had several viewers around, apparently. Hinchley wants us to ensure it wasn't any of them before making any accusations.'

I frown. 'But all the viewings were accompanied. How could anyone have...?' My mind whirls.

'What?' James is nothing if not perceptive.

'Reynolds was helping show them around. He was there when Rob and Ben viewed. What a good way of covering up a theft.' I can't believe the man could be so damn sneaky.

James shrugs. 'Well, that's it then. We're never going to prove it. Which means she'll never get her stuff back. He's hardly going to admit to anything now he's already bang to rights. He's got nothing left to lose.'

'What about the insurance?'

'They're not going to pay up knowing that she's had strangers wandering around her home while she was living with a criminal, are they?' James shakes his head. 'It's hopeless. She had some expensive pieces, too.'

I feel sorry for him—and me. Tonight was going to be so magical, our first really intimate night together and now it's all been spoiled. And by Suzanne, of all people. This is just so typical.

'I assume it was all jewellery and money that was taken?' I ask with a huff.

'Mostly.' James looks really fed up. 'A few items of clothing and some shoes, too, I believe.'

My ears prick up. 'Shoes? What shoes?' Suzanne must be devastated.

He gives a little grin. 'Not the type you'd be interested in. Just some trainers, I believe.'

I frown. 'I can't see Suzanne in trainers, to be honest. Was she into keep-fit?'

He smirks. 'She was going to take it up, apparently. Bought all the paraphernalia but then couldn't find the trainers. Quite expensive ones, seemingly.'

'No doubt.'

We hear the buzzer and James gets up. 'That'll be dinner.'

I stand up to help. He's ordered a lovely selection and we leave it all in its foil containers, just spread them all out on two trays, then grab a couple of plates and forks.

'This looks lovely,' I say, my tummy rumbling with anticipation. We take it all through to the living room, along with another bottle of wine, and tuck in.

It's absolutely delicious and we sit back for a while enjoying the meal.

'So, she hadn't missed these expensive all-singing, all-dancing trainers, then?' I ask incredulously before biting into a battered chicken ball.

'She hadn't thought any more about losing them until Reynolds was arrested. She said she thought she must have just misplaced them. When I heard—from you, incidentally—that she'd been seeing him, I told her to check all her belongings. It was only when she realised that some of her jewellery and clothes had gone that she added two and two about the trainers. A few other trinkets were missing, too, but they were more pretty than valuable. He might not have known that, of course.'

James reaches over for some beef in black bean sauce and I'm treated to a waft of his heavenly cologne.

'That must have been awful for her,' I say. I dislike the woman with a passion but can't help feeling sympathetic.

He nods while eating.

I frown as a thought occurs to me. 'Do you know what make of trainers they were?' I ask, reaching for my phone.

He raises his eyebrows. 'I've got it written down somewhere.' He takes a crumpled list from the side table and checks it. 'Nikes,' he says. 'Suzanne said they were the latest style.'

'Of course, they were.' Who would expect anything less?

'You've got a point there,' he concedes. 'According to this, they were Nike Air VaporMax Flyknit 2, whatever they are.'

I scroll down my phone. 'Anything like these, do you know?' I show him the picture of Millie Reynolds being led away by the police after her arrest at the back of Hanover Heights. 'This was the day Millie threatened Oliver with the bread knife,' I explain. 'I knew those trainers looked out of place on her.'

He looks closely at the picture, then at me. 'So, if we can prove Reynolds took these he'll have a hard job proving he didn't take the rest.' He grins.

'His wife might know more than we think,' I suggest. 'I'll send this over to your phone.' I guessed that would be his next question.

'Great. I'll send it to Suzanne for verification.' He looks a lot brighter than he did, his eyes shining.

'And then would someone else be able to follow it up?' I ask, hopefully. 'Unless it can wait until Monday?'

He grins. 'I'll get Alex to deal with it. He's on duty all weekend.'

I beam back. 'I'll clear this up,' I say, gathering the empty cartons while he gets on his phone.

'You were right,' he says, when I return a few minutes later. 'Looks like they *were* Suzanne's trainers. And I've passed it all over to Alex.' He looks much more relaxed and as gorgeous as ever.

'So, the evening's all ours?' I ask, snuggling next to him.

'Every minute,' he promises. 'And I can't think of any way I'd rather spend it than with you in my arms... or maybe my bed.'

His eyes are almost black with lust as he takes me in a passionate kiss, the likes of which I've never encountered. His hands roam up and down my back, making me tingle and glow hot. His body feels hard and warm under my ministrations as I stroke his neck while he holds me tightly against him.

'Shall we go to the bedroom?' he murmurs after a few minutes.

A thrill of excitement zips through my body like an electric current and I stand up, holding his hand as he leads me through.

Moments later, we're under the covers of his king-size bed, all naked and warm and... you know.

My heart's thumping wildly and my whole body feels alive, on edge. It's actually happening. We're here, about to do this at last. James holds me in his arms, his lips inching closer for a sensual kiss.

Suddenly, a cacophony ruins the moment.

'Shit!' James thumps the mattress in frustration, then grabs his dressing gown. Someone must be leaning on the damn buzzer as it won't stop ringing. 'I'll sort it,' he promises, clenching his jaw in frustration. 'Just don't you move.'

'I'm not going anywhere,' I promise with a giggle.

I can't let him see I'm as frustrated as he is. Whoever it is has impeccable timing that's all I'm saying.

When James doesn't return after a few minutes, I pull his shirt on and open the bedroom door. I can hear raised voices. One is his and the other... I don't bloody believe it.

'What the hell are *you* doing here?' Suzanne glares at me as soon as I walk into the living room.

I fold my arms, lean casually back against the doorframe, and raise my eyebrows in a 'what do you think?' sort of way.

Her mouth gapes open as she takes in the sight of me in James' shirt and him in just his gown. 'You've been...?'

Chance would be a fine thing!

'As you can see, you *have* disturbed me,' James tells her curtly. 'Maybe next time you could just send a text.'

'But I'm a woman in need!' she explodes. 'I told you, the house is flooded, I've nowhere to go. You *have* to let me stay here! I'm your ex-wife, for God's sake, and it's the middle of the night, what do you expect me to do?'

'Book into a B and B?'

She glares at him. 'What with? You know that man took me for every penny I had!' She gulps as though about to start crying and James rolls his eyes.

'And almost every penny *I* had, too,' he points out, angrily. 'And all because you lied to me about needing money for the house. I gave you the money for that pipe when we first noticed a tiny crack. Just because you chose to give it to your boyfriend instead, doesn't mean I should have to put you up now it's burst.'

Suzanne looks flustered as well as annoyed.

'You *have* called a plumber, I take it?' I ask her, almost afraid of the reply.

James stares at her.

'I didn't have any money,' she wails.

'Suzanne, are you telling me our house is currently being flooded and you've done absolutely nothing to stop the flow of water?' James' eyes are wide with horror, and I feel my stomach churn.

'I told you. I didn't know what to do,' she whimpers.

'Don't you even care about your own home?' I snap, outraged.

She looks sheepish. 'Th-that's another thing,' she says timidly, 'there were these forms Oliver asked me to sign and... the house might not be ours anymore. Can I move in here?'

THE END

May I ask a favour?

I really hope you've enjoyed this book. If so, would you be so kind as to leave a review (one word is enough) at:
https://www.amazon.com
https://www.amazon.co.uk
https://www.goodreads.com
https://www.bookbub.com
Thank you so much.

The following trademarked items appear in *Stepping It Up*. The author acknowledges the trademarked status and trademark owners of the following wordmarks mentioned in this work of fiction:

Christian Louboutin: Christian Louboutin Ltd

Manolo Blahnik: Manolo Blahnik International Ltd

Kurt Geiger: Kurt Geiger Ltd

Karen Millen: Karen Millen Ltd

McDonald's: McDonald's Corporation

McMuffin: McDonald's Corporation

Big Mac : McDonald's Corporation

Radley: Radley & Co Ltd

Marc Jacobs: Marc Jacobs International LLC

Jovani: Jovani Fashions Ltd

Selfridges: Selfridges Retail Ltd

Harvey Nichols: Harvey Nichols & Co Ltd

Ford Focus: Ford Motor Company

Mercedes: Daimler AG

Mars bar: Mars Incorporated

Net-a-porter: Net-a-Porter Group

Coke : The Coca-Cola Company

Sherlock Holmes: The Sir Arthur Conan Doyle Literary Estate

Miss Marple: Agatha Christie Ltd

KitKat: Nestle SA

eBay: : eBay Inc

Christian Dior: Christian Dior Ltd

Chanel: Chanel International B.V.

Nike: Nike Inc

Nordstrom: Nordstrom Inc

Yorkie: Nestle SA

Mint Aero: Nestle SA

Monsoon: Monsoon Accessorize Ltd

Dorothy Perkins: Arcadia Group

Jimmy Choo: Jimmy Choo Ltd

Estee Lauder: The Estee Lauder Companies Inc

L.K. Bennett: L.K. Bennett

Stella McCartney: Stella McCartney Ltd

Starbucks: Starbucks Corporation

Ted Baker: Ted Baker plc

J'adore: Christian Dior Ltd

Quality Street: Nestle SA

Roses: Mondelez International

The Running Man: Stephen King (as Richard Bachman)

Pretty Woman: Uptown Wink LLC

The New Avengers: Walt Disney Studios (written by Brian Clemens)

Chloe: Chloe S.A.S.

Kate Spade: Kate Spade LLC

Victoria Beckham: Victoria Beckham Ltd

Vivienne Westwood: Vivienne Westwood Latimo S.A.

Diane von Furstenberg: DVF Studio LLC

Jasper Conran: Conran, Jasper

Heat Magazine: Bauer Media Group
Louis Vuitton: LVMH
IPad: Apple Inc
Bluetooth: Bluetooth Sig Inc
Deichmann: Deichmann SE (Company)
Nora Gardner: Nora Gardner LLC
Asics: Asics Corporation
Cosmopolitan: Hearst Corporation

As a courtesy, the author would like to acknowledge the following celebrities mentioned in *Stepping It Up*:

Lindsey Kelk
Hugh Grant
Olivia Newton-John
Julia Roberts
Mo Farah
Martin Lewis
Joanna Lumley
James Dyson
Ellie Goulding

About the Author
BEA STEVENS

Author of Chick Lit, lover of chocolate (and doesn't think it's pure coincidence that the two sound similar!) Has a penchant for shoes, bags, clothes (the usual necessities), and socialising with friends, family and anyone else who gets dragged along.

Hopes you enjoy her books, get her humour, don't object to her use of British spellings and keep in touch.

Please feel free to sign up to her newsletter at:
http://eepurl.com/dnI9bv

And/or follow her on:
https://www.facebook.com/AuthorBeaStevens/
https://twitter.com/beastevensbooks
https://www.instagram.com/authorbeastevens/
https://www.bookbub.com/authors/bea-stevens
https://www.goodreads.com/author/show/17444011.Bea_Stevens

And check out her website at
https://www.beastevens.com/

Also by Bea Stevens

BEST FOOT FORWARD
(The Liberty Lawrence Series Book 1)
http://mybook.to/BestFootForward

IF THE SHOE FITS
(The Liberty Lawrence Series Book 3)
http://mybook.to/IfTheShoeFits

RUNNING IN HEELS
(The Liberty Lawrence Series Book 4)
http://mybook.to/RunningInHeels

HERE'S A TASTE OF 'IF THE SHOE FITS'...

Think nice thoughts, I tell myself over and over as I hop about from one foot to the other, my knuckle poised millimetres from the door. I'm trying hard. Right. Concentrate. I stare down at my shoes. Louboutins. You can't get nicer than those. These are shiny, black courts. Expensive. Not quite as expensive as they would have been had I not bought them on eBay, but still a lot more than I had told James they were.

And talking of James, another nice thought just pops into my head. We actually did it… Friday night believe it or not. He has been in such a foul mood with all that business with his ex-wife Suzanne that I didn't expect it to happen at all. The cow's only gone and moved into his flat. He was livid, but there wasn't much else he could do under the circumstances. If he hadn't let her stay at his place, she would have only made him pay for a hotel—and Suzanne doesn't do cheap.

She obviously knew he'd say yes as she'd brought all her stuff. James promptly packed a bag of his own, and after we'd gone over to their house in Richmond, he came back to mine—well, mine and Cassie's. Cassie Beaumont is the best flatmate and friend anyone could ask for. She didn't bat an eyelid when I explained that James was staying for the weekend. She did wink, though.

Suzanne had neglected to get a crack mended in a pipe in their bathroom, and the damn thing had burst, sending water cascading all over the first floor of their gorgeous home. It wouldn't have been so bad had she bothered to turn off the water before gathering her belongings and heading over to Fulham to disturb James and me at a most inopportune moment. By the time we got over there, the living room ceiling was already sagging, and the upstairs carpets were ruined.

James switched off the water, but it was too late to do anything about the mess. We just locked up and went back to my place. It was great. The whole weekend, I mean, not just… you know. Although that was amazing, too. More than amazing, actually, it was…

'Arghh!'

Someone just opened the door in front of me, scaring me half to death.

'Did you want something?'

My hand's still in the air, mid-knock. I quickly put it back to my side, clearing my throat while I scramble my thoughts.

'Good morning. I heard you wanted to see me.' Phil Peerless frowns at me. Nothing new there. 'Right. Yes. Come in.'

He looks as flustered as I feel.

'Thank you.'

I straighten my back and walk into the office, taking deep breaths to steady my nerves.

He looks out the door, and I can't help suspecting he was probably on his way to the loo. Now, he'll have to quickly decide whether to keep me waiting or delay his visit. I read somewhere that people make their best decisions while bursting for a pee. It's something to do with the urgency, I believe that doesn't give you time to over-think, so you just impulsively choose the best course of action.

'Is everything okay?' I ask, not wanting to sit down in case he thinks me rude, but at the same time, not wanting him to disappear and have time to think about sacking me. Not that I've done anything wrong, exactly. Well… not really.

All I did was solve a mystery—well, several actually. But I thought my boss, Dave Chandler, was a crook and nearly got him into trouble with the police. Well, how was I to know he had an identical twin brother? And then I inadvertently threatened to take my story to the press if the *Daily Chronicle* gave me the sack because of it. I hoped I'd get away with it, but the management decided to wait until after the weekend to make their announcement about my fate. And so here we are.

He jerks around to face me. 'Yes, of course.'

He closes the door and walks around to his side of the desk. 'Sit down, Libby.'

I do as he says. *So far so good!*

I'm about to ask him if he had a good weekend but think better of it. If he didn't, he might dwell on it and be in a bad mood and much more likely to sack me—especially if he thinks it's my fault. Which it isn't. Wasn't. Can't have been. Or he might ask how mine was, and if it was better than his, he'll be even more annoyed. And I have a feeling mine was *much* better than his. After all, I'll bet he and his wife didn't spend nearly all their time in bed and… No, I don't think he'd still do any of that at his age. If ever.

'Mr Stratton and I had a long talk on Friday evening,' he says.

I lean forwards, trying to read his expression. When that fails, I try for his mind. Even emptier.

Mr Stratton is the owner of the *Daily Chronicle*, the newspaper I work for. Or, at least, I *hope* I still do.

'Right.' I can't think of anything else to say.

He clears his throat before taking a sip of water from a crystal glass on his desk. 'We've decided to move you to work on *Woman Matters*, the ladies' supplement.'

My stomach lurches, and I want to jump up and give him a hug, but I refrain. Not just because he might change his mind, but he smells a bit weird. Sort of old manish.

'Right.' I try not to sound too thrilled, but inside, I'm doing cartwheels—which is a bit of a miracle because I could never do them on the outside. I swallow hard, keeping my hands firmly clasped over my knee.

'Siobhan O'Leary will be your mentor, and your chief editor will be Valerie Fulton-Coombes. The position will be for a trial period of one month. After that, we'll see how things stand.'

See how things stand? I think he'll find me standing firmly rooted to the department—maybe even running my own section. I'm just imagining it when I remember he's awaiting a response.

I nod. 'Thank you.'

'Melanie will be starting her maternity leave next week, so you can begin over there today. Hopefully, she'll be able to hand over the reins before she goes.' Phil looks very stern, and I wonder if he would have preferred to sack me after all. I can't help wondering just how much say he had in the matter.

'Right, thank you.' I stand and lean over to shake his hand like the true professional I am.

He raises his eyebrows but shakes my sweaty palm as he gets up. He follows me out the door, and I walk to the lift as quickly as I can. Once inside, I fist pump the air. That's when I realise, I'm not alone. Kevin Stratton is standing behind me with a couple of very important-looking ladies.

They all glare at me. I smile and give a nervous little laugh. I actually hear one of the snooty women tut. I stare at her just to let her know I've heard and turn to face the door, willing it to open soon.

The women are both well-dressed, one in a bright-green Prada suit, which brings out the colour of her eyes, and the other in a navy shift dress I think I recognise from Monsoon. It doesn't excuse their lack of manners, though.

I desperately want to text James, but I daren't get my phone out with the big boss standing right there. *Damn!* I know he'll be worried about me, too, despite how optimistic he was this morning. I honestly don't know how anyone can be so cheerful first thing on a Monday. He never ceases to amaze me.

To my horror, I let out a giggle. I was only thinking about how amazing James was and out it came. And now, I can't stop. I feel them all staring at me from behind, but I daren't look round. The more I try to stifle it, the worse it gets. I think I'm about to burst. Suddenly, a loud snort overtakes me. Gosh, this is awful. That woman's just tutted again, but I daren't stare at her this time. Just the thought of those stuck-up faces makes me worse. I'm praying for the doors to open so I can escape. What if I get sacked for this? Oh, no, just when it looked like it was all going so well. Even that idea doesn't stop the onslaught, and suddenly, I do a laugh-snort-cough thing just to really finish it off.

As soon as the doors open, I hurl myself out of the lift, bumping headlong into a couple of photographers.

'Hey, watch out!'

'Sorry.'

I hear another tut behind me and spin around to see that Kevin po-faced Stratton and his women have followed me out. Oh, no. I was only getting off here to escape them. I don't even know which floor I'm on. Taking a deep breath, I head down the corridor until I see a sign for the ladies' loo and dive in. Surely, those annoying, tutting women won't follow me in here? I don't even look back to check. I just find an empty cubicle and lock myself in.

I sit down with a massive sigh. Oddly enough, now that I'm away from that lift, I don't feel like giggling at all. It must have been nerves that caused it. And relief. I'm so glad I've kept my job—for now. I can't believe they're putting me on a month's trial, though. What does that mean? If I don't fit in, they'll move me? Or sack me anyway?

A lead weight sinks to the pit of my stomach. I'm not out of the woods yet. But there's hope. If I keep my nose clean and do well in the women's supplement, they're bound to want me to stay. If not, I dread to think what'll happen.

I stand and straighten my dress. It's my black Karen Millen skater with the white trim. It's a bit loose as I must have lost weight with all the running around I had to do while working in the newsroom. I've teamed it with a white jacket and a little black shoulder bag borrowed from Cassie. The bag's a Gucci. That just shows how good a friend she is.

I'm on a mission now to make everyone in the new department like me. That way, they won't make me leave when my month's up. In fact, I'll be so popular, they'll beg me to stay.

I wash my hands and check my hair and make-up. Apart from being a little flushed, I look okay. Now, if I can just work out which floor I'm on, I might be able to find the office, which is on the fourth floor. As I turn to leave the room, I hear a tut behind me and swing round to glare at the culprit. It's the woman in the green Prada suit. I frown at her.

'Is there a problem?' I ask as politely as I can manage. She raises her perfectly shaped eyebrows, looking quite taken aback.

'I beg your pardon?' She sounds very posh.

'That's the fourth time you've tutted at me today,' I tell her. 'I wondered if you have a problem with me?'

She shakes her head disparagingly. 'My dear girl, I don't even *know* you. However, I do find your behaviour more than a little… shall we say… *distracting*? I don't know which part of the building you work in, but in my department, I expect my staff to show a lot more decorum.'

With that, she rolls her eyes at me and leaves.

No decorum? How dare she say I have no decorum? I'm filled with bloody decorum. Well, the rum bit anyway, James and I drank quite a bit of it over the weekend. I want to go after her and give her a piece of my mind, but I don't. I need all my mind pieces to impress my new boss. It's a good job she's left, though, or she would have heard exactly what I think if her.

'Snooty, stuck-up bitch!' I mumble, staring at the closed door.

A tut from the washbasin makes me jerk around, and I stare at the woman in the Monsoon navy shift. Shit. I hadn't realised anyone else was in here. She looks down her nose at me, daring me to retaliate. Instead, I huff loudly and leave the room.

Looking up and down the corridor, I don't recognise this area at all. I head back towards the lift and discover I'm on the fifth floor. Luckily, the lift is empty this time so I quickly text James on my way to the fourth level.

Hi, James. I'm going to work with Siobhan! Hope you're okay. Lxx

There's no need to worry him about the temporary bit. With any luck, it won't be an issue anyway. I'm determined to make a go of it.

I smile as I open the door to the large office where Siobhan and her team work for the fashion section of the *Daily Chronicle's* female supplement, *Woman Matters*. There's a large table in the middle of the room with desks all around the wall. It's very light and spacious, and everyone's bustling around excitedly. Rails of clothes line one end of the room, and a couple of women are looking through them. Someone else has laid an outfit on the table and is frowning at it. I recognise one of the girls as Tammy. We met on a night out recently when I joined Cassie and her boyfriend, Rob. There was a gang from the newspaper with them, and we all got on famously. Her gorgeous, dark-red hair is shorter than the last time I saw her. It now bounces in natural waves on her shoulders, looking lovely. Her Prada glasses make her look very intelligent and enlarge her bright-blue eyes. She carefully pins a dress onto a mannequin, her tongue hanging out in concentration.

'There you are! I thought you'd got lost,' Siobhan calls over to me with a smile. She has an immaculate black bob and perfect make-up. Utterly stunning. She's with Francesca, the girl I met the other day. Francesca's much more natural looking, with tight, orangey curls cascading over her broad shoulders.

I grin at them, not wanting to admit that I *did* actually get a bit lost.

'Hi.' I go over, suddenly feeling a little nervous.

'Welcome to the mad house,' Siobhan says, gesturing to the room. She even smells gorgeous.

'Thank you. I'm so excited to be here.'

'We're just waiting for a new collection to come in,' she goes on. 'It's called 'Fame' and is all about brandishing your name on your clothes. You know, getting your name out there, sort of thing. It ties in with the current trend of selfies and self-promotion. I think it's supposed to encourage confidence and self-esteem.'

My stomach flips with excitement. 'Sounds great. I love the idea.'

'The delivery's been a bit delayed but when they arrive, I want you and Francesca to work on them. Melanie's had to go home poorly, so it's great that we have you. I need to know all about the quality, workmanship, and wear ability. It's something that's taken off in a big way over in the States, and we're the first to see it over here. Apparently, the collection's set to make a lot of money.'

'Right.' Sheer joy bubbles up inside me. This is what I wanted to do all along. This job is just perfect. I'm right on the cusp of something massive.

'First, let me introduce you, though,' Siobhan says. She raises her voice, looking very efficient in her royal blue bodycon dress. I've no idea how she can walk properly in something so fitted, let alone work in it, but she looks great. 'Okay, girls, listen up. This is Libby, who's come to join us. I know you'll all make her welcome and give her any help she needs.'

There's a chorus of hellos as everyone looks over and smiles at me. They look like a bunch of models—they're all so pretty. I smile back. This is so lovely, although a little intimidating. I didn't get anything like this in the boring old newsroom.

'I won't go through all the names now, as it can be a bit overwhelming, but you'll pick them up as you go along. And don't be afraid to ask questions, Libby.'

'Thank you.'

'Come on, I think Valerie's back in her office. She's the boss. I'll take you in.' Siobhan ushers me towards the corner where another office hides behind a glass door. The door has blinds pulled down, and I notice this place has windows overlooking the main room. Again, the blinds are down at the moment. I can imagine it'll be a great way for the boss to be included with what's going on without being intrusive. There's a good sense of cohesion about it.

Siobhan knocks, and a voice calls for us to go in.

'Hi, Valerie. I just wanted to introduce you to our new recruit,' Siobhan says, as I follow her into the large office. 'Valerie Fulton-Coombes, meet Libby Lawrence.'

Valerie stands to shake my trembling hand. Her eyes flash at me and widen. My stomach churns as I take in the green Prada suit, the immaculate hair, and the disparaging look. Judging by her expression, she's recognised me, too.

Oh, shit!